Murder in Little Venice

ALSO BY PHILLIP STRANG

MURDER IS ONLY A NUMBER
MURDER HOUSE
MURDER IS A TRICKY BUSINESS
MURDER WITHOUT REASON
THE HABERMAN VIRUS
MALIKA'S REVENGE
HOSTAGE OF ISLAM
PRELUDE TO WAR

Copyright Page

Copyright © 2017 Phillip Strang

Cover Design by Phillip Strang

All rights reserved. No part of this book may be reproduced, stored in a retrieval system, or transmitted in any form or by any means (electronic, mechanical, photocopying, recording or otherwise) without the prior written permission of the publisher, except by a reviewer who may quote brief passages in a review to be printed by a newspaper, magazine, or journal.

All characters appearing in this work are fictitious. Any resemblance to actual events, locales, or persons, living or dead, is coincidental.

All Rights Reserved.

This work is registered with the UK Copyright Service
ISBN: 9781549600449

Dedication

For Elli and Tais who both had the perseverance to make me sit down and write.

Chapter 1

To those who lived on the houseboats that lined either side or the cyclists and the walkers who regularly used its towpaths, the Regent's Canal was a place of beauty. Only a few would know of its history, and that two hundred years previously it had been busy with barges shipping cargo from the seafaring vessels that docked at Limehouse on the River Thames, to connect with the Grand Canal, and then up through England.

Even fewer would know that it was named after Prince Regent, a frivolous man, the son of a mad King. He was better known for his grossly expensive tastes in decorating palaces and wasting money, although some others may have known of his penchant for mistresses, including the infamous Mrs Fitzherbert.

Such history was far from the mind of Mary Harding as she walked her dog along the towpath between Westbourne Terrace Road Bridge and Harrow Road in an area of London known as Little Venice. It was still early, and it was only her and her dog, a sprightly Jack Russell. She had walked that stretch of the canal many times before and still enjoyed the atmosphere. She looked up at the elegant Regency houses as she walked; wished she could afford to buy one but knew she probably never would. She glanced over at the water, and sometimes into the open windows on the houseboats: some were modern and luxurious, others were run-down. The smell of early morning cooked breakfasts pervaded the air.

Mary Harding maintained her pace, trying to rein in the dog as it tugged on its lead. *A waste of money for dog training*, she thought.

'Stop barking,' she said, knowing full well that people were still sleeping in their boats no more than six feet from where she was. She had had problems with the dog before in the flat she shared with two others, just two hundred yards from the canal, although separated from the houses close to the canal by several million pounds in real estate value. The dog, of which she was uncommonly fond, would have to go, she knew that. A good home in the country where its barking would not offend anyone.

Mary Harding moved forward to grab the dog and to scurry away with it in her arms. The dog took one step forward, peering into the water, barking incessantly.

'Shut that damn dog up,' a voice bellowed from within the confines of a houseboat. A nervous woman, Mary Harding apologised as best she could, but the dog continued to defy her.

Looking into the water, the woman could see why. There, in the water, wedged to the rear of the belligerent man's houseboat, was what appeared to be a dead animal.

She found a stick nearby and prodded the carcass; it turned over. Stricken with horror, incapable of using her phone, she hammered on the side of the houseboat. 'Help, help!' she screamed.

The man who had criticised the dog came out within seconds. 'What the –?'

'There, behind your boat.'

Still barefooted, and only wearing a tee shirt and shorts, the houseboat owner looked over into the water where the dog had been barking. Then, still half asleep, he rushed back to the houseboat, picked up his phone and dialled the emergency services on 999.

***

'It's enough to turn your stomach,' Crime Scene Examiner Windsor said. They were the man's first words apart from the pleasant early morning courtesies on arriving at the scene. The former towpath, now a footpath, had been blocked off at both ends from upstream at Westbourne Terrace Road Bridge down to Harrow Road – the people who would normally walk down there relegated to Warwick Crescent. From there the curious could watch the investigation unfold.

'What do you reckon?' DCI Isaac Cook asked. It was still early, and he would have preferred to be in bed, but when the phone rang, he had been out of the door within five minutes. After apprehending the murderer in his previous case, the psychotic Charlotte Hamilton, he was once again the shining star at Challis Street Police Station, especially after she had stabbed him in the shoulder, although he wondered if the murders in the area would ever reduce in numbers.

'What's left has been in the water for less than a day,' Windsor's reply. Gordon Windsor had been assigned to Challis Street for some years, and the man knew what he was talking about. Isaac Cook knew that the on-the-spot analysis from the CSE would be enough for him to bring the full team together. The pathologist and the autopsy would reveal more about the body, or what remained of it, on the towpath by the rear of the houseboat.

Jim Parsons, the owner of the houseboat, and Mary Harding, the dog's owner, were both sitting down at the other end of the boat drinking cups of tea. Larry Hill, Isaac's DI, was interviewing them. Parsons, previously annoyed with the barking dog, was patting it.

'White, male, age uncertain,' Windsor said.

'Any chance of an identity?' Isaac asked.

'DNA, missing persons. It may be possible, but there's not much to be going on with here.'

Isaac looked at the body, shielded from public view by a hastily-erected crime scene tent. He could see the CSE's reluctance to be more precise. It was clear that whoever had done it had been a butcher. It was evident why the woman had thought it was a slab of meat that was bobbing up and down in the water.

Apart from a torso, nothing else remained: no head, no legs, no arms. Even Windsor had felt a lump in his throat on seeing the body for the first time, and some of the other police officers, uniforms, had vomited into the canal.

'The cause of death?' Isaac asked.

'I'd have thought having your head cut off would have been as good a way as any,' Windsor replied.

'Dead before decapitation?'

'Pathology may be able to tell you, but I can't be more precise. I'd say after death, but don't quote me on that.'

'Any injuries to the body?'

'None that I can see.'

'Murder?'

'It hardly seems to be an accident, does it?'

The two people integral to the discovery could not help with the details about the body; one was walking her dog, the other was asleep. Both Isaac and Larry stayed at the crime scene for two hours before returning to Challis Street. The uniforms had commenced interviewing people walking past, and Wendy Gladstone, Isaac's sergeant, would conduct a door-to-door later in the day down Warwick Crescent and then up Delamere Terrace, although it was a long shot. Unless the team knew how long the body had been in the water, and the flow of the water in the canal, it would not be possible to ascertain where the body had entered it. It was believed, not certain, that what had been found at the rear of the houseboat had come from upstream, but where? DCI Isaac Cook and his Homicide team needed to meet.

***

Detective Chief Superintendent Goddard put his head round the door of Isaac's office to give the obligatory words of encouragement before leaving. 'I've total confidence in the team, hopeful of an early result, keep up the good work.'

Isaac could only reflect on the insincerity of the man. Goddard had always been his mentor, but now the man's political manoeuvring, his attempts to ingratiate himself with the commissioner of the London Metropolitan Police, his ability to suck up to politicians had started to grate.

Sure, on the previous case with little progress on catching the killer he had held on to Isaac for as long as he could, but in the end he had been dumped as the SIO and supplanted by a downright miserable sod of a man by the name of Seth Caddick. Isaac knew that if he hadn't played his hunch right and arrested the serial killer, he would no longer be at Challis Street. Almost certainly out of London, maybe a remote station in the country or demoted.

Mid-morning, the key members of his team gathered in Isaac's office: Larry Hill, his DI, Sergeant Wendy Gladstone and Constable Bridget Halloran, the department's case prosecution officer. 'An update, sir?' Wendy asked.

'I've already started work on the paperwork,' Bridget said.

'This is what we have,' Isaac said. 'At 6.05 a.m. a body was discovered in Regent's Canal at Maida Vale. The woman who found it was walking her dog.'

'And the woman now?' Wendy asked.

'Once she'd given her statement, she was taken home. Also, the owner of a houseboat gave a statement as the body was wedged under the rear of his boat. There is no suspicion attached to either person.'

'Any indication as to how long the body had been there?'

'According to Gordon Windsor, the condition of the remains indicate that it had not been in the water for long so we must assume it had drifted down the canal. As for a more precise time? That's up to Pathology, but it may prove difficult.'

'Why?' Bridget asked.

'The body had been dismembered, and there is no head.'

Both Wendy and Bridget looked shocked.

'Murder?' Wendy asked after clearing her throat.

'That would be the logical conclusion. Gordon Windsor assumes it would have been a blow to the head or a bullet, but with no head, there's no way to prove it.'

'How do we establish the identity?' Wendy asked.

'DNA may help, or at least it may give us an approximation of its background: Anglo-Saxon, Asian.'

'African?' Bridget suggested.

'The body's white.'

'Where do we go from here?' Wendy asked.

'Missing persons. You and Larry can do some checking. In the meantime, we need someone who understands river flows, especially the Regent's Canal. Camden Lock is about three miles downstream, there are no locks upstream, at least none that should affect the flow. We need to put together some names of possible victims, and hope Pathology is able to do some reconstruction analysis: height, age, ethnicity.'

'Long shot, sir,' Wendy added.

'Agreed, but let's go with what we have.'

'We're dealing with savages here,' Larry said.

'That's understood, unless there was a reason for concealing the identity.'

'It's still savage, and if the body's not been there for long, then maybe he's not been missed yet.'

'Regardless, we have a murder case. No easier, no harder than our previous cases, and we managed to solve all of those. We'll solve this one, I'm sure of it,' Isaac said.

He had to admit he was becoming tired of the endless succession of murders. London crime figures, especially murders, were down, yet his area of London was continuing to accumulate the numbers. True, he knew that he and his team had solved them all, even when the odds were not stacked in their favour, and when others within the Met were looking for them to fail, or at least, him. Not that it concerned him unduly. He knew how it worked, although it was a distraction. The best he could do was to get on with it and prove to his doubters that they were wrong.

***

Larry observed prior to entering the Canal and River Trust's building located next to Westbourne Terrace Road Bridge on the western side of the canal at Little Venice that the water flow was negligible.

Once inside, George Ashburton, one of the Trust's employees, confirmed his observation. 'Minimal. Just enough to keep the water flowing towards the Thames, although if there's a lot of water upstream, then it'll flow a little faster.'

'If an object was thrown in the water, let's say within the last twenty-four hours?' Larry asked.

'We always have to deal with that problem. The locals are the worst, but so are some of the tourists with throwing in plastic drink bottles, stolen bikes. You'd be surprised what turns up if we drain part of the canal.'

'Do you do that often?'

'It's necessary sometimes. The canal silts up, and the banks need restoration work. The canal's been here for two hundred years, so it's bound to require maintenance.'

'And the houseboats?'

'They need to find somewhere else, but there are precious few places for them to go.'

'You've heard about the discovery in the canal today?' Larry asked.

'Who hasn't? It's not every day a body is fished out.'

'It was hardly a body.'

'What do you mean?'

'It was only a torso.'

'No head and limbs?'

'Precisely.'

'It's a first for the canal, although we've had the occasional body in there; some murdered, the occasional drowning. It's not deep, no more than six feet in most places, but it can be mighty cold sometimes. They jump in after a drunken night out, sometimes for a dare, at other times because they're too daft not to, and what happens? The water can be close to freezing under the surface, and then they find out they're not as good a swimmer as they thought they were.'

'Expensive around here?' Larry asked. He had admired the houses as he parked his car.

'That's why there are so many houseboats. They're in the best part of London at a fraction of the cost of a building on land. Mind you, they still have to pay for mooring, and the maintenance can be expensive, but all in all they're an excellent way to live.'

'You live in one?'

'For the last thirty-five years. Once I retire, I intend to travel the canals of England in my home.'

'If we could come back to the body in the water,' Larry said. 'Could it have come from one of the houseboats?'

'It's possible, but if, as you say, it's been dismembered, it would make an awful mess. Have you been inside a houseboat?'

'No.'

'There's not a lot of space. It's more like a long caravan than a house. I wouldn't be looking there for an answer, and besides, why?'

'Why someone dismembered the body, instead of taking it to the Thames and weighing it down with concrete blocks or burying it in the ground?'

'I see what you mean.'

'That's a question we need to answer,' Larry acknowledged.

***

Meanwhile, as Larry was discussing the case at the Canal and River Trust, Wendy was moving up and down the road adjacent to the murder site. Warwick Crescent, affluent and expensive, with an elegant Regency terrace house on the corner which fronted onto Westbourne Terrace Road at the western end close to the bridge. Next to it was a large block of flats. To Wendy, they looked to have been built fifty years previously, an attempt to blend into the surroundings by painting the exterior off-white and affecting a fake Regency styling. The real estate signs in the area indicated that they were for sale, but she knew they would be outside her price range. The signs plastered on the railings outside stated that any bikes chained to them would be removed and disposed of. Wendy was not sure if they were strictly legal, but she was there to ask questions, not debate a point of law. There appeared to be over one hundred flats. She had been joined by a couple of uniforms, although without a time of death other than in the last day, she felt that their efforts may well be wasted. She was adamant that this one road was to be the limit of her knocking on doors until she had more specifics.

***

Isaac busied himself in the office. It had been rough for a while on his previous case when he had been sidelined, but now he was back in his seat, safe and secure. Or, at least, as confident as anyone could be with a commissioner who'd had his nose put out of joint after his man, DCI Seth Caddick, had failed to make his mark. Isaac had only spoken to Caddick on a couple of occasions and neither time had been an enlightening experience. Still, the man had not disturbed his office too much; even managed to water the plant that Bridget and Wendy had bought him in the past when he had been going through a difficult patch in his love life. Even now, that was patchy, almost non-existent, if he was honest.

Larry Hill had told him to find a good woman and settle down, and he had wanted to with Jess O'Neill, but it had not worked out. They kept in contact, met up occasionally for a social drink, but there seemed no way they could rekindle the previous intensity: too much water under the bridge, too many unspoken truths, or at least one, Linda Harris. Not that he had heard from her for a long time, and Isaac still did not know for sure whether she had committed a murder or not, but it was moot, as the case had been closed, and there was no way the current government would allow it to reopen.

Isaac, too long a DCI, and with enough experience and ability to make detective superintendent, knew that forces beyond his control were holding him back, as well as his superior, Detective Chief Superintendent Goddard. The man had been marked for a commander's position, but people in high places had ensured he would have to wait a few more years.

Not a man to reflect for too long, Isaac decided to phone Gordon Windsor, the crime scene examiner. It was still too soon to expect a result back from the pathologist, although the time of death would help. Larry had a fair idea of the canal's flow rate, and it should be possible to hazard a guess as to where the body had entered the water. With that information, Wendy and her uniforms could focus their door-to-door more precisely.

'I'm heading over to the pathologist now. Meet me there in twenty minutes,' Windsor told Isaac. That was what he liked about the CSE: A man always enthusiastic, always willing to go the extra mile, and always affable. They were not comments Isaac could level at the pathologist, whom he had met before on several occasions, usually when a body was being cut open.

The pathologist, Graham Pickett, a tall, thin man in his late fifties, did not say much, and when he did, it was direct and to the point. So much so that Isaac had learnt to say little in his presence other than to ask the questions for which he needed answers.

'Four hours in the water,' Pickett said as Gordon Windsor and Isaac entered his office. 'That's what you want to know, isn't it?'

'Yes,' Isaac replied.

'No sign of maceration of the skin, no water ingestion into the lungs, and a massive loss of blood, although that's to be expected.'

'What else can you tell us about the man?'

'There's a tattoo on the back of the shoulder. It appears to be in the shape of a spider's web, but it's crude.'

'Your guess as to when and where?' Windsor asked.

Pickett sat down in his chair and leant back. 'Five years, at least. As to where? Either in prison or else in the far east.'

'Any assessment of height, age, physical condition, at least while he was alive?' Isaac asked.

'Height would need one of the major leg bones, the femur or the tibia, at least to allow any accuracy. Regardless, judging by what remains, I'd hazard a guess at between five feet six and five feet nine inches, but that will not be in my report, other than with a disclaimer. I don't want to be held accountable in court as to why I gave a height when I cannot guarantee the accuracy. With no legs, no fingerprints and no head, there's not a lot more I can tell you, although based on my examination and assessment of the clavicle, the pubic symphysis and the sternal rib end, standard and verifiable tests, I would give the man's age at between thirty and thirty-nine.'

'Caucasian or Asian?' Isaac asked.

'DNA will confirm, but the body is Caucasian, probably European. The body's not been long in the water, so the colour of the skin is fairly accurate.'

'Is it possible to ascertain when he was killed?'

'Ten hours maximum, although the immersion in water caused more rapid blood loss. It must have been a hell of a mess; the serrations around the neck and the top of the limbs were caused by a chainsaw.'

'It would need somewhere industrial,' Isaac said.

'You're the detective, but yes, that seems possible. There would have been a horrendous amount of blood, as well as the noise of the chainsaw.'

'Would there have been a lot of blood loss in the water?'

'Probably not as much as you would expect, and there was not a lot left in the body when I examined it; also, no signs of drugs or alcohol. As you can appreciate, a dismembered torso doesn't give a lot to work with. No signs of injuries either: broken bones, that sort of thing.'

'Is it possible to tell if this is terrorist related, crime gangs, sexual deviancy?' Windsor asked.

'Don't ask me,' Pickett said. 'Ask the DCI. I've told you what I've determined, and whoever did it was sick, but as to why and whom, I've no idea.'

'One final question,' Isaac said.

'What is it?'
'Was the body alive at the time of dismemberment?'
'Impossible to tell,' Pickett said.

Chapter 2

With the time in the water estimated at four hours, and with assistance from George Ashburton from the Canal and River Trust, the possible entry points were established. As it had been dark when the torso entered the water, the possibility that the person or persons responsible would have been seen was negligible.

And there was the unknown of how long the torso had been wedged under the houseboat. Isaac and Larry realised that the most likely scenario was that the body had entered the water no further upstream than the Westbourne Terrace Road Bridge. Although that was only thirty yards, the crime scene tape was extended as far as the junction of Chichester Road and Delamere Terrace on the southern side of the canal, and the junction of Bloomfield Road and Clifton Villas on the northern side. Isaac felt that near to the bridge was more likely, as both banks up from Westbourne Terrace Road Bridge were lined with houseboats stem to stern.

Windsor and his team, plus a contingent of eager uniforms, would be checking on the streets adjoining the canal: down on hands and knees if that was needed, looking for the minutiae that a crime scene invariably reveals.

Isaac reflected on what a thankless task they had in front of them. He well remembered his time on the beat, proudly wearing his police uniform. There had been some good times, some not so good, and being pulled in to walk or crawl slowly down the road or through the vegetation, occasionally planting a knee in dog excrement, did not qualify as good. And today, those out searching would be feeling the first throes of winter.

Wendy would be assisting, as would Larry, and any updates would be funnelled back to Isaac, who had the unenviable task of meeting with Richard Goddard, his senior. At least once a week they would meet, and on most occasions it was a pleasant affair, but the previous murder case had almost cost Goddard his job and had seen Isaac replaced as the senior investigating officer. Both men were naturally reluctant to allow a repeat, and although they were only one day into the current murder investigation, they knew that others within the Met would be observing, looking for the first sign of inaction and waiting to pounce and claim their jobs.

***

It was fortunate that it was the weekend and the usual heavy traffic in the area of Little Venice was moderated. The closure of the bridge over the canal at the closest point to where the body had been found would not present a problem, although it would need a few officers to redirect the traffic over the Harrow Road bridge not far away.

'You know what we're looking for here,' Gordon Windsor said, his team of twenty gathered around him. They stood on the road closest to Jim Parson's houseboat. Larry thought the small, balding man looked like Napoleon giving his officers their orders. 'We've checked around the houseboat down below, and we know the body, or what remained of it, did not enter the water at that point,' Windsor said.

'Where should we start looking?' one of his investigation team asked.

'Upstream, no more than three hundred yards. You've all been briefed. What we're looking for are signs of a body being placed in the river: blood, disturbance of the canal bank, cigarette ends; but mainly blood.'

'It could have been in a bag, and the body was removed from the bag over the water,' one of the assembled group said.

'That's always a possibility, but if they brought the body in a bag, it would have dropped blood. If they had thrown the bag into the water, then where is it? The water moves slowly, and if it was plastic, then it should be close by. Any more questions?'

No one put their hand up, and they all moved off to their nominated locations: ten police on either side of the canal. The first group was at the junction of Delamere Terrace and Chichester Road, the other at Bloomfield Road. Access on the Delamere side was through gates along the canal edge, although there were iron railings elsewhere if someone wanted to pass a body over them. On the other bank, a brick wall separated the road from the canal, and it was high enough to dissuade anyone from climbing over.

Slow and steady was the order of the day, and both teams moved slowly forward; the occasional houseboat occupant sticking their head out, wondering what was going on. The police, ever polite, asked them to stay where they were, at least until they had been given the all clear. Most had complied; some had moaned and taken no notice. One who had been particularly obstructive had to be reminded that interfering with a police investigation was an offence. The police officer involved made a note in his diary, adding the comment high on drugs, suspected marijuana, in case the man took it further. Some of the boats were gently rocking with the occupants indulging in early morning lovemaking. *That's what I should be doing*, Constable Reading thought, his feet cold and his mood distinctly downbeat as he searched in the undergrowth next to one of the boats. One owner on the Delamere Terrace side prepared ten piping hot cups of tea which was much appreciated. So far, there had been no rain, and the chance of success was looking good, so much so, that Windsor had phoned Isaac with an update.

***

'They're still after your blood,' Richard Goddard said. He sat in a leather chair behind his desk in his third-floor office at Challis Street Police Station.

Isaac sat on the other side of the desk, not sure as to the mood of the meeting. Sure, Goddard had been polite on his entering, shaking his hand warmly, but Isaac knew the detective chief superintendent had felt the heat as much as he had in the previous case. After so many years of working with the DCS, Isaac was still not sure how the man would react if the cards were played by their superiors: would he throw him to the wolves, or would he support him. Isaac wanted to think the best of a man who outside of the office he regarded as a friend, but...

'I remain optimistic that we'll wrap up the Regent's Canal case soon enough,' Isaac said, although he realised that he was saying it for the audience.

'Optimistic you may be, but you've no identity, no motive, and certainly no suspects. How do you progress on this one?'

'The only identifier is a tattoo on the man's shoulder.'

'Ten a penny,' Goddard replied.

'We're looking into its significance. It could just have been tattooed after a drunken night out, or it could be a gang's mark.'

'You know this one will be lapped up by the media?' Goddard reminded Isaac.

'Yes,' Isaac said. Even now, he had noticed on Facebook and Twitter that the body in the canal was ranking. The news organisations were not fully onto it yet, although Larry had phoned earlier to say that a television crew was out at the canal, and they were being kept at a distance. Some of the houseboat occupants, principally Jim Parsons, had been on talkback radio recounting his tale; no doubt receiving some payment for his time.

Isaac remembered in his early days in the force, before the advent of social media, that it had been easier. Now everyone wanted a result immediately, and there were plenty of armchair critics, or critics on buses, on the train, or in the office with a smartphone, updating on recent events, offering advice on how they would do it. And, of course, passing judgement if there wasn't instant gratification, but this was a murder case with a dead man, not frivolous entertainment for the masses. Isaac imagined the blood and gore, the state of mind of a person who could commit such an atrocity. And if it was a bloodlust, was it sexual, an obscure religious cult, a warning from one gang in London to another gang?

Isaac knew that without an identity they were going nowhere. He hoped the team out at Regent's Canal knew that. The visit that morning had been the first time he had been there for some years. As a child, he had walked with his parents from Camden along the towpath, and enjoyed lunch at the Waterside Café, no more than fifteen feet from the murder scene.

***

The early morning search at the furthest point on the Delamere Terrace side of the canal had revealed nothing of interest. The discarded cigarette they had found, Turkish in origin, had interested Gordon Windsor at first, with its connotations of a crime syndicate, but it had soon been discounted when the owner of one of the houseboats admitted to throwing the cigarette end out on the towpath, rather than in a rubbish bin. 'It's my wife. She can't stand the smell of it,' he said. 'I bought it on holiday in Istanbul.'

The team on the Bloomfield Street side found nothing.

Constable Jenny Arnett, a newcomer at Challis Street, newly trained and still young and enthusiastic, not jaundiced as some of the others after previous searches on a cold morning, made the first discovery. 'There's blood here,' she shouted.

Gordon Windsor arrived within two minutes. The area next to the towpath was quickly sealed off, even to the other police in the area.

Windsor brought up his trained investigating officers. The blood, just visible on the top of the brickwork lining the edge of the canal bank, looked recent, but until it had been checked, it was circumstantial.

'It's a good place to conceal a crime, under a bridge' Larry Hill, Isaac's DI, said.

'Even so,' Windsor reminded him, 'they would have had to walk up to here, either from the entrance of the Warwick Crescent side of the bridge or by the gate next to the Canal and the River Trust's offices on Delamere Terrace.'

With a confirmed possibility, all of the police on that side of the canal removed themselves from the immediate vicinity and reassembled downstream of the murder scene. From there they continued searching, although it was no longer blood that interested them, but anything that may have been discarded or lost by those disposing of the body.

After so many years as a crime scene examiner, Gordon Windsor was confident that what had been discovered was relevant and would be tied in to the body.

Grant Meston, one of Windsor's team, knelt down by the blood. The temperature under the bridge was still markedly colder than outside where the sun had briefly deemed itself worthy to show through the clouds. 'I can take a sample first, and if I'm careful, I can remove the brick and take it back to the laboratory,' Meston said.

Gordon Ashburton, arriving at work to find the Canal and River Trust building surrounded by policemen, watched horrified as part of his precious canal was removed.

'Don't worry,' Larry Hill said. 'You'll get it back when we're finished with it.'

With the blood sample removed, Grant Meston and Gordon Windsor looked for further traces of blood. Further down towards the Waterside Café, they found another bloodstain on the metal railing on the footpath leading up to Westbrook Terrace Road. The weather was turning nasty, and rain was in the air; the worst possible scenario for the work still to be completed.

Several crime scene tents, already erected, were brought down to the immediate area and secured in position. Some of the houseboat owners, blocked from the most direct entry to their boats, complained. They had tried to reason with Larry, but he was resolute, and he could not allow them to traverse an area of investigation. One of the owners, an angry man, said that he would talk to his local member of parliament, but Larry knew it was just bluff. And besides, the inconvenience would not last for more than a few days.

Meston, assisted by Rose Denning, whom Larry knew from a previous case, methodically worked his way back from under the bridge where the first blood sample had been taken and down towards the Waterside Café, before turning up the walkway to the bridge. The blood sample on the metal railing at the bottom of the walkway had already been taken. Larry, at first enamoured by the idyllic lifestyle that living on the water represented, realised that come winter when the water was cold and the towpath was slippery, or on rare occasions was covered in snow, it would not be so agreeable. He admitted that his small semi-detached, basic as it was, without the romanticism of a houseboat, represented normalcy, sometimes boring normalcy. However, it was what he wanted; apart from his wife's faddish diets, which tested his resolve sometimes.

After three hours of painstakingly checking the area, Grant Meston and Rose had to admit that no more evidence would be found.

However, at 2 a.m. or thereabouts in the morning, a person carrying a heavy bag down the path and then under the bridge could possibly have been seen by someone. Wendy knew it was back to knocking on doors.

Chapter 3

Confirmation had been received from Forensics: the blood retrieved at the site was from the body.

'It was early when the body was dumped. It must have been well wrapped as the blood discovered at the two locations was minimal,' Isaac said.

'But we found no sign of wrapping where the body was placed in the water,' Larry said.

'Which means they were careful in holding the body and the packaging over the water.'

'The divers?' Wendy asked.

'They're scouring the canal floor looking for anything, but the visibility is virtually zero, and the water's cold.'

'Could the packaging still be in the water?' Larry asked.

'Possible, but we're assuming it would have been plastic, more likely a heavy-duty rubbish bag, and they float. No way to hold them down, at least not without heavy weights.'

'Assume the divers will not find anything,' Isaac said. 'Focus on the neighbours, see if they saw anything suspicious: vehicles parked nearby, any noise.'

With little more to be said, Wendy headed back to the murder site.

Larry decided to follow up on the tattoo found on the back of the torso. He believed it was significant, and if the man had been a local, then someone may remember doing it. The area around Notting Hill seemed the best possibility. It was still early when he arrived, only a ten-minute drive from Challis Street. He decided to treat himself to an English breakfast in a café, hoping that his wife would not find out.

It's a long day, I'll need the energy, he thought in an attempt to justify his actions, knowing full well that she had packed two meals for the day in a lunch box, even if they were macrobiotic and devoid of meat.

The waitress at the café – he had been there before – asked him what case he was working on. Larry, always ready for a chat, told her. She expressed horror when he revealed some of the details and left him and his breakfast to each other.

Wendy was already out on the street. She had eight police officers to brief. 'We know where the body was taken down onto the towpath, which means a vehicle would have had to park near the corner of Westbourne Terrace Road Bridge and Warwick Crescent,' she said, as she stamped her feet attempting to stimulate her circulation.

The morning was cold, the first frost of the year, and her arthritis was giving her hell. She longed for a hot bath, but she knew that was not going to happen until much later in the day.

'It could have been carried here,' Jenny Arnett, the young constable who had discovered the blood on the towpath, said.

Smart woman, Wendy thought.

'Constable Arnett is right. It could have been carried here, but there are no signs of blood other than what we have found so far. It would have needed to be well packaged.'

'Bulky then,' another young constable said, although he had a cocky manner about him that Wendy did not warm to.

'Bulky, not easy to carry, and then there is the disposal of the packaging. We've found nothing so far.'

The weather was worsening, and a light drizzle fell on the assembled group. No one looked pleased to be there, especially Wendy, but she would do her duty. However, Jenny Arnett looked excited. Wendy decided to keep a look out for her, maybe bring her in with the Homicide team.

The team was divided into twos: the first two would continue down Westbourne Terrace Road as far as the junction of Delamere Street, a distance of eighty yards. The second team would check Delamere Terrace up as far as the junction of Bloomfield Villas, a distance of seventy yards. The third team would cross the bridge and move up Bloomfield Street, as far as the junction of Clifton Villas, a distance of one hundred and sixty yards; there were only houses on one side of the street. The fourth team would cross the bridge and turn right down Bloomfield Street heading as far as the junction of Warwick Avenue. Wendy and Jenny Arnett would focus on Warwick Crescent, which to Wendy seemed to offer the best possibility, as it was adjacent to where the body had been discovered. If the five teams returned a negative result, then the area of investigation would be expanded, possibly talking to the houseboat owners in the area, although Wendy did not see that as the priority. Apart from Jim Parson's houseboat, the only boats in between there and under the Westbourne Terrace Road Bridge was the Waterside Café, a former houseboat, but at two in the morning it had been locked up and empty, as had another boat moored in front of Parsons'.

***

DI Hill revived after his breakfast, feeling guilty that he would have to lie to his wife that night. He found that there were three tattoo shops in the area. He knew the possibility of finding the tattoo shop responsible was slim, especially after the pathologist had said that the spider's web had been crudely tattooed on the man's shoulder.

Harry's Tattoo Studio was eerie on entering, with the sound of the pens buzzing, the expression of the hapless person feeling the pain, regretting their decision. Some of the patrons displayed eagles on their backs; one young woman was having a butterfly engraved close to her breast. 'Not much I can tell you,' Harry said in between inflicting pain and wiping the area with a clean cloth.

'You've seen the design before?' Larry asked, showing the man a photo.

Harry, in his late fifties, covered in tattoos, even on his face, was an agreeable man, willing to talk. Larry liked the man, even if his appearance was unusual. 'It's common enough. I do it myself.'

'This one was crudely done,' Larry said.

'Then it wasn't me. I've won awards for my work.'

'Who would be most likely to have done it?'

'Crude?'

'Yes. That's what we believe.'

'Two options.'

'And they are?' Larry asked after the young woman had thanked Harry for her butterfly, paid her money and left the shop.

'You wouldn't want to know where some of the women want tattoos,' Harry said.

Larry could only surmise but decided not to ask the man to elaborate. 'Two options, you said.'

'Either the man has been in prison, the number of strands indicating how many years he's been inside, or he was a member of a gang, each strand representing a murder, a crime, or a rite of passage.'

'Rite of passage?' Larry asked.

'Not that I know a lot about gangs, although we get some in here from time to time, but a rite of passage would imply a murder or killing a member of a rival gang.'

'It's murder on both counts.'

'Not to them.'

'What do you mean?'

'Killing a rival gang member is not murder, only retribution. That would be a reason for celebration, not regret. You need to study up if you think the body was a gang member. And whatever you do, don't confront them unless you have a backup. They hate the police. They'd not hesitate to kill you,' Harry said. Larry knew how the gangs operated, their code of behaviour, but he decided not to mention it to the tattoo shop owner. And besides, another person was waiting for his leg to be tattooed. Larry had seen the design, wondered why someone would want a picture of a cartoon character.

Larry phoned Isaac on leaving the shop, the smell of burning flesh in his nose. 'What do you reckon?' Larry asked.

'We can check prison records, but I've not much confidence there. How many prisons, how many tattoos, and do they keep records?' Isaac said.

'They probably do from medical examinations, but a spider's web in prison: there are probably thousands.'

'Gangs in London?'

'No idea on that,' Larry said. 'I've come across them over the years. They're usually harmless, but in a group, they'll knife anyone who gets in their way. I had to deal with a gang war a few years back. Four deaths before it calmed down. Mind you, none of them would have been sorely missed; not many brain cells between the lot of them.'

'Dumping the body in Little Venice required some intelligence or at least a reason.'

'Are you discounting the gang member option?' Larry asked.

'Not entirely, just thinking out loud,' Isaac said. He was still in the office dealing with reports. Bridget Halloran was assisting. 'It required brain power to conceal the torso and then dump it. And why? Why not just dump it on a rubbish tip, bury it in a park? It's as if someone wanted it to be found; as if they wanted to send a message.'

'A message or just bragging?'

'Wendy's out knocking on doors. You obviously have an area of investigation.'

'And you, DCI?'

'Damn paperwork, and then I'll go and meet up with the pathologist again. From what you've said, he may be able to offer some more insight into how the tattoo was applied, what type of ink, type of pen.'

***

'Did you see anything between the hours of 1 a.m. and 3 a.m. yesterday?' Wendy asked for the twentieth time. The answer each time in the negative.

'I was fast asleep,' said the woman at the last door, the twenty-first. She was still in her dressing gown. Wendy could feel the heat radiating from inside the flat. 'You look cold,' the woman said. 'Fancy a cup of tea?'

Wendy entered the ground floor flat, glad of a respite from the biting cold. She was soaked from the constant drizzle.

'Take your shoes off and get yourself warm. I'm Marge Gregory, by the way.'

A cat jumped up on Wendy's lap. 'I've got two at home,' she said.

Jenny Arnett was down the other end of the street asking questions. Phone updates from the other teams had revealed nothing of interest. Wendy knew that if they drew blanks today, there would be another day on the street; the idea did not appeal to her.

'Here you are. I've put in two spoons of sugar. You look like a person who likes their tea sweet.'

Wendy did not comment that she used sweetener, and sugar was definitely off the agenda. *This one time won't matter*, she thought.

Twenty minutes later, Wendy was back out on the street. Jenny met her soon after. 'Nothing,' she said.

'It's not unexpected. Even if they're awake, they're distracted by a visit to the toilet, or checking emails.'

Before the two policewomen resumed their door knocking, the woman where Wendy had spent a pleasant break from policing duties opened her door. 'There was a car outside last night,' she said.

Jenny and Wendy went back into the ground floor flat. Jenny gladly accepted a cup of tea.

'The cat wanted to go out. I opened the door, and there was a car on the other side of the road. I never gave any thought to it, as most nights there are cars up and down the road.'

'Why didn't you remember before?' Wendy asked.

'Forgetful sometimes. My daughter wants to put me in a nursing home. I nearly burnt this place down once after I forgot to switch off the oven.'

Jenny realised the woman was describing the early signs of dementia.

'Mrs Gregory, tell us about the car,' Jenny said.

'It was blue.'

'Anything else?'

'It was the same as my daughter's. Although hers is a prettier colour.'

'Your daughter. What type of car does she drive?' Jenny asked.

'You'll have to ask her. I don't know anything about cars, never even learnt how to drive.'

'Do you have a phone number for your daughter?' Wendy asked.

'It's on a pad on the kitchen wall.'

Wendy went out to the kitchen, noted the daughter's number and dialled. The phone was answered: 'Lynn Gregory.'

Wendy explained the situation, obtained the details of the daughter's car. Lynn Gregory said she would be over within ten minutes to take her mother out of the house. Given her close proximity to a murder, as well as being a potential witness, the daughter did not want her mother to be on her own. Wendy could only concur.

'Blue Toyota Corolla,' Wendy said on her return.

'How many of those are there in London?' Jenny said.

'Thousands, but it's a start.'

'I saw a man,' Mrs Gregory said.

'And?' Wendy asked, exasperated that if Jenny had not been outside when she left Mrs Gregory's flat, and she had walked down the road to meet her, vital information would have been lost.

'He didn't see me.'

'Can you describe him?'

'It was dark. I remember a short man wearing a leather jacket.'

Wendy asked for another cup of tea, aware that in time the woman would remember some other piece of information: trivial to her, vital to the police investigation.

Twenty-five minutes later came a knock at the door. Lynn Gregory identified herself and kissed her mother on the cheek. She pulled Wendy over to one side. 'She's getting old. Her memory plays tricks on her.'

'We'll verify what she told us in due course.'

'Good. Just don't place too much credence on it though.'

As all four left the house, Mrs Gregory fussing over leaving her home, she looked over at the road. 'That's the colour,' she said, pointing to a car parked in front of her daughter's.

'Is that the car?' Jenny asked.

'Oh, no. The car was smaller, more like Lynn's.'

Wendy realised that it may not have been a Toyota Corolla that the old woman had seen, but the colour and the size were significant. Very early morning there would not have been too many vehicles on the road, and once outside of the residential area, there would be surveillance cameras, especially in areas of traffic control.

The teams reassembled close to the Waterfront Café to debrief. Apart from Wendy and Jenny, no one had any further information. Wendy declared the search concluded for the day.

As she was leaving, the owner of the Waterfront Café came over. 'I'm losing money,' he said. It was evident to Wendy that he was not in a good mood, but how he was losing money was unclear. The weather was atrocious, and of those walking along the street above, none were tourists looking for a coffee and a meal.

'It's a crime scene. If you've an issue, you'll have to take it up with our public relations department.'

'I will need compensating.'

Wendy gave him the number. *Fat chance*, she thought.

Chapter 4

'The tattoo interests us.' Isaac stood in Graham Pickett's office. The pathologist was sitting down behind his desk, the top of it covered in X-rays and reports.

'Why?'

'It may help to identify the body. Is it possible to determine how it was applied, the type of pen, the ink?'

'Forensics is working on it,' Pickett said. Isaac realised the man was almost friendly; the first time he had seen the man's countenance with anything closely resembling a smile.

Pickett phoned Martin Wallbridge, the forensic scientist who had been entrusted with analysing the tattoo. Wallbridge came over to Pickett's office and introduced himself to Isaac. To Isaac, he represented the nerdish scientist with pens in the top pocket of his white lab coat.

'We're one step ahead of you, and frankly, your people are always pushing for an early result,' Wallbridge said.

'You must be used to it now,' Isaac said.

'It's still irritating,' Pickett said.

'Sorry about that, but what can you tell us?'

'Crudely applied. The ink used was graphite mixed with water. It was done in prison,' Wallbridge said.

'That's what we thought. Are you certain?'

'Unless he was there on a day visit and decided to get a cheap tattoo,' Pickett said, reverting to type.

Wallbridge, a gentler man, answered straight after Pickett. 'In prison they have problems with the inks as well as the equipment necessary, so they improvise. Graphite, they get it from a pencil, and then they crush it and mix it with water. It works well enough. It's not the best quality, but in prison they don't have much choice.'

'What about colours?' Isaac asked.

'A pencil only comes in black. For colour, they'd need a gel roller pen, but they'd need to be careful. No metallic content or acrylic, and it has to be water soluble.'

'And the equipment?'

'They make their own: a motor from a play station, a biro, a bent toothbrush or a spoon, some electrical tape, and a needle.'

'Where would they get the needle?'

'Guitar string, sewing needle. As I said before, it's crude, but it works.'

'It sounds unpleasant,' Isaac said.

'It is,' Wallbridge replied.

'Does that answer your question?' Pickett asked. The man had a disinterested look as if he wanted his office back.

'Almost. Just one more question. Is it possible to tell which prison?'

Wallbridge looked up into the air before answering. 'Somewhere where the smuggling's under control, or else it would have been in colour.'

***

Isaac, back in the office, had another job for Bridget, once she was free from working with Wendy. Bridget was still the best CCTV viewing officer at Challis Street Police Station, and now there was a car to find.

Isaac spoke to Wendy. 'Any luck?'

'We're accessing the cameras now,' Wendy replied.

'Where are you looking?'

'The main entry points into the area. It was early, so we should be able to isolate the vehicle, assuming our source is reliable.'

'Is it?'

'Hard to say. The woman was vague, but she was adamant on the size and the colour. Anyway, we'll know soon enough. How about you, sir?'

'Some success. The man had spent time in prison.'

'That's a lot of people.'

'If you can identify a vehicle, as well as a registered owner, it might help to identify the body.'

'We'll try our best.'

'And once Bridget is finished with you, I need her to research prison databases.'

Isaac then phoned Larry. 'Where are you?'

'I'm checking out gangs in the area,' Larry replied.

'Are there many?'

'There's enough, mainly Jamaicans.'

'Forensics is sure the tattoo was done in prison.'

'Most gang members would know what the other side of prison bars looks like.'

'The spider's web indicates a lengthy term in jail.'

'It could still represent a rite of passage even if it was tattooed inside.'

Isaac could only agree with his DI's analysis. 'It may be a gang out of the area,' he said.

'I know a local gang leader who'll talk to me.'

'Why?'

'I've known him a long time.'

'Dangerous?'

'He owes me. I'll be safe with him.'

'Do you want me there?'

'Not a chance. He knows me, not you. If you're there, he'll clam up. Mind you, you could speak to him in Jamaican.'

'You mean English?'

'Yes, English.' Isaac knew what Larry meant. The gangs in London affected their own style of talking, and with Jamaicans that would mean the patois of their parents' home country.

***

Rasta Joe, not his real name but the only name the man with the dreadlocks answered to, was friendly on meeting Larry in the pub at midday.

'Mine's a pint,' the undisputed leader of his gang in Notting Hill said.

Larry knew that Rasta Joe had been born in London and that his parents were decent, upright citizens.

Larry wondered how Isaac had avoided being drawn into the gangs; he assumed his parents had been tenacious in keeping him away from their influence.

Most gang members were benign, only causing trouble when they were in a group or high on ganja. Larry knew that Rasta Joe was one tough Yardie, the colloquial Jamaican for a gang member, and he ruled with an iron fist, or a sharp blade, or, as Larry knew only too well, sometimes with a bullet.

The man had killed, would kill again, but he had been innocent of the crime for which he had been arrested. Larry had been the arresting officer when Rasta Joe had been charged with murder, although subsequent investigations had revealed that the man had been shacked up with his girlfriend that night; the evidence indisputable.

There were some in the police station who had wanted to let him be convicted, knowing full well that he had killed others before, and the streets would be better without his offensive presence. However, Larry had gone out on a limb and had stood up in court and confirmed that the man was innocent of the crime. Not that it helped the girlfriend, as the day after giving her evidence and proving Rasta Joe's alibi, her other boyfriend shot her. For that crime, there was no alibi, and the man was serving a life sentence in prison.

'Rasta Joe, you know about the body in Regent's Canal?'

'What's it got to do with me.'

'I never said it did.'

'And besides, that's not how we work. We're peaceful, law-abiding.'

Larry had heard it before. He knew that Rasta Joe was a drug dealer, a local villain, and he ran a few women down in Paddington. Regardless, Larry needed his help, even if the man was a villain of the first order.

'We know the dead man had served time in prison.'

'Is it true that he had no head?' Rasta Joe asked. He had his glass in front of him. If Larry wanted him to keep talking, it would cost another pint.

'No arms and legs, as well.'

'Whoever did it must have been a callous bastard.'

'Why do you say that?'

'To cut someone up like that.'

'Your people cut up others with knives.'

'Not my people.'

'Hypothetically,' Larry said.

'Some gangs might.'

'But not your gang?'

'Right-on,' Rasta Joe replied.

'Could the man in the canal have been a gang member?'

'Not from around here.'

'Why?'

'He was white.'

'Somewhere else?'

'It doesn't look to be a gang to me,' Rasta Joe said. 'They'd want to make sure the body wasn't found.'

Two more pints later, and Larry was feeling queasy, having matched the man pint for pint. He phoned Isaac. 'It seems unlikely to be gang related.'

'I didn't think it would be. It was worth checking,' Isaac said.

'Any luck with the vehicle?'

'Not yet. Bridget and Wendy are still working on it.'

***

Wendy, her arthritis better for sitting in a warm office with Bridget, watched the videos around the area of Little Venice. The primary locations that interested them were the junction of Harrow Road and Warwick Crescent, the junction of Harrow Road and Warwick Avenue, the junction of Bloomfield Road and Westbourne Terrace Road, and the intersection of Westbourne

Terrace Road and Warwick Crescent. Both Wendy and Bridget realised that they had not included all possible entries to the area, but there was not much they could do. A myriad of cameras were installed across London, but they were there for traffic flow, to catch errant speeders and cars running red lights; not to investigate a murder.

Still, the women were upbeat about the possibility of success, although it could be a couple of long days ahead.

Isaac was anxious for a result, as was Larry, who having exhausted his gangland killing theory was waiting for a new avenue of inquiry, although there was always paperwork back at the police station.

DCS Goddard kept up his regular phone calls, but so far he had kept his presence in the Homicide office to a minimum.

Bridget methodically worked her way through the video recordings. So far, she had seen several cars that matched the information received from Mrs Gregory, although they had been discounted as they had either pulled into a driveway or had transited the area.

'What about that one?' Wendy asked the one time that she had squinted her eyes to focus on the computer monitor. Bridget, if she had not been her friend, would have asked her to let her concentrate.

'It's possible,' Bridget had to admit. A blue car could be seen at the intersection of Harrow Road and Warwick Avenue; the time was 1.42 a.m. Its colour was the same as described by the old lady, a street lamp illuminating the vehicle.

Bridget checked the junction of Harrow Road and Warwick Crescent, a distance of sixty yards. The blue car was clearly visible. Forwarding the video slowly, the car could be seen turning into Warwick Crescent.

Realising that the car represented their best possibility, Bridget looked for cameras closer to where the body had been dumped. There were none. Undaunted by the temporary setback, Bridget and Wendy continued to check. Eleven minutes later, the vehicle could be seen at the roundabout of Clifton Villas and Warwick Avenue.

'That's the car,' Wendy said. 'It's had time to dump the body.'

'It's not a Toyota,' Bridget said. 'More likely a Hyundai.'

'Don't worry about that. It's our vehicle. I'm sure of it. Any chance of a registration number?'

A traffic light camera on the junction of Edgware Road and St John's Wood Road had picked up the number plate four minutes later, although it had taken Bridget another three hours to find it.

'GK52 YJQ. It's a blue Hyundai i30,' Wendy said on the phone to Isaac.

Isaac quickly called Larry who put out an all-points warning for the vehicle. Within fifteen minutes, all police cars within London equipped with automatic number plate recognition cameras were focussed on looking for the Hyundai. The legal owner, a vicar in Maidstone, Kent, where it had been first registered, was soon contacted. 'In my driveway at home,' he said when the police phoned his mobile. At a religious retreat in Cornwall, he was surprised when told about his car being in London; shocked when informed that it had probably been involved in a serious crime. Larry did not tell him that it had transported a dismembered body in the boot.

One hour later, the vehicle was pulled over by a police car, the driver was taken into custody, the vehicle sent to Forensics.

After a short period in the cells at a police station in Surbiton to the south of the city, the driver was transferred in handcuffs to Challis Street.

Vicenzo Pinto, a short man wearing a leather jacket, preferred to be called Vince. Isaac read him his rights in the interview room and offered him legal aid and a free lawyer, which he declined. 'I've done nothing wrong,' he said.

Both Isaac and Larry were confident they had their man, although his mild-mannered appearance and his disarming politeness belied a man capable of mutilating a body.

'On the night of the twenty-ninth of October at approximately 1.48 a.m. in the morning, you drove up Warwick Crescent in Little Venice,' Isaac said.

'Not me, DCI.' The man who was close to being charged with murder sat on his chair with a broad smile.

'We have photographic evidence that a blue Hyundai i30, registration GK52 YJQ, did travel along Harrow Road and turn into Warwick Crescent.'

'I've never been to Little Venice. The big one, yes, many times.'

'This is a serious matter,' Larry said. 'The vehicle you were driving had been stolen. Also, subject to Forensics confirming it, the body of a male between the ages of thirty and thirty-nine was in the boot of the car. We have been told that there are traces of blood.'

'I bought the car,' Pinto replied.

A knock on the door. Bridget entered. 'Gordon Windsor is on the phone,' she said.

Isaac paused the interview and left the room with Larry.

'Confirmed?' Isaac asked on the phone.

'It's the same blood group. Subject to DNA, I'm almost one hundred per cent sure that you have the right vehicle.'

Isaac and Larry re-entered the interview room.

'We have confirmation that the vehicle you were apprehended in did transport the dismembered body of an adult male. You do realise what this means?'

'I didn't know what it was.'

'Were you curious?'

'I had to do it.'

'Unless you are able to convince us that you did not kill the man or dismember him, then I will be charging you with murder. You do understand what this means?'

'I understand, but I didn't kill him.'

'Then why did you put the body in the canal.'

'I had to, or else it would have been me.'

'They would have killed you?'

'Yes.'

'Are you ready to give a written statement?'

'I need a lawyer.'

'Legal aid?'

'I've got no money.'

Isaac adjourned the interview for two hours while a lawyer was found. Pinto was returned to the cells. A pizza was delivered to him. His smile had disappeared.

***

Bridget and Wendy were basking in the glory of a personal phone call from Detective Chief Superintendent Goddard to each of them.

'Good work,' Isaac said when they walked in.

'Something else, sir?' Bridget asked.

'We need to know the identity of the body.'

'The man in the cells?' Wendy asked. 'Won't he tell you?'

'He's not the killer,' Isaac said.

'He may still know who he was.'

'We need to know the history of the dead man. We know that the spider's web tattoo on the man's shoulder was done in prison. The ink was graphite. What we need to know, assuming our man down below doesn't, is which prison and who he was, as well as known associates.'

'Any ideas how we should do this, sir?' Bridget asked.

'Two suggestions: prisons that maintain a rigid control on smuggling, and amateur tattooists who are locked up.'

'Why the interest in smuggling?' Wendy asked.

'The tattoo is black, which indicates that either the man did not want colour or they were unable to smuggle it in. Check for confiscated special tattoo inks or gel roller pens. It's a long shot, but prison records are extensive. An amateur tattooist, strictly illegal but probably known by the authorities, would have needed to construct a tattoo pen. Yet again, not difficult, but the parts would need to be sourced.'

Chapter 5

At 2.30 p.m. the interview with Vicenzo Pinto, alias Vince, resumed. Katrina Hatcher, his lawyer, had spent one hour with her client briefing him on his rights. She had also been given the file documenting his arrest, and the murder enquiry to date.

'Vicenzo Pinto, are you ready to make a statement?' Isaac asked.

'Yes.'

'I have a written statement from my client,' Katrina Hatcher said. 'I would like it added to the records.' Isaac noted that she was a smartly-dressed woman, obviously sharp as a tack, and well in control of the situation.

'Please continue,' Isaac said.

'My name is Vicenzo Pinto. My date of birth is the 3rd July 1975, and I was born in Verona, Italy. I came to England in 1977 with my parents. I am innocent of all crimes. I admit placing an item in Regent's Canal. I was unaware as to what it was as it was dark. I was following instructions.

'The car, which you tell me was stolen, was given to me for that job. I did not look in the boot before arriving in Little Venice. At Little Venice, I removed the package, carried it down to the water's edge under the bridge, opened the plastic bag, and released the contents. I then returned to the car and left. That is the end of my statement.'

Isaac looked at the lawyer. 'It won't hold up in a Court of Law.'

'My client has made a preliminary statement to confirm his innocence. He is open to further questioning, but let me remind you that he is innocent until proven guilty.'

'Your client is about to be charged as an accessory to murder. I hope that has been explained to him.'

'My client will make a full disclosure of all that he knows.'

Isaac once again focussed his eyes on Pinto. 'You are aware of the seriousness of this?'

Larry sat quietly to Isaac's side. He could see that his DCI was trying to break through Pinto's smugness.

'I am aware,' Pinto replied sombrely.

Isaac continued. 'On the night of the twenty-ninth you dumped the torso of a man in Regent's Canal.'

'I never knew what it was.'

'What else could it be?' Larry said, his tone less friendly than Isaac's. The lawyer said nothing, only observed and listened.

'I had to do it,' Pinto said.

'Why?'

'They'll kill me if I tell you.'

'And if you don't, how many years in prison?' Isaac posed a rhetorical question. 'Ten years as an accessory. And if the jury believes you were involved in the murder, then it's life. Do you understand?'

'Prison is better than what they'll do to me.'

'Are you saying that you would rather spend the rest of your life in jail.'

'I know what they did to him.'

'Him? Does he have a name?'

'They'll kill me if I tell you.'

'You've already said that,' Larry reminded Pinto.

'My client will not respond to you two playing the good cop, bad cop routine.'

Isaac smiled. He and his former DI, Farhan Ahmed, had had the patter off to a tee; Larry had not yet perfected the technique.

'I suggest,' Isaac said, 'that you inform your client of the seriousness of this matter.'

'My client is well aware. However, he is frightened for his life.'

'We can ensure that he is protected.'

'Not in prison, you can't,' Pinto said.

'It may be possible to avoid prison if you assist us.'

'If they know that I've told you anything, then I'm a dead man, and I don't want to end up like him.'

'Him? Who is he?'

'I'm not talking.'

'And if you walk out of here now, free as a bird?'

'They'll know I've talked.'

'Unless you speak now, I'll ensure that I will personally escort you out of Challis Street Police Station and thank you for your assistance.'

'You wouldn't do that!' an alarmed voice said.

'This is unacceptable,' Katrina Hatcher said. 'You're threatening my client.'

'I agree,' Isaac said. 'He's free to go. I'll escort him out of the police station now.'

'You can't do that,' Pinto said.

'Once you've gone, I'll put the word out on the street that we have a name for the torso, and a list of potential murderers.'

'I'll be dead within an hour, chopped up like he was.'

'He?' Larry asked, realising that the man was about to crack.

'I only knew him as Dave. That's the honest truth.'

'Why was he killed?' Isaac asked.

'He cheated on them.'

'Them?'

'I can't tell you.'

'Okay, that's fine. Thanks for your assistance. You're free to go.'

'You're sending me to my death.'

'Have you seen a photo of Dave's body, or what remained of it?' Larry asked.

'No. It was dark under that bridge, spooky even. I just did what I was told and left.'

Isaac realised that some gentle questioning would disarm the man further. 'What was the significance of Regent's Canal?'

'They wanted to send a clear message.'

'Why?'

'If you cheat them, that's what happens to you.'
'And Dave cheated?'
'Yes.'
'So why were you given the job of dumping him?'
'We were both cheating, only they decided to kill one of us, scare the other.'
'Are there others involved?' Larry asked.
'There are a few.'
'Were you there when Dave was killed?' Isaac asked. Pinto's lawyer was observing intently, saying little. Isaac and Larry were conducting the interview of the now-nervous Pinto according to police procedures.
'I saw him die.'
'Was he alive when they chopped him up?'
'They shot him in the head first.'
'Any idea where the head is now?' Isaac asked.
'No. That's the truth. Don't put me in prison, please,' Pinto said.
'There's only one chance for you: the full truth.'
'It's too late.'
'Why do you say that?'
'If you catch some of them, there'll always be more. They're like ants scurrying across the ground. They're vermin.'
'Who are they?'
'Charge me, lock me up in your prison cell. I've no more to say.'
'Miss Hatcher, I suggest that you consult with your client. We will take a ten-minute break,' Isaac said.

***

'What do you reckon?' Larry asked outside the interview room.
'Who or what could scare a man like that?' Isaac asked.
'A crime syndicate probably, but do we have any that vicious in London?'
'We've got everything here. We need to dig deeper, find someone who understands the dark underbelly of the city.'

The two men drank coffee from the machine in the hallway; it tasted awful, but there was no time to go out for anything better. A police officer had taken in drinks for Vicenzo Pinto and his lawyer. Katrina Hatcher had asked for a ten-minute extension. Isaac took the opportunity to phone DCS Goddard with an update, and to call his sergeant, Wendy Gladstone.

Goddard, as expected, was full of praise, looking for an early wrap-up on the murder case. Wendy, more circumspect, was anxious for a clear direction.

'According to Pinto, the dead man's name was Dave.'
'Did he give you a surname?' Wendy asked.
'He said he didn't know.'
'Do you believe him?'
'Not sure. The man is frightened to tell us more.'
'Bridget has been checking prison records, but a spider's web tattoo is nothing special. I don't think Dave will help her much,' Wendy said.
'Just keep trying.'

***

Thirty minutes passed before the interview recommenced. Isaac could see that Vince Pinto was calmer.

'My client wishes to make a statement,' Katrina Hatcher said.

'Dave and I became involved with a crime syndicate. I only knew him for six months, but we were friends. He came from Liverpool; that's all I ever knew, and I never knew his real name. He sometimes called himself Dave Simmonds, other times it was Doug Fairweather. He did not talk about himself, and I had no idea if he had been married or had children.

'We'd just done a run, decided to cream some off the top for ourselves. There was plenty, and we thought no one would notice. However, we didn't count on a snotty-nosed accountant they employed. They picked us up as we were enjoying a quiet drink at a pub. Although with Dave it was never quiet.'

'Why do you say it was never quiet?' Isaac asked.

'Dave was not a drinker, no more than a couple of pints, but he was sociable and loud.'

'The pub?'

'It varied, but most times it was the Pride of Paddington, down on Craven Road.'

'I know it,' Larry said.

'You have no criminal record. Why were you involved with a crime syndicate?' Isaac asked.

'You'll find out soon enough. I'm a gambler, not very good either. It's an addiction. I've been to Gamblers' Anonymous, but it makes no difference.'

'What type of gambling?' Larry asked.

'Horses, greyhounds, cards, poker machines. Most of the time it's under control, but occasionally…'

'A lot of money?' Isaac asked.

'More than I could hope to cover.'

'Were you set up?'

'Probably. That's how they get people to work for them.'

'Do they have a name?'

'Those in charge remain hidden. The only people I ever saw were the underlings. Whoever is behind this is very secretive, possibly very powerful and influential.'

'What happened?'

'I'm down nearly one hundred thousand pounds and no way to cover my debt.'

'Where was this?'

'Down near Camden, a seedy gambling joint. I was playing poker and badly. Anyway, there I am, and there's no way I'm leaving, at least walking.'

'They would have killed you?'

'A dead man can't be bled for money, but they would have smashed my knees.'

'You're still walking,' Larry said.

'The club sold my debt. I was there for two hours with two heavies breathing over me, threatening to pummel me, roughing me up. I even peed in my trousers; I was that frightened.'

'Why are you telling us this now?'

'I'm dead whatever happens. If I leave here, they'll know I've spoken. At least in prison my death won't be the same as Dave's.'

'Did you see him die?'

'Yes.'

'And when he was cut up?'

'I was there, but I didn't take part. There were two of them who went at him with a chainsaw.'

'Why the dismemberment?'

'A warning to those who disobeyed or cheated on them, and also to anyone who talks to the police.'

'Coming back to the club,' Isaac said. The lawyer said nothing.

'After two hours, a man comes in. He's dressed in a dark blue suit, or at least I think it was, as he remained partially hidden. He spoke with an educated accent.'

'And then what?'

'He made me an offer. If I came and worked for the organisation that he represented, my debt would be absolved.'

'You accepted?'

'What could I do? I knew I was not leaving there in one piece if I refused.'

'Then what happened?'

'He pushed some documents across the table, and I signed the last page, initialled the others.'

'What did it say?'

'Are you kidding? I just signed, that's all.'

'After that were you free to go?'

'They kept a watch on me. There'll be someone outside this station.'

'Do you have a name for the man in the suit?'

'He kept his face hidden, and no, he did not give a name.'

'Would you recognise him again if you saw him?'

'The voice maybe.'

'Describe him?'

'Average height, well dressed, spoke with an educated accent, and his nails were manicured. That's all I can tell you.'

'Do you know his position in the crime syndicate?'

'No. I assume he was someone paid to deal with people like me. As I told you, the big men remain hidden behind a veil of invisibility. Catch them, and you've caught some big fish, but they'll be able to wriggle out of it.'

'Why do you say that?'

'That's what the suit said, and he wasn't a man to mince words.'

'What kind of criminal activity are we talking about here?'

'Drugs, more drugs than you can imagine.'

'Dave was a gambler?' Isaac asked.

'He was just a man down on his luck. He said he'd been in jail for a crime he didn't commit, but I didn't believe him.'

'That he'd been in prison?'

'No, I believed that, but a crime he didn't commit. If you let out all the prisoners in jail that said that, you wouldn't have anyone left inside. He could be a violent bastard sometimes.'

'You saw this violence?'

'Once. We were drinking, minding our own business, when a drunk comes over and tries to pick a fight with Dave.'

'Did Dave provoke him?'

'No, he minded his own business. Anyway, the drunk is getting difficult; Dave's ignoring him. The drunk grabs Dave by the collar, aiming to pull him around. Dave loses his temper and smashes the guy in the face. Ten minutes later, Dave's as calm as a leaf, drinking a pint.'

It was six in the evening. Isaac did not intend to postpone the interview until the next day, but everyone was in need of food. Pinto was talking, and there were still more questions to ask. Isaac called a halt to the interview and ordered food for everyone: the standard diet for a long night in the police station, pizza.

Once everyone was fed, Isaac was back into his questioning. He could see that Pinto was falling asleep, the result of a good feed and a long day. Not that Isaac intended to ease off. This was his arena, somewhere he had succeeded many times in cracking the toughest nut. And from what he could see, Pinto was a very tough nut.

Vicenzo Pinto had no criminal record, apart from a succession of speeding fines and parking tickets, but no history of violence, and certainly nothing to suggest that he was any more than a minor functionary in the drug syndicate. The most the man had achieved in life was to work in a burger bar, and as for educational qualifications, there were none.

If the crime syndicate was as well organised as Pinto had said, then it needed smart people, and there was the man who had thrust the papers in front of Pinto to sign. If he was only another employee, then who was in charge? Who was Mr Big?

Isaac had grown weary of arresting the minor players, having them charged and convicted, only to know that the main culprit remained free and at large. In a previous case two of the murders had been government sanctioned, yet an abused woman resided in prison for the killing of another. She had had a reason to hate the man, not that it abrogated her from the crime, but there had been two other murders and those responsible for the assassinations had no doubt received a pat on the back for a job well done.

'Let me come back to the syndicate,' Isaac said. 'You've told us that they are involved with drugs.'

'That's what I said.'

'What type of drugs?'

'Heroin, and lots of it. Sometimes cocaine.'

'What was your function in the syndicate?'

'It varied, but most times I was transporting it from one place to the next.'

'In the UK?'

'Mainly, but sometimes in France.'

'Let us start with France. We are aware that you made three trips there in the last six months.'

'If I tell you, they'll kill me.'

'And if you don't, they will anyway. Your only hope is to place your trust in us.'

Katrina Hatcher leant over towards her client. 'The DCI is right.'

'I know that,' Pinto said.

'If you work with us, we'll ensure that your prison sentence will be lenient.'

'You want me to grass?'

'For a man with no criminal record, you've certainly picked up the lingo.'

'That's Dave. He had a colourful turn of phrase. No doubt from all the time he spent in prison.'

'How long was that?'

'He said eight years, but I don't know if it was true. He said he was going to get the bastard who put him there.'

'What did he mean? The man who stitched him up, the police officer who arrested him, or the judge who put him in jail?'

'After a few pints, he would talk, but it was never very much. I've no idea, and that's the honest truth.'

'Let's return to France,' Isaac said.

'I would go there, pick up a truck and bring it back.'

'And the trucks were loaded with drugs?'

'Well hidden.'

'Customs checks on entering England?'

'They were only interested in case we'd picked up some Afghans in Calais. Anyway, if they had stripped the vehicles down, they would have been hard pushed to find anything.'

'Why?'

'I saw how they did it once, a welded compartment inside the transmission housing. Also, they had welded on extra parts that looked like the chassis. It was dead easy.'

'How much would you carry?'

'At least fifty kilos of heroin, as well as cocaine,' Pinto said.

'That's five million pounds on the street,' Larry, who had left the questioning since they had resumed to Isaac, said.

'Each trip had that much heroin?' Isaac asked.

'I only saw what they took out that one time.'

'If you made three trips, that's close to fifteen million pounds.'

'Maybe it is, but I was only concerned about the money I owed them and my life. I knew they were vicious.'

'How? Apart from threatening you when you owed money due to your poker playing, you've not mentioned any other violence.'

'They were always threatening.'

'But you and Dave still decided to cheat them?'

'We were desperate. Dave had driven a truck over from France. He phoned me up from Dover, let me know that one of their hiding places was visible, and would I be interested in going halves with him.'

'You agreed?'

'I needed the money. I wanted to go back to what I was doing before.'

'Flipping burgers?' Larry said.

'With the drugs we took, there was enough to buy my own business, even go to Italy; get away from those bastards.'

Isaac looked up at the clock; it was 8.30 p.m. The questioning had been going for eight hours. All the participants were exhausted, but he was determined to continue. Pinto appeared not to be guilty of murder and had been compromised due to his gambling debts. However, Dave seemed to have been someone in need of a job and money. If the eight years in prison was correct, it might be possible to trace him.

'Did you ever take a photo of Dave?' Isaac asked.

'On my phone.'

'Where is it?'

'Outside. One of your officers took it before I was slammed up in here.'

Isaac halted the interview, and he and Larry went to find the phone. Pinto and his lawyer waited in the interview room. A cup of tea was given to both of them.

The two police officers retrieved the phone and returned to the interview room. 'Show us,' Isaac said.

Pinto scrolled through his photos. 'That's him.'

Larry forwarded the image to Bridget who was still in the office with Wendy.

'Interview concluded at 8.50 p.m. We will resume tomorrow morning at 8 a.m. prompt,' Isaac said.

Pinto was returned to his cell. Katrina Hatcher left the building ten minutes later, but not before speaking to Isaac. 'My client is innocent of murder,' she said.

'He's admitted to drug smuggling, disposing of a body.'

'You cannot charge him with murder.'

'Let's see,' Isaac said.

Chapter 6

Isaac and Larry walked up the two flights of stairs to the Homicide office. It was late. Isaac remembered that he had arranged to meet with Jess, an attempt to rekindle their romance. He phoned her. 'Forget it,' the only two words she said. He knew by the way it was said that she was referring to the romance, not the fact that he was standing her up again. It seemed to him that a normal life with the woman he wanted was not possible.

'Bad day, sir?' Wendy asked. She had seen the look on her DCI's face as he walked in the door.

'Personal issues,' Isaac's reply.

'You need to find someone else. It's not going to work out, you know that.'

'I suppose I do, but…'

'If she can't put up with the hours you work, there's no more to be said. It's best to call it quits and for her to get on with her life; you to get on with yours.'

Isaac was thankful for his sergeant's concern, but now there was a more pressing issue. Who was Dave?

'We have a name, the time he spent in prison, a tattoo and a photo,' Isaac said to the team.

'I've already instigated a database search on the picture. I'm sure we'll have a result within a couple of hours,' Bridget said.

'Why don't you go home, sir?' Wendy said. 'We can always phone you.'

The idea appealed to Isaac, but his mood was not conducive to relaxing after another bust up with Jess, his on-again, off-again girlfriend. He still wanted her, but it had happened yet again: the chance of a romantic interlude and he had chosen a murder investigation. It was inevitable in that it would always be the same as long as he stayed with the police force. Maybe when he made detective superintendent he could back off a little, but that seemed to be a few more years in the future, and Jess O'Neill, broody and wanting a child, would be gone by then.

Isaac knew he would not be going home. He looked at the paperwork in front of him, he spoke to Larry, he looked over the shoulders of Bridget and Wendy, but mostly he sat quietly, pensively waiting for a result: the result that would drive the case forward.

If the crime syndicate was as vicious as they appeared to be, then who were they, and why hadn't he heard of them before?

'Larry,' Isaac said as he went over and sat at the desk next to his, 'we need to find out about large shipments of drugs into this country. Who's the best person to talk to?'

'We could get someone from Serious and Organised Crimes Command.'

'Agreed. What about your gang leader?'

'He'll know about the distribution of the drugs on the street, but he's not likely to be able to tell us much else. He's only small fry, a local hustler.'

'Talk to him anyway. He'll have his ear to the ground.'

'He won't talk to me too openly, you know that.'

'He will if he believes the syndicate is threatening him.'

'Are they?'

'Who knows. The body was meant to be discovered.'

'To frighten others involved in the crime syndicate?'

'I'll meet up with Rasta Joe again,' Larry said. 'You can't believe the earbashing I received the last time at home after I came in smelling of beer, and he likes to drink.'

'At least she's there for you,' Isaac said.

'I've found him,' an excited voice shouted from the other side of the room.

Both Isaac and Larry moved over to Bridget's desk. The woman had a broad smile on her face. 'Wandsworth Prison.'

'Do you have a name?' Isaac asked.

'Dougal Stewart.'

'What else can you tell us?'

'He served nine years for armed robbery. A man was killed, although Stewart was not responsible. They released him six months ago.'

'Great work,' Isaac said.

Thirty minutes later, close to midnight, the four police officers left the station.

Isaac would phone his DCS as he drove home.

***

'We have a name for your friend Dave,' Isaac said after the interview with Pinto had reconvened at 8 a.m. Katrina Hatcher was sitting alongside her client.

'I only knew him as Dave,' Pinto replied. The man looked as though he had had a restless night.

'Dougal Stewart spent nine years in Wandsworth Prison.'

'Was that his name?' the lawyer asked.

'We have prison records to confirm that Dave and Dougal Stewart were one and the same person.'

'That's the first time I've heard Dougal,' Pinto said.

'You stated that you had both been cheating,' Isaac said.

'I told you that before.'

'Did you not realise that they would have records of what was being transported?'

'There's always some cheating, especially with drugs, so we assumed they'd not be concerned with a short shipment.'

'But they were?'

'Yes. They found us at the pub.'

'What happened?'

'Two men we've seen when we delivered the merchandise came into the pub. They were friendly. Dave bought them each a pint.'

'After that?'

'We stayed there drinking with them. They bought some drinks; we bought some. After a few hours, we left the pub. As we were about to get into Dave's car, he had an old four-wheel drive, they grabbed us.'

'I thought Dave was a strong man.'

'They coshed him over the back of the head and bundled him and me into the back of Dave's vehicle. We had our hands behind our backs, tied with cable ties. They also had cable ties around our ankles. We're there trussed up like turkeys. I'm freaking out until one of the two men turned around and smashed me over the head with a cosh. I'm out for the count, and I don't remember any more until we arrive at this warehouse.'

'And then what?' Isaac asked.

'There's Dave to one side of me. They have him strung up, his hands tied by a piece of rope hanging down from the ceiling.'

'And you?'

'I'm tied to a metal beam. They've made sure that my feet are barely touching the ground. I'm in terrible pain. There's a man in the corner. He's hidden from view.'

'Did he speak?'

'Oh, yes. He spoke.'

Katrina Hatcher looked apprehensive, almost as if she knew what Pinto was going to say. Isaac could see the colour draining out of her face.

'What did he say, the man in the corner?' Isaac asked.

'"You know what happens to those who steal from us."'

'What did you say?'

'I said I was innocent. Dave tried to blame me.'

'They didn't believe you?'

'Of course not. We were guilty, we knew that. All I could think of was to protect myself. Trust me, I regretted my miserable life at that point. I could see our two previous drinking friends were anxious for some action. Dave was protesting his innocence repeatedly. One of the two heavies smashed his fist into Dave's ribs. I swear I could hear them breaking. One of the heavies comes over to me. "Are you innocent?" he asked.'

'What did you do?'

'I confessed, told them where we had hidden the stolen drugs. I begged them for my life.'

'They let you go?'

'No. They left me tied to the beam.'

'And Dave?'

'One of the heavies shot him in the head. I wet myself. The two heavies laughed. After that, they cut Dave down and went at him with a chainsaw. There was blood everywhere.'

Katrina Hatcher excused herself from the room; she was holding a handkerchief over her mouth. Isaac halted the interview for thirty minutes until everyone had revived after Pinto's graphic description of Dougal Stewart's murder.

***

It was evident to Isaac they were dealing with some very nasty people. He assumed that if they killed with such brutality, they would have no aversion to killing a police officer. He warned his team to be careful. Wendy had found out the last known address of Dougal Stewart. Isaac asked her to wait for Larry, another hour at least.

The interview with Pinto resumed, his lawyer still looking the worse for wear.

'You've mentioned a warehouse,' Isaac said. Pinto sat glumly, the initial cockiness long gone.

'I didn't see where it was on the way there; they had coshed me. I was out for the count.'

'But you took the body or what was left of Stewart from there.'

'Yes.'

'So you know where it is.'

'Do you want me dead?' Pinto asked.

'You know that your best hope of survival lies with us,' Isaac said, although he did not believe it. Whoever was behind the crime syndicate ruled by fear, not idle threats. Out on the street, Pinto was a dead man. Inside the secure walls of a prison, he was dead as well.

Isaac knew that he had to solve a murder and break a crime syndicate which, on the face of it, was extensive, well funded, and well hidden.

Pinto discussed the situation with his lawyer. She advised a frank and open disclosure of all that he knew. Pinto did not agree, although he had no better solution. He still hoped for his future; realised that it might not last for very long.

'The warehouse was in Ladbroke Grove,' Pinto said.

'Address?' Larry asked.

'Canal Way. You can't miss it. It's the only place there.'

Isaac halted the interview and left the room. 'Canal Way, Ladbroke Grove,' he said on the phone to Wendy. 'Make sure you take sufficient uniforms. Be prepared for a lot of blood, and ensure the place is secure before entering.'

'Is that where Dougal Stewart died?' Wendy asked. She had been sitting in the office waiting for instructions.

'It is according to Pinto. Once secured, get Gordon Windsor and his CSE team down there, and don't let anyone destroy the evidence with their flat feet.'

Wendy did not need instructions on what to do, although she could judge that Isaac was pumped with success. After the warehouse had been checked, there was Stewart's flat to visit.

Isaac returned to the interview room. 'Is that where they gave you the car with Stewart in the boot?' he asked Pinto.

Pinto was aware that once the police were swarming over the scene of his former drinking pal's dismemberment, there would be no way that he could conceal his confession to the police. He was a troubled man.

'Yes,' Pinto said.

'And you drove from there to Regent's Canal?'

'Yes. The two heavies kept me company at the warehouse for an hour or so, told me what would happen to me if I didn't do what they said.'

'This mysterious man, what happened to him?'

'He left.'

'Did you get a clear look at him?'

'No. Only that he drove a late model Jaguar.'

'How do you know?'

'I saw it out of the window.'

'The two heavies, what can you tell us about them?' Larry asked.

'The more aggressive of the two was an Irishman by the name of Devlin. The other one, hard as nails, called himself Steve. Apart from that, I don't know much about them, other than they drink in the Pride of Paddington on a Friday night, the same as we did.'

Isaac realised they had almost concluded the interview, and there was plenty to follow up on. One last question remained. 'Why was there so little blood at Regent's Canal?'

'They put what was left of Dave in a freezer for some time. I suppose that must be the reason.'

'The packaging? What did you carry the body in?'

'A garbage bag, one of those heavy-duty ones you put in your dustbin.'

'And where is it now?'

'I dumped it in a rubbish skip not far from the canal.'

'Do you know where?'

'Not the address.'

'Could you find it again?'

'Yes.'

'Larry,' Isaac said. 'Take a couple of cars, some uniforms and our friend here. See if you can find it.'

'No problem,' Larry said. 'It won't do us much good though.'

'Agreed, but it may help to corroborate Pinto's story.'

'What about me?' Pinto asked.

'You will be charged with aiding and abetting in the murder of Dougal Stewart. There will be a further charge of drug trafficking.'

'Is that it?' Katrina Hatcher asked.

'I am willing to believe that your client was not involved in the murder of Dougal Stewart. However, he will be remanded in prison awaiting trial.'

Pinto's lawyer looked over at him. 'I may be able to get you bail,' she said.

'Don't bother. I'm a dead man walking,' Pinto replied.

***

By the time Isaac and Larry returned to the office, Wendy was preparing to leave. Pinto had been formally charged and would be transferred out of the cells at Challis Street Police Station to a prison, pending trial. Before Pinto's transfer, Larry needed to take him to find the plastic bag that Stewart's torso had been wrapped in, although the visit out to the warehouse described by Pinto was more immediate.

Three vehicles converged on the warehouse on Canal Way. Larry had driven with Wendy in the passenger seat. The other two unmarked cars carried four men in each, all armed in case of trouble. The first of the two vehicles entered the forecourt of the warehouse after breaking the chain securing the metal gates at the front with hydraulic bolt cutters. The second car then drove through with the first car following. Larry and Wendy remained outside on the street at a secure distance.

Five minutes later, Larry's phone rang. 'It's all clear.'

Larry moved forward and drove through the front gate of the warehouse. It looked modern but unused. A police officer, a gun still in his hand, let them in. 'No one here,' he said.

Wendy phoned Gordon Windsor first. 'You need to bring your team over,' she said.

'Any sign of blood?' Windsor asked.

'We're securing the area for you. It's a big place.'

'Keep everyone out of there.'

'Some of our men needed to check it out, but they've been careful.'

'Thirty minutes and we'll be there.'

Wendy and Larry, careful to ensure they were wearing foot protectors, moved around the warehouse. Two uniforms were securing the area. One of the two cars that had accompanied them had left.

It was evident that the building had been empty for some time, a clear indication of the downturn in the economy. In one office, they found signs that it had stored furniture at one time. The place was as hollow as a grave, their voices echoing as they spoke. A lone pigeon sat high up on a beam. At the back, close to a rear entrance, they found their proof.

The floor in a rear store room was covered in blood. A piece of rope hung from the ceiling. 'That must be where they strung up Dougal Stewart,' Larry said.

Wendy surveyed the scene, smelt the blood and the dead flesh. She left and found an open door out to the rear of the building and vomited. Larry remained at the scene, careful not to move in any closer. He could see a chainsaw, and what appeared to be a bloodied mess; he knew what he was looking at. He left and went to join Wendy. He needed fresh air and plenty of it.

'Sorry, DI. Too much for me,' Wendy said. She had a cigarette in her mouth. 'I haven't had one for two weeks.'

'If you've got another one…' Larry replied.

Gordon Windsor arrived shortly after with Grant Meston and Rose Denning. Windsor took one look at the scene. 'Pretty grim,' he said.

Another three crime scene investigators were checking the rest of the warehouse.

Windsor moved into the crime scene, taking photos as he went. Rose Denning was documenting, taking fingerprints, shoe prints. Grant Meston confirmed that the chainsaw was almost certainly used in the dismemberment of Dougal Stewart.

To Larry that was stating the obvious. The chainsaw was barely recognisable, covered as it was in dried blood. Meston picked it up, tagged it and ensured it was ready to transport to Forensics. 'We'll check that it's Stewart's blood later,' he said.

Larry could see the beam that Pinto had described. The smell in the room was horrendous, so much so that he retreated again. Wendy stayed outside, not willing to return.

Rose Denning moved around the scene, oblivious to the carnage, the barbarism that had occurred.

'How can you take it?' Larry asked.

'I'm just focussed, that's all. Don't come looking for me later in the day,' she said.

'Why?'

'I'll have my head over a sink, blubbering like a child.'

'Delayed reaction?'

'Yes. That's it.'

Windsor moved around the outside of the room, careful where he stepped. He looked at the bloody mess that Larry had seen earlier from a distance. 'Good God!' he said.

'What is it?' Grant Meston asked.

'It's a head.'

'Dougal Stewart?' Larry asked.

'We'll need to get it to Pathology. Not much I can tell you here.'

Chapter 7

Larry and Wendy returned to Challis Street. Gordon Windsor and his team were occupied at the warehouse in Ladbroke Grove.

Vicenzo Pinto was led out of the police station later that morning and placed in the back seat of a marked police car. His hands were cuffed at the front. Larry sat on his right side. Wendy sat in the front passenger seat.

'Which way?' Larry asked.

'Go back to where I threw Dave in the canal,' Pinto said as the car exited the car park at the rear of the police station. A man sitting in a café on the other side of the road took note. He made a phone call.

The police car drove to Warwick Crescent and pulled up outside the flat of Mrs Gregory, their first witness. 'Up there, cross the bridge, and then turn left,' Pinto said.

The vehicle crossed Westbourne Terrace Road Bridge and turned into Bloomfield Road, before turning right again two blocks later into Clifton Villas. 'That's where I dumped it,' Pinto said.

The garbage skip was close to overflowing with builder's rubble from a house renovation. 'We're about to take it away,' the foreman said.

Larry flashed his police ID badge. 'It's a crime scene now.'

'My boss will be furious.'

'There's not much I can do about it,' Larry said. After dealing with the foreman's concerns and with an irate house owner, he phoned Windsor.

'I'll get a couple of my people over there within the hour,' Windsor replied.

Larry and Wendy stayed at the scene for another fifteen minutes, before two uniforms arrived and secured the area with crime scene tape. They also put up some barriers directing pedestrians to the other side of the street. A few complained, but most complied.

Once the area was secured, Larry and Wendy, along with Pinto, went back to Challis Street. Pinto was returned to the cells, awaiting transfer to prison. His lawyer had applied for bail, the charge for aiding and abetting in a murder reduced to drug trafficking.

***

DCS Goddard was full of praise when Isaac entered his office later that day. He shook his DCI's hand vigorously. 'Soon have this one wrapped up,' he said.

Isaac let the man have his moment of glory.

'I've phoned Commissioner Davies to let him know that we're moving forward. He's delighted.'

'There's still a dangerous group of individuals behind this,' Isaac said.

'That's not your concern. From what you've told me, one of the two heavies killed Stewart and then cut him up.'

'We know where they'll be on Friday.'

'Then what's the problem?' Pinto will give evidence that they killed Stewart and we've wrapped up the case.'

'What about the drug trafficking? And what about this mysterious man who gave the heavies an order to kill Stewart?'

'That's up to Serious and Organised Crimes Command,' Goddard said.

'We should inform them as to what we're involved with,' Isaac said.

Of course. Follow agreed procedures, but remember we're Homicide. We deal with murders, and you know the two men who killed Stewart. That's what I want, a conviction for murder.'

'We'll deal with that first, but I can't help thinking that it will not be as easy as all that,' Isaac said.

'DCI, that's your problem. Always looking to stir up a hornet's nest. Our job is to apprehend a murderer and ensure he's convicted. Those behind the murder are not for us to go chasing. Think of your career: another case solved, and in record time. It's a win–win for both of us. Let's show our commissioner what we're made of.'

Isaac left his superior's office feeling disconsolate. The man was not interested that someone had been murdered and dismembered; he was only interested in his career and his cushy life. Isaac realised that the man he had admired since he was a sergeant had sold out. Richard Goddard in his estimation was a man who lacked a soul.

Isaac knew that he had not reached that situation and wondered if he would. Was it necessary to be shallow and political to rise to the top in the London Met? What about competence and professionalism?

***

With his DCS more interested in a conviction for murder than a resolution to the crime syndicate, Isaac felt the need to check further. One man had been found dismembered so far, but were there others, or could there be more in the future? He also had concern for the well-being of Vicenzo Pinto, so much so that he had requested special security for him in the prison where he was to be confined.

Pinto had grassed, and those who had killed Stewart would regard his confession as tantamount to betrayal. Isaac had to agree with Pinto's estimation of his precarious situation, but there was a murder to solve, and two men to be arrested. One had committed the murder; the other had assisted with the chainsaw.

Larry intended to visit the pub in Paddington on Friday, where the two heavies who had killed Stewart were known to drink, knowing full well that his wife would be giving him the cold shoulder on Saturday, and there'd be no chance of an early morning cuddle. *How I suffer for the London Met*, he thought.

The initial plan had been for him to go on his own and to check out the two men, but he was known in the area. Also, he had to meet up with Rasta Joe, the dreadlocked Jamaican again, although he was not involved, certainly not as a member of the syndicate. However, the man had his ear to the ground.

'Do we have enough for an arrest?' Isaac asked in the office.

'There are some fingerprints at the warehouse,' Larry said. 'Windsor and his team found them easily enough.'

'But whose are they?'

'Certainly Pinto's, and the others, or at least some of them would be Stewart's.'

'Have you checked Stewart's accommodation yet,' Isaac asked.

'Not yet,' Wendy replied.

'Then you'd better do it today. I want an arrest on Friday, not surveillance. And besides, where are these two men now?'

'They've not been seen for the last few days,' Larry replied. 'We assume they're lying low.'

'Which means they may not be at the pub on Friday.'

'That's a possibility.'

'Okay, check out Stewart's flat and get some fingerprints.'

Wendy and Larry left the office soon after. Stewart's flat, they knew, was in a tenement building close to Notting Hill, not far from the expensive houses in Holland Park. However, as they knew from the address, there was nothing fancy about Stewart's place of residence. It was definitely downmarket, and for a man who had supposedly been paid well to transport heroin and cocaine, there was little to show for his efforts. The flat was on the third floor, the lift did not work, and Wendy was puffing after the climb. Two of Gordon Windsor's team had accompanied the two police officers. A uniform was already standing on duty outside the door and not enjoying himself. 'I don't go much for his neighbours,' the policeman said.

'Giving you trouble?' Larry asked.

'Scum from God knows where. It's the kids who hurl abuse at me. They know I can't retaliate.'

Larry could sympathise. Where Stewart lived was low income, full of welfare recipients with little chance at the big game. Most of the young children would be on the street and into crime soon enough; a fair proportion would become members of gangs, menacing society, trading drugs. Statistically, Larry knew, between five and ten per cent would be dead before their twentieth birthday.

Wendy was in the flat with the CSIs. A small television stood in one corner, an old chair had been placed six feet away from it. The kitchen was compact, with one of the cupboard doors hanging haphazardly on its hinges. In the sink, there were still some dirty dishes.

'Not much to look at,' Grant Meston, one of the CSIs, said.

'His housekeeping is no worse than mine,' Wendy replied. The place felt eerie to her, but she did not mention it. The flat may have been unloved, and definitely not desirable, but it had been the residence of a man, not a torso dumped in a canal.

'There's plenty of prints,' Meston said.

'Stewart's?'

'The most reliable will be in the bathroom: toothbrush, razor. And from what we can see, he lived here on his own; no sign of a woman.'

Rose Denning, Meston's assistant, was in the bedroom. She called out, 'No woman in here.'

Wendy looked through the door of the bedroom. A double bed, its headrest broken, a sheet crumpled and pulled back.

'No action in here,' Rose said.

'How do you know?' Wendy asked.

'Look at the sheet. One side is more crumpled than the other.'

'Both sides look well used to me.'

'They've not been changed for a while. Mind you, I don't think many women would want to come up here, do you?'

Wendy had to agree, but they were not there to discuss Stewart's love life. They were there to obtain his fingerprints and to check out the flat. Larry looked around the main room. He opened the doors of a sideboard. Inside he found some ganja, almost certainly supplied by Rasta Joe. There was no sign of heroin or cocaine. On a table, there was a photo of a woman. She looked old enough to be Stewart's mother. It was known that Stewart had come from Liverpool and his mother was still alive. A local detective had dealt with the difficult task of informing her that her son was dead.

'There's not much here,' Meston said.

'Fingerprints?' Larry asked.

'Enough. We'll isolate Stewart's and Pinto's at the warehouse.'

Another policeman was left guarding Stewart's flat as the team left. Crime scene tape had been applied to the door, but Larry and Wendy knew that as soon as there was no police presence, the flat would be vandalised.

***

'It's Stewart's head,' Gordon Windsor, the CSE, said over the phone.

'Arms and legs?' Isaac asked.

'Not at the warehouse, although Meston's working on the fingerprints from Stewart's flat.'

'What else can you tell us about the head?'

'Bullet through the brain.'

'That killed him?'

'Yes.'

Isaac knew that Pinto's confession had been one hundred per cent accurate. Isaac could see that it was an easy route for someone with an addiction to become involved with serious crime. He had a friend at school who after smoking some hash had become addicted, and ended up on the street with a dirty needle and heroin. Isaac remembered trying hash once, the result of a stupid dare at school. He had seen no benefit in it. After that, he had smoked cigarettes for a few months, but even that had stopped soon enough. To him, some people, Pinto as an example, although his vice was gambling, are susceptible to addiction, others are not.

Pinto's bail application was due to be heard. The charge for drug trafficking remained in place.

Katrina Hatcher had been busy doing her homework and had compiled an extensive list of precedences as to why her client should be released on bail.

Isaac was aware of the bail hearing, scheduled for the following Tuesday. Unless there were reasons to the contrary, he would attend, but would not make an impassioned plea for bail to be refused. Pinto was unlikely to cause trouble, he had no prior convictions, and he would return to live with his parents.

The garbage skip in Bloomfield Street had been removed and taken to Forensics. Three of the department's juniors had been given the task of methodically emptying it. It had been outside the house in Bloomfield Street for builder's rubble, not as a local tip, but that was what it had become. The three CSIs stood inside the skip, masks on their faces to minimise the smell of the contents: old bricks, wood with nails still protruding, rotten food, and dog faeces. One of the juniors had taken umbrage at the task, but Rose Denning had taken him aside and given him a good talking to; told him that she had had her fair share of unpleasant jobs when she had first joined the department, but now she was involved out at crime scenes. The junior went back to his job, and found the plastic bag ten minutes later.

Once it was removed from the skip, the Forensics team checked it out. Inside there was some blood, but not as much as expected, which, yet again, aligned with Pinto's statement that the torso had been placed in a freezer before being dropped into Regent's Canal.

Chapter 8

'Somebody is supplying you with heroin,' Larry said to Rasta Joe as they sat in a pub on Portobello Road in Notting Hill.

'I don't use heroin,' the English-born Jamaican said.

'I'm not here because of that. We know someone is behind the large-scale importation of heroin and cocaine into this country; someone who'll not hesitate to use extreme violence, even against you.'

'Whoever he is, he scares us.' Now Larry knew why the Jamaican was so keen to meet him, not that it meant that Rasta Joe would be buying the drinks.

'What do you know?' Larry asked.

'There are others who trade in drugs.'

'Not you?'

'I just clean a few windows, turn a few cars to make money. I don't mess with heroin.' Larry only smiled at Rasta Joe's statement.

'These others, what do they say?'

'They say their previous suppliers are either not selling or they've disappeared.'

'Disappeared?' Larry queried.

'Dead.'

'Any proof?'

'One day they're there. The next they're gone.'

'How long ago?'

'One disappeared three weeks ago.'

'A name?'

'I've never met the man, but those who've dealt with him say his name was Rodrigo Fuentes.'

'It sounds Brazilian.'

'It is.'

'Where can I find this man?'

'I told you, he's disappeared.'

'And you believe he's dead?'

'That's the word on the street. Someone killed him because he never listened.'

Larry could see the fear in Rasta Joe's face, at least when he didn't have a glass of beer to his mouth. Larry matched him pint for pint, knowing full well what his wife would say when he got home. Another night on the couch in the living room seemed a distinct possibility, the only company the family cat.

'And those who used to buy from Fuentes are now forced to buy from someone else?'

'It's the someone else that's got everyone scared. We, sorry, I mean they, are compelled to pay more money or else.'

'Or else?'

'Dead.'

'You, sorry, I mean they,' Larry threw back Rasta Joe's previous slip of the tongue, 'are using the deaths of Fuentes and Dougal Stewart as a warning.'

'Fuentes mainly, but there have been others.'

'Where are these new suppliers?'

'They move around.'

'Rasta Joe, we need to work together on this. I know you're involved in selling drugs, but I'm with Homicide. Whoever these new players are, they're organised and extremely violent. They could kill again without warning. If you make one wrong move, say the wrong word, or argue their prices, it could be you in the canal minus your head and your genitals.'

'They didn't cut off Dave's balls,' Rasta Joe said.

'You knew him?'

'We used to drink at the same pub.'

'And you knew that his genitals were intact?'

'It was in the newspaper.'

'No, it wasn't. You know more than you're telling me. What is it?'

'Okay. I'll need your word that I'm safe from prosecution.'

'From me, you are.'

'I'm down the pub. I recognise the two men that we're forced to deal with sitting not far away. They're hitting the whisky really hard. One is named Devlin, a miserable, tough bastard. The other one calls himself Steve, fancies himself with the women. Anyway, there I am, minding my own business with my girlfriend, hopeful she'll be receptive to my charms later in the night.'

'What happened?'

'I'm getting progressively drunk, as is my girlfriend.'

'What about the two men?'

'They're getting louder. I'm sitting there overhearing what they're saying.'

'What did they say?'

'Devlin starts bragging about how he shot the man in the head. Steve, the other one, recounts how they went at the body with a chainsaw.'

'You've known this for how long?'

'Just a few days. I thought the men were talking nonsense. It was before you fished the body out of the canal.'

'They weren't bragging, and they'll do it again.'

'That's what I'm worried about.'

'Would you testify? Make a written statement.'

'Are you serious? With those bastards on the loose?'

'If we put them out of business?'

'We'll see,' Rasta Joe said.

***

Pinto's bail hearing was a formality. Katrina Hatcher had prepared well, and Isaac, who had made a plea for the man to remain in prison, as much for his own security as anything else, could not sway the judge.

Conditions were imposed: residence at his parents' house, a weekly visit to his local police station to report in, and a detailed account of his movements. Isaac could see that the situation was not ideal, but there was no more he could do.

Pinto looked to be both pleased and worried as he descended the steps outside the court house.

'Glad to be out on bail?' Isaac asked.

'For the time being.'

Katrina Hatcher came over and wished Pinto well. He accepted her wishes with a smile and a kiss on the cheek. Pinto's parents were there, and he got into their car.

The bail application and the speed of it being processed concerned Isaac. The two who had killed Dougal Stewart and then chopped him up were still free.

Larry had intended to arrest them on the previous Friday, but they never showed up. He had taken a couple of plain-clothes with him, just in case the two hard cases caused trouble.

The word on the street was that they had left the area. Not that this pleased Larry and Isaac. The drug trade was still operating, so if it wasn't Devlin and his offsider Steve, it was someone else, or was it?

Isaac thought that maybe the fear within the criminal community had caused everyone to clam up. The full details of Dougal Stewart's gruesome death were now common knowledge, and even the newspapers and social media were reporting it correctly.

DCS Goddard was a worried man again. His nemesis, Commissioner Alwyn Davies, was on his back again. Three weeks had passed, the alleged murderers were known and yet no arrests.

Isaac had received a phone call from the disagreeable DCI Caddick intimating that he was coming back to show him how to run a murder investigation. Isaac had to admit he did not like the man. Discreet enquiries into Caddick had revealed a history of low achievement, yet the man always came up smelling of roses.

Isaac, disillusioned as he was with his DCS, had to admit that he had protected him in the past, and besides, Isaac knew, he had a good track record, whereas the man aiming to take his place did not.

It seemed incongruous that the commissioner of the Met would compromise his position by protecting Caddick, who was only marginally competent. Unless there was a reason, some event in the past where Caddick had saved Alwyn Davies's career and reputation. Isaac had to admit it was idle speculation and not relevant to the current case.

Serious and Organised Crimes Command had been in touch to confirm that they were concerned with the escalating drug problem. Apart from that, they had said little, and after a quizzing from Isaac, they had reluctantly agreed that there was a significant operator in the city, and so far they had had little success in tracking down the ringleaders.

It seemed to Isaac that his team was doing better than those with a fancy title and a well-funded operation at Scotland Yard.

***

Larry was out on the street aiming to find out what he could about the men he wanted to arrest. His regular informers had clammed up, even when he offered more than the going rate. Rasta Joe, a man who was a criminal but at least relatively open with him, was saying nothing either. Larry sensed a palpable fear in the criminal community. For once, he was frightened. These people were dangerous, and he had no idea where to look.

Devlin, the person who had shot Dougal Stewart, had accommodation in Bayswater. It had taken some time, but Wendy had found the place. The man's full name was revealed to be Devlin O'Shaughnessy, and he had an extensive criminal record, mainly for armed robbery. Larry was surprised that he had not heard of the man, but his crimes had been committed in Ireland. Steve, the other villain, was still being elusive. Wendy thought she had found his place, but it was not correct.

Gordon Windsor and his team had been out at O'Shaughnessy's terrace house. It was expensive, and according to the landlord, O'Shaughnessy paid without fail on the first of the month.

'Always cash,' Alex Hughenden said.

'Illegal money,' Larry informed him. Hughenden was taken aback, considering that he was a lay preacher in his local church and the curse of illicit drugs worried him greatly.

'That's the last time I'll take money from him,' Hughenden said.

It seemed a moot point to Larry as it was clear that Devlin O'Shaughnessy was not coming back. The house had been filled with expensive furniture and reflected a man of good taste, yet the tenant was capable of extreme violence. Nothing was apparently missing when Windsor and his team had gone over the place, other than there were no clothes, no personal belongings, no money to be found.

'You must have known he was a dubious character,' Larry said to Hughenden, a small, well-dressed man who sported a bowtie.

'He was remarkably articulate considering.'

'Considering what?'

'The tattoos on his arms.'

'Distinctive?'

'There was just a lot of them, yet he could discuss art and literature. I liked the man, even if I would not have wanted to introduce him to my circle of friends.'

'They would have disapproved?'

'Almost certainly, but quite frankly he was more knowledgeable than most.'

'What else can you tell me about him?' Larry asked.

'He said he had come over from Ireland and he was involved in a cash business.'

'And you didn't suspect?'

'Not really. A lot of people are cash only round here. If you get down to Portobello Road on a Saturday, they're cash in hand.'

'But they wouldn't be able to pay you cash on a monthly basis for your place in Bayswater.'

'You're probably right. No doubt I've sinned in accepting the man's money.'

'Probably, but that's between you and your maker,' Larry said, knowing full well that the man had placed greed over his religious ideals.

At least he can ask for forgiveness, Larry, a man with no strong religious conviction, thought.

'He's gone now. Any idea where? Any forwarding address?' Larry asked.

'He paid me in advance, and no, I don't know where he's gone.'

***

Isaac paced up and down Homicide's office at Challis Street. The case was starting to get to him. The anticipated quick arrests, with certain convictions due to the fingerprints at the warehouse where Dougal Stewart had been butchered, as well as Vicenzo Pinto's evidence, were not materialising.

Katrina Hatcher had phoned him not two minutes earlier to tell him that Pinto was missing. 'He failed to report,' she said.

Pinto's parents, it was known, lived to the west of the city, and it was thought that he would be safe there. Now there was a concern that he had done a runner, the same as Devlin O'Shaughnessy and his offsider. But why Pinto? The man was likely to get off with a shortened sentence, probably two years maximum, especially if he gave evidence against O'Shaughnessy and Stewart.

Larry returned to Challis Street; Wendy was already there. Ten minutes later they were out of the office and in the car and driving west.

'He was all right,' Pinto's father said. He still had the strong accent of Napoli when he spoke. His wife, a typical Italian Mamma, said little. She obviously enjoyed the pasta that she made.

'We need to find him,' Larry said.

'He's been a bad boy,' Pinto's mother said.

'If he works with us, we'll keep him out of trouble,' Wendy said. The smell of Italian cooking pervaded the small house; her stomach rumbled.

'What has happened to him?' the father asked.

'That is why we are here. Has he been gambling again?' Larry asked. He had also smelt the food being prepared in the kitchen.'

'He said he had given it up but…'

'Addicted?'

'Yes. We know he tries, but it's hard for him.'

'Why?'

'A family trait,' the father said. 'I was the same at his age. Eventually he'll grow out of it.'

Larry realised the son may not have that opportunity. And with the two heavies not around, there was a strong possibility they were related.

The two police officers left the Pintos' house, but not before they had sampled Italian home cooking. They visited the local police station where Pinto had been reporting. The duty officer stood behind the counter as they entered. Larry and Wendy showed their police identification. The locked door through to the offices opened when the officer pressed the button for the electronic lock. Inside, Inspector Pritchard introduced himself.

'You think he's dead?' Pritchard, a slovenly dressed man, asked.

'He's an important witness.'

'Maybe, but dead is dead. There's not much you can do if we find his body.'

Wendy did not like the man's attitude. They had only just entered the police station, and Pritchard was already defeatist, as if he always expected the worst. Larry thought he was a half-empty, not a half-full man.

'We need him found,' Larry said.

'And you want me to find him?'

'Yes.'

'It's a lot of work just for one man.'

'This man is an important witness in a murder investigation. His whereabouts are critical. Are you able to help?'

'Why not? We'll put out an APW. If someone sees him, we'll soon know.'

'We'll need more than that.'

'We're undermanned here.'

'We will need a thorough investigation of all gambling clubs, legal or otherwise, all pubs, all brothels, and it will need to commence within two hours,' Larry said.

'Who the hell do you think you are? You come in here and start giving me orders. I'm not your lackey.'

Wendy leant over to Larry, ensuring that Pritchard heard. 'Phone DCI Cook. Get DCS Goddard to call the officer in charge of this station. And make sure that the DCS mentions that he is becoming involved due to unnecessary delays being incurred by junior officers.'

'Okay, I don't need threats. Give us three hours to check,' Pritchard said.

He rushed out of the office where all three had been sitting; Larry and Wendy could hear him giving orders and raising his voice.

'A man eager to please,' Larry said sarcastically.

Five hours later, Pritchard phoned Larry. 'We can't find him.'

Chapter 9

Katrina Hatcher, Pinto's lawyer, was noticeably upset when Isaac phoned her with the latest developments. 'I worked hard for that man,' she said.

'He may turn up yet,' Isaac said.

'You don't believe that.'

'I'll remain optimistic for the present.'

Larry and Wendy were back in the office within ninety minutes of receiving the news regarding Pinto. Isaac convened a meeting.

'It's not looking good,' Isaac said. Larry chose to stand in the corner of Isaac's office. Wendy was sitting down, not willing to admit to the soreness in her legs.

'For Pinto?'

'For the whole damn case, and now Alwyn Davies is after our DCS's blood.'

'Which means you as well, DCI,' Wendy said.

'What can you tell me about Vicenzo Pinto?' Isaac asked, choosing not to respond to Wendy's comment.

'Unless we receive advice to the contrary, Pinto is a missing person,' Larry said.

'Is he dead?' Isaac asked.

'It's a possibility.'

'Then we'd better find him or those who may have killed him. What's the deal with your friend Rasta Joe? Doesn't he know what's going on?'

'He may do, but he's scared. The same as everyone else on the street. Something's going on.'

'But what? You need to squeeze Rasta Joe,' Isaac said.

'It would help if you could speak to him,' Larry said.

'He'll not talk to me.'

'I'll ask him. He may open up more with you.'

'A fellow Jamaican over from the Caribbean, is that what you mean?'

'I suppose so. You understand his culture.'

'Maybe, but we go back a long way.'

'What do you mean, sir?' Wendy asked.

'I've known Rasta Joe since childhood. Back then he was Joseph Brown. His parents came from Montego Bay.'

'Criminal then?'

'He sang in the church choir.'

'What changed?'

'Ganja and gangs.'

'And you, sir?' Wendy asked.

'Joining a gang was for losers.'

Larry changed the subject. 'There's still Rodrigo Fuentes. According to Rasta Joe, he got on the wrong side of the syndicate. We should still follow up on him. It may lead somewhere.'

'Pinto had mixed feelings when he was granted bail,' Isaac said. 'The man had given us valuable evidence. The syndicate would want him dead.'

'That's the word on the street,' Larry reminded him. 'So far, Dougal Stewart's death is the only one we can confirm.'

'Rodrigo Fuentes. What do we know about him?'

'Not much. According to Rasta Joe, he operated in the area, importing drugs from South America, and selling to whoever was willing to pay his price.'

'And he's believed dead?' Isaac asked.

'May not be true, but we should check.'

'And Devlin O'Shaughnessy and his offsider, Steve. Did we ever get a name for that man?'

'Steve Walters. Bridget identified him off a photo that Pinto had. We've an APW out for both of them, but they could be anywhere.'

'Even six feet under,' Isaac said.

'Or floating down the Thames,' Wendy added.

***

Rasta Joe, a man who had deliberately distanced himself from the police before, was now very accessible. Larry had suggested meeting with Isaac, and the man had agreed. Not that Isaac was pleased when he had been informed that they were to meet that day, but out of the city. 'It's too dangerous for me to meet you in public,' Rasta Joe had said.

'You can always come down the police station,' Larry said.

'They'll have someone watching. No one's safe, not even me.'

'Why? What have you done?'

'I've met you.'

'Have they contacted you?'

'I can sense they're watching.'

'Sense them?' Larry asked.

'You'd not understand.'

Larry knew that a Rastafarian believed in the power of ganja to discover their inner consciousness, but he supposed that if Rasta Joe was feeling the effects of the drug, he might well have thought he had the ability to sense something that was not there. Not that it concerned Larry. He had the all clear to take Isaac with him.

The three men met in Guildford, a small town to the south of London.

'Rasta Joe, this is DCI Cook,' Larry said as the men met in the back room of a local pub.

'How are you, Isaac?'

Fine. And you, Joseph?'

'DCI Cook said that he knew you.'

'We were friends back then,' Rasta Joe said.

'And now?' Larry asked.

'A lot of water under the bridge since then,' Isaac said.

'Your boss is right,' Rasta Joe said, talking to Larry. 'We don't see eye to eye.'

'Now's not the time to rake up the past,' Isaac said.

'Did you find the man who grassed on them?' Rasta Joe asked.

'Not yet.'

'The word on the street is that he's dead.'

'What else does the street say?'

All three men had a pint in their hand. Isaac remembered the last time he had met Joseph Brown, the choir boy. Back then he had been a decent person, but now he was scum. Isaac did not like his fellow Jamaican, but this was not the time to show ill feeling. Whatever the future held for Isaac and the current case, it seemed that Rasta Joe was to be an integral part of it.

Rasta Joe waited for Larry to bring him another pint. The frightened man was still able to enjoy himself at the police's expense. 'Whoever's running this organisation, he's got powerful friends, and nobody's safe, not even the police.'

'What do you interpret that to mean?' Larry asked.

'You need to be scared, the same as me.'

'Were we mentioned directly?'

'That's not how they operate. It's by veiled threats, intimidation, a dead body in the canal.'

'But they mentioned Pinto?'

'Not directly. Only that the person who had grassed had been dealt with, and anyone else that crosses them can expect the same.'

'Did they say where he had been killed? What had happened to the body.'

'You'll find him soon enough,' Rasta Joe said.

'I thought Rastafarians didn't drink alcohol,' Isaac said. He had left the majority of the conversation to Larry; he had not forgiven his fellow Jamaican for what had happened in the past.

Larry had noted his DCI's disdain for the man sitting opposite. He would ask him later what it was about.

'I don't hold with all their views.'

'You're heavy on the ganja,' Larry said.

'I happen to like it.'

'Coming back to your earlier statement, that we'll find him soon enough,' Isaac said.

'They intended to make an example of Pinto. A warning to others.'

'I would have thought Dougal Stewart would have been sufficient.'

'Short memories out on the street. They need reminding on a regular basis.'

'Every two weeks?' Isaac said.

'Maybe not so often, but Pinto's a special case.'

'Why are you frightened?' Larry asked Rasta Joe.

'As I said, I've been seen with you.'

'Did they contact you?'

'I received a phone call.'

'Who was it?'

'That bastard Devlin.'

'What did he say?'

'He told me not to take out any life insurance.'

'Where did he phone from?'

'No idea.'

'We may be able to trace it,' Isaac said, anxious to get back to London. If Pinto was dead, they needed to find him soon, as well as Rodrigo Fuentes. He knew that if they didn't act quickly, Rasta Joe might be added to the list as well as his DI, Larry Hill.

***

DCS Goddard was in Isaac's office on his return. He was not in a good mood, which was not unusual since Commissioner Alwyn Davies had assumed the top position at the Met. Isaac would have preferred not to have seen his DCS. There was a phone number to trace. Larry had taken the details of the phone call made to Rasta Joe, the number clearly visible on the screen. Bridget could trace where the phone call was made from, as well as other phone calls from O'Shaughnessy's phone. And there was the issue of Rodrigo Fuentes. Who was he? Where was he?

Fuentes' death didn't ring true. No body and the syndicate's warning was diluted, and supposedly there had been others, but who were they?'

Challis Street Police Station was responsible for the area, and there was a lot more crime going on that they didn't know about, or at least they didn't know about in the Homicide Department.

There had been a time in the past when a visit from Richard Goddard was always welcome, but those times were long past. 'What's this I hear about Vicenzo Pinto?'

'What did you hear, sir?'

'That your star witness is dead.'

'We have no proof.'

'Yet again, a laughingstock. You have a witness to the murder, and he walks out of the courtroom.'

'He satisfied the requirements for bail.'

'Only because you watered the charge down. It's not that lawyer of his, pretty and female, is it?'

'I resent that aspersion,' Isaac responded.

'We've had this conversation before. Did you go easy on Pinto because of her?'

'No.'

'Very well, but why didn't you charge him with murder?'

'The man had no criminal record, and he checked out. I could hardly charge him with murder, knowing full well that any half-smart lawyer would have had him out of here in twelve hours.'

'You could have held him for longer.'

'We still don't know he's dead,' Isaac said.

'You believe him to be dead though.'

'I'm willing to concede that possibility.'

'Good God, man. How can I protect you?'

The man's interested in his own future, not in justice, Isaac thought.

Wendy, sensing the mood in Isaac's office, kept her distance. She had news to tell him, but it could wait.

'What are you doing to find Pinto?' Goddard asked.

'We have an APW out for him.'

'What are they looking for, the man or a body?'

'Both. Unless confirmed otherwise, we'll focus on both.'

'And if he's dead?'

'We're back to square one.'

'This Jamaican friend of yours, any help?'

'He's no friend of mine.'

'What's he got to say?'

'Pinto's dead. Another drug dealer is also probably dead.'

'They're not corpses down the morgue?'

'No.'

'I need this wrapped up,' Goddard said before storming out of the office.

'Rough, sir?' Wendy asked when she came into Isaac's office.

'All the time,' Isaac replied.

'He's under a lot of pressure.'

'So are we. Anyway, what do you have?'

'A trace on O'Shaughnessy's phone.'

'And?'

'O'Shaughnessy's phone call to Rasta Joe was made five days after DI Hill intended to arrest him.'

'Where was the call made?'

'Local.'

'Can you be more precise?'

'Bayswater. Only accurate to within fifty metres.'

'A needle in a haystack,' Isaac said.

'There are literally hundreds of potential locations, and tens of thousands of people.'

'Any more calls from O'Shaughnessy's number?'

'We're going through them now. He's not made any calls for the last few days.'

'Which means?'

'He's using another phone.'

'Trace all his phone calls; see if you can find any reference to Pinto. Also, any phone calls to his boss.'

'A long night for Bridget and I,' Wendy said.

'A long night for all of us,' Isaac replied, knowing full well that the murder of Dougal Stewart, the assumed murder of Vicenzo Pinto, were not to be the last.

***

Vicenzo Pinto, strung up as if he was a piece of meat, was barely conscious. The savage beating had almost killed him. 'Please, let me go. I never told them anything.'

'So how did they find out my address?' an angry Devlin O'Shaughnessy said.

Outside it was late, and Pinto did not know where he was, although it was only four miles from the sanctity of his parents' house. He had not enjoyed himself there, what with his mother fussing and his father lecturing about how he had wasted his life. Pinto, if he had been in a position to contemplate it, would have said that his father was a right one to talk, knowing his father's predilection for gambling in his youth.

Steve Walters, Devlin's offsider, stood to one side of Pinto. 'You remember what we did to Dave?'

'Please. I told them nothing.'

'How come you're out on bail?'

'My lawyer, she was excellent.'

'I would have said she was a miracle worker,' O'Shaughnessy said. 'I rob a supermarket, and I'm slammed inside for ten years, and there's no bail for me. Either your lawyer's screwing the black police inspector or you've done a deal.'

'I swear that I've not made a deal,' Pinto said. The derelict warehouse was cold and miserable, even O'Shaughnessy and Walters would admit that, but they had the benefit of clothes; Pinto did not.

'We want the full story.' Walters, a shorter man than his dismembering colleague, worked out at a gym in Notting Hill. His muscles bulged under his shirt.

'I did nothing,' Pinto panted. His feet were barely touching the ground, his arms were stretched, his wrists securely bound. 'They had nothing on me.'

'Their Forensics department took the car we gave you apart.'

'They knew about Dave and that I threw him in the canal.'

'Then why release you?'

'I'm still charged with drug trafficking and the illegal disposal of a body.'

'No one gets bail for drug trafficking,' O'Shaughnessy said, punching his fist into the desperate man's chest.

'Before you die, you'll tell us everything,' Walters said.

'Please let me down. I'll talk.'

'What we want is the truth. Once down, you will lie, but believe me, strung up there you will tell only the truth. All you need to worry about now is whether your death will be soon, or whether we'll keep you strung up for another two days. A few cuts to the body and then the insects will find you.'

'You wouldn't do that?'

'Why not, and besides it will be fun,' O'Shaughnessy said. 'That bastard Brazilian was fun. You're a gambler. Do you want to place a bet? What do you reckon? Two days, three, maybe four before you die.'

'Let me down, please.' Pinto, frightened and alone in a warehouse with two murderous men, was ready to talk.

'Not until you tell us something.'

'And then you'll let me down?'

'It depends if you tell us the truth.'

'The police don't believe I killed Dave.'

'That may be true,' O'Shaughnessy said. He released the rope slightly to allow Pinto to stand flat footed on the concrete floor. 'You help us, we help you.'

'Did you tell them the truth about what had happened to Dave?'

'No.'

Walters wrenched on the rope, pulling Pinto's feet firmly off the ground. There was an audible pop as one of his shoulders dislocated. 'I hope you aren't left-handed,' Walters said.

Pinto moaned and said nothing. O'Shaughnessy shook him violently. 'Are you still with us?'

'Yes.' A weak murmur.

O'Shaughnessy turned to Walters. 'Don't do that again. My money is on him lasting for three days. If you keep doing that he'll only last one before he's dead, and besides I want to see what happens when the flies find him.'

Walters looked towards O'Shaughnessy, ensuring that Pinto was aware of the repartee between the two men. 'Sorry. I'll be more careful next time.'

O'Shaughnessy turned back to Pinto. 'What did you tell them about Dave's death?'

Pinto knew only too well what would happen if he lied again. 'I told the police that I had seen him die.'

'That's sounds right. You're there trying to save your skin. What do your friends matter?'

'I never mentioned your names.'

'Pinto, you must think we're stupid.'

Vicenzo Pinto realised that the moment they had their truth, he was a dead man. He wanted to curse that smart-arse lawyer for getting him bail; he wanted to curse the police inspector who had not objected strongly enough. He wanted to curse his miserable life, but the pain that he was suffering was too intense.

'It's the truth. I never mentioned your names.'

'And out on bail within a week. We know they had a warrant out for our arrest,' O'Shaughnessy said.

'That wasn't my doing.'

'How did they find the warehouse where we cut him up?'

'I don't know.'

'You're lying. Do you want to hear your other shoulder dislocating?'

'No. I've told you the truth. Honest.'

'We don't trust you,' Walters said. 'And now we're hiding out, thanks to you. Are you keeping in contact with the police? Letting them know how our organisation works? Are you giving names and places in exchange for bail and a cushy prison? Should we let you live or should we make an example of you, the same as we did with Dave?'

'I'll tell you all I know if you'll promise…'

'Steve, let him down. He may as well be comfortable while he tells us the full story.'

Pinto, released from the rope, sat on a wooden chair in the middle of the warehouse. Walters leant against a dirty wall; O'Shaughnessy sat on an old desk that had been left when the previous tenant had vacated.

'Now tell us the truth,' O'Shaughnessy said.

Pinto had no option. His only hope was to be open and honest. The rope strung over a beam was hanging loose. Walters maintained a firm grip on one end of the rope; the other was still binding Pinto's wrists.

'I told them about the warehouse. They were going to charge me with murder.'

'To save yourself you told them about the warehouse and us.'

'Yes.' Walters pulled on his end of the rope.

'Did you tell them about your trips to France and the vehicles you brought back.'

'Some, not all.'

'And now our whole operation is jeopardised.'

'Why? I don't know how it operates.'

'The police interest is cramping our normal operation,' O'Shaughnessy said.

'They had cameras. They saw me dump Dave.'

'Did you tell them about the man in the blue suit?'

'Yes, but I never knew who he was.'

'And they've released you on bail for being a good boy. Are you in their pay?'

'No.'

A voice in the office to one side could be heard. 'Enough. I don't need to hear any more. The man's a liability. You know what to do.'

Walters grabbed his end of the rope and pulled hard. Vicenzo Pinto felt his body being yanked from the chair and pulled upwards. He knew he would not be coming down alive.

Chapter 10

Isaac had finally met up with Jess O'Neill. The evening had gone well, and she had spent the night at his flat. The two had discussed moving in together again but decided to wait and see. She was still the executive producer of the country's most successful nightly TV drama. The older actors had all been replaced by younger, unknown actors after market research had shown that the programme needed an update and fresh blood, and the accountants had decreed that they had to keep down costs.

Isaac had to admit that whereas their night together had been great, he still had a problem in that he tended to take his work home with him.

The case of the death of Dougal Stewart, the possible deaths of Rodrigo Fuentes and Vicenzo Pinto, was baffling. The drugs were still being sold on the street, so someone was still running the trade, and it was evident from Rasta Joe that it was the syndicate in which O'Shaughnessy and Walters were only minor functionaries.

Inspector Len Donaldson of Serious and Organised Crime Command had come over to the office in Challis Street to brief the team. An agreeable dark-haired man with a distinctive Scottish accent, he fitted in well.

'There's always one organisation or another attempting to take control,' Donaldson said. The team were seated in a conference room. 'We're aware that the new player is exerting force on the others.'

'And killing those who resist?' Larry asked.

'That's how they deal with the opposition. Either you're with us, or you're dead.'

'Devlin O'Shaughnessy and Steve Walters,' Isaac asked. 'Are they known to you?'

'They've been around for a while.'

'Who's behind the syndicate?' Larry asked.

'That's what we'd like to know,' Donaldson said.

'It's important.'

'I realise that, but every time we get close to an answer, they go underground. We've come close on a couple of occasions, but nothing's eventuated. A confirmed murder should make it easier to put them out of business.'

'You've seen our reports?' Isaac asked.

'You've had more success than us,' Donaldson acknowledged.

'Apart from O'Shaughnessy and Walters, we're only aware of a man in a blue suit. Any idea who he is?'

'We've had surveillance on O'Shaughnessy's landlord.'

'The devout churchgoer?' Larry asked.

'That's him.'

'You've brought him in for questioning?'

'We have nothing against him.'

'Then why is he a suspect?'

'Profiling. The man professes to be pious, yet during the week he's in the company of O'Shaughnessy, and then on Sunday, he's down the church asking for forgiveness.'

'O'Shaughnessy and Hughenden are together during the week?' Isaac asked.

'Hughenden's not a drinker, so you wouldn't see him down the pub, but apart from that the two men are very friendly.'

'Gay?' Wendy asked.

'Hughenden may be, but not Devlin O'Shaughnessy. Every Friday night after the pub he visits one of the local whores.'

'Apart from a suspicion, what else do you have?'

'Not a lot really; more supposition than anything else. We know that Hughenden spent time in prison when he was a lot younger.'

'What for?'

'Passing forged cheques. Since then no convictions.'

'He's got money,' Larry said.

'Inheritance. Strictly above board, although he's amassed a lot more since then.'

'If he's involved, there's no apparent sign of drug money.'

'Have you been in the house?'

'Yes.'

'You've seen the paintings on the walls?'

'Some were very good.'

'Some are extremely expensive. Some are even worth more than the house.'

'Hughenden said that the furniture and the decorations were O'Shaughnessy's.'

'It's possible some are, but the paintings are all Hughenden's. We've checked out the purchases. He used a different name and paid cash. They're better than money in the bank.'

'In that case, we'd better bring him in,' Isaac said.

'I want to be present when you interview him,' Donaldson said. 'The bastard knows me.'

***

Three men met: Devlin O'Shaughnessy, Steve Walters, and Alex Hughenden. The location was outside London, another property owned by Hughenden; the address known only to those present.

'We're in trouble,' Hughenden said. 'The police are looking for you, and I've been summoned down to Challis Street Police Station.'

'They've got nothing on you,' O'Shaughnessy said.

'Nothing they can prove, but I've got my reputation to protect.'

'With the money you're being paid, why should you care?' Walters said sneeringly. It was evident he did not like the precise, elegantly dressed man.

'That may be so, but I like it here. I don't want to move to Thailand and hide out in Phuket with a woman young enough to be my daughter.' It was clear that the dislike between the two men was mutual. Walters spoke poor English, whereas Hughenden was particular with his pronunciation.

Regardless of their mutual disdain, they needed each other. In fact, all three needed the other, as much as they needed the man who remained unknown, a voice at the end of the phone, a bank account generous in distributing its funds. Unknown to everyone except Hughenden.

Hughenden pondered what to do about the two heavies: one he liked, the other he did not.

The two men had become a liability, and although they had carried out their tasks successfully, they had become too well known in the community, and O'Shaughnessy's friendship with him was known.

The man who Hughenden communicated with sat in another part of London. He listened in on the conversation, unknown to O'Shaughnessy and Walters.

Hughenden was playing his cards carefully, well aware that his life was in the hands of a man that he had met once. He knew that the man would protect him at all costs.

After all, hadn't he taken the rough ideas and formed them into a credible drug trafficking organisation for the man, Hughenden thought.

He had to admit that without the man's money, it would not have been successful. But Hughenden knew that he had been putting himself in the spotlight, incurring the interest of Inspector Len Donaldson of Serious and Organised Crime Command, but the police officer had nothing on him, nothing that could be proven.

Hughenden knew he had covered his tracks well, and, as far as the local community and his local church were concerned, he was a pious man who gave to charity, helped out with the church services. Walters did not understand what he had achieved, he knew that. But what was Walters? Just another thug with a passion for maiming people and then cutting them up.

Hughenden had to concede that the two men had done a good job dealing with those who had threatened the syndicate. Fuentes had been dealt with, he knew that, although his body would not be found. The murder of Dougal Stewart had sent the right warning, but after the trouble it had caused, he was not sure it had been worth it.

Alex Hughenden had believed it was necessary to frighten those who threatened their well-being and their bank accounts. Hughenden knew that the money in his account was exceedingly healthy, and the joy of buying masterpieces to adorn the walls of his property in Bayswater excited him. Not that anything else did, he had to admit. He knew he was a solitary man, fussing over the old dears at the church, giving his time to hopeless causes.

'What are we going to do?' O'Shaughnessy asked.

Hughenden, brought back to reality, asked, 'What about Pinto?'

'Stiff as a board.'

'He's still complete?' Hughenden asked.

'We couldn't chop him up there.'

'That may be as well.'

'What do you mean?'

'Pinto dumping the torso in Regent's Canal was probably not the best idea.'

'Are you admitting that you were wrong?' Walters asked. He had advised against it in the first place. He had killed before, never been charged with murder, and why? Because the body had never been found, and there was no way of connecting it back to him. Fuentes had disappeared, and no one, at least no one official, had come looking for him. He had heard of a woman who had been enquiring after him, as well as some drug peddlers, but the woman was no longer around and the drug peddlers were now buying from them.

'Has there been any trouble with anyone else trying to muscle in, attempting to cheat us?' Hughenden asked. He knew the man on the phone would be listening to his reply.

'Everyone is behaving themselves,' O'Shaughnessy said.

'I just think we could have disposed of him somewhere else; somewhere that didn't focus police interest in our part of the city.'

'Hindsight,' O'Shaughnessy said.

'That's true.'

'What about Pinto? What did he tell the police?'

'You were there. You heard him.'

'He told them all that he knew. He told them about you two.'

'And you're still in the clear,' Walters said.

Alex Hughenden looked over at Walters. *Your day will come*, he thought.

The man on the other end of the phone listened intently. He did not intend to reveal himself to O'Shaughnessy and Walters. He pondered what to do about Alex Hughenden, a man now directly on the police radar. The man had performed well and protected him, but for how much longer?

The man knew that Hughenden was a sadist and had enjoyed watching the two men carve up Dougal Stewart. He also knew that if the police had any proof against Hughenden, he would grass on them all. The man knew that his position in society was more important than Hughenden's, and the concealment of his identity was paramount.

***

A meeting of the board in the city was not unusual, although the topic was. Behind the veil of respectability, four men met. One was an MP, a member of parliament, another a well-respected businessman, another a peer of the realm. The fourth man, the mastermind who had put the business plan to them two years earlier, had been persuasive. He knew of the others' vices. The MP had a penchant for expensive whores, the businessman needed to stave off a competitor, and the peer of the realm needed to save his family's fortune.

It had been a pact that the four had formed when they had been at Eton College; an agreement that still held them together. Whenever one of them had an idea to float, he would put it to the others first, and if they rejected it, then they would respect that person's confidence, no matter how ludicrous or criminal the idea.

Miles Fortescue was the MP for a constituency in the north of England, although he did not like the area, having only moved there because it was a secure seat and he was desperate to be in Westminster. Not that he saw his constituents very often, as his party could have put up a half-educated donkey and kept the seat. He had won fifteen years previously with fifty-five per cent of the vote, and he had only bought the run-down house there to satisfy the locals. As long as he went up there once a month to show his face, say a few words, kiss a few babies, he knew he would continue to be their local member in Westminster. Any more than that and he wasn't interested.

His wife interested him more as she had money, but not much else. He would admit to the other three in the room that she was as exciting as an old prune and that he did not like her. To everyone else, she was the beautiful wife on the arm of an MP, and their open signs of affection were almost embarrassing at times.

'You screw who you want,' she had said after two years of marriage, 'but no scandal. In public, we'll be the perfect married couple, even if you are odious and contemptible.'

Fortescue, once free of the pretence, had turned to what he enjoyed more: expensive women who demanded overseas trips and luxury cars and upmarket accommodation. His latest, at the time when the fourth member of the group had put forward his plan, came with the need for a credit card with no limit. She had been bleeding him dry, and he knew he could not stop indulging her. He had been the first to embrace the idea of illegal drugs.

Fortescue had known then, as he had always known, that his wife had been right; he was odious and contemptible, and whatever was required to allow him to live the life he wanted, there were no issues about it.

Jacob Griffiths had done well in life. In the twenty-five years since the four had left Eton, he had been the most successful. A chain of supermarkets up and down the country, an adoring wife, three children and a sixteenth-century manor house, an hour from London. It had all come about through sheer hard work and talent.

The day that the fourth man had put forward his proposal had been a dark day for him, as an overseas competitor with even more supermarkets was undercutting prices, even below wholesale. Griffiths knew their game. He had even done it occasionally, aiming to drive a local competitor out of business, but the overseas supermarket chain was doing it throughout the country. He knew what they wanted; they wanted him out of business, and they were going to succeed. There were three options: accept their ridiculous offer for his business, match them on prices, or close up and accept defeat. Griffiths knew that two of the options were unacceptable, but a price war cost money; money he could not afford to risk just in case the competitor didn't back off.

The fourth man had come along at the right time with his business plan. 'Fifty million pounds for each of us the first year. By the second year, it should be up to eighty million.'

Lord Allerton, the third man in the quartet, had not been successful in life. There was the stately home, the wife and family, his position in society, and enough money to survive as long as they let in the tourists at the weekend to gawp at them. He had joined an investment bank on leaving school; his title had ensured a good salary, but he had not been successful. A weakness in mathematics meant that deal after deal went wrong. He had tried his hand at writing a history of the family, tracing it back for eight centuries, but the book had been poorly received. His father had been a war hero, his grandfather an admiral, but what had he achieved? Nothing, and it irked him.

The fourth man's proposal, abhorrent as it was, promised untold wealth for little effort on his part. The peer knew that he was an honest man, but he had seen enough honest men with little to show. He threw his hand in as well.

The fourth man outlined the details. Each of the four would put in one million pounds. He, utilising his criminal connections, would do the rest. The other three knew that he had embraced crime as a profession, white-collar crime, and he had been successful. His name was not well known, not even to those who worked for him, nor to the criminal community in general, and very few had met him.

He reflected after listening in on the phone conversation of Hughenden, O'Shaughnessy, and Walters that one man did. He knew that Alex Hughenden had done a good job, and he did not have anyone to replace him, not yet, but the man was to be interviewed by the police, and what if he grassed, the same as Pinto? What then? Hughenden did not know his name, but it would not take a competent police officer long to find him. He knew what he had to do.

***

For a week there had been no sign of police activity. It was as if the heat was off. Devlin O'Shaughnessy knew only too well the crimes he had committed; he was after all an intelligent man who had been slammed up in prison for a crime he did not commit, although there were plenty that he had. It had seemed at the time that the police wanted him behind bars, and if they couldn't get him for one crime, they'd get him for another.

A friend of his in Bayswater had told him that no police had been seen close to where he had lived. O'Shaughnessy, who had become interested in art in part due to the influence of Alex Hughenden, in part due to his innate desire to better himself, needed to visit his home.

After two weeks of living out of a suitcase, moving every few days just in case, he needed to reacquaint himself with his personal belongings. He knew the risk. Steve Walters, his offsider and a man who had no interest in the better things of life, thought he was crazy and told him so plainly enough.

'You'll never understand,' O'Shaughnessy said, as he drank a pint of beer with Walters.

'You're in for life if they catch you.' Walters, not an educated man, knew the realities.

O'Shaughnessy and Walters had met a year ago. A chance meeting, although fortuitous for all three. Hughenden, owner of a small shop in Notting Hill trading in antique jewellery, knew when the two men had entered his shop by the rear door that he could use them. Hughenden, respectable and beyond reproach at the front door; crooked at the back door.

A small lane by which those who had stolen from the rich to give to the poor, in that case Hughenden, had increased his wealth.

Those who came in the front door paid well; he made sure of that, but they were always arguing over the price and the quality and the state of their finances. Little did they know that after Hughenden had reworked what others had stolen, those items often ended up in the front of the building.

He had taken great pride when one tiresome woman had walked out of the shop thinking that she had purchased a bargain. *Only five thousand pounds*, she thought.

Hughenden, who knew her through the church, could only smile, knowing full well that what she had just purchased had been stolen from her six months previously and extensively reworked. Hughenden knew he was a master of his trade, and in the years that the store had been open, he had only been visited by the police once. And that was not about stolen goods, at least not his, just assistance in appraising a gold bracelet that had been found under the floorboards in the home of a thief now in custody.

O'Shaughnessy had been the easiest to win over, as Hughenden realised that notwithstanding his heavily-tattooed appearance, he was a man who appreciated the finer things in life. That was why he had let the ex-prisoner stay in one of his investment properties. Hughenden knew that it would be safe. Walters, strictly criminal class, had given him concern initially, until O'Shaughnessy, who had spent many a night drinking with him, told Hughenden that he trusted the man.

'He's rough round the edges, but apart from fancying himself with the women, we can trust him,' O'Shaughnessy had said.

'If you vouch for him,' Hughenden's reply.

'Outline the plan,' O'Shaughnessy asked.

The drug trade, especially in heroin and cocaine, was burgeoning, and they intended to take control of their part of the city. Hughenden had outlined the plan in all its simplicity: make sure we're the only supplier.

O'Shaughnessy liked a simple plan, and he liked violence and Bach and expensive paintings.

'You've no aversion to dealing with anyone who interferes?' Hughenden asked.

'None,' O'Shaughnessy replied, which had not been entirely truthful as he had not killed a man in cold blood before, expect for a Taliban in Afghanistan when he had been a soldier, but that didn't count. The tribesman had been standing in front of him with a Kalashnikov pointing at him.

O'Shaughnessy knew that an innocent man had died when he had been involved in an attack on a supermarket to steal that night's takings. It had been close to Christmas, and the standard procedure of emptying the tills and transferring the money with adequate security was not in place.

Then, he knew that it had been a complicated plan: wait until you get the signal, check that the store's security is distracted, and there are no customers close to the till. Then check and check and when you're ready, the four of you go in and empty all the cash registers, and remember the safe in the manager's office. It's bound to be full of money.

An old-time criminal had meant well when he put the plan together, making the four that were to rush the store practise over and over again, even setting up desks in the room where they met to simulate the supermarket checkouts. Even at the time, O'Shaughnessy thought it elaborate. He would have just waited till they transferred the money to a security van later that night. Then they could have rushed the guards carrying the money and forced them to the ground, or smashed them around the head with a cosh. But the old-time criminal had won out. His plan was to be implemented.

The men waited for the right moment that fateful night. They entered full of bravado, only to be spotted by the manager of the store. 'Stop. I've called the police.'

One of the other three raised his rifle and pointed it at the man. The manager kept coming forward; the gun man, a timid youth of nineteen, pulled the trigger. The manager fell to the ground, dead.

In the pandemonium, all four of the robbers rushed for the exit. O'Shaughnessy remembered tripping and two men holding him down until the police arrived. He had not fired the shot, but he was guilty by association. A ten-year sentence, although he was out sooner, had curtailed his activities. No, he thought, a simple plan works better.

Chapter 11

A dredging boat was not how Duncan Fogarty had imagined his life at sea. He had dreamed of sailing the seven seas aboard his own yacht, or a life with the merchant navy, but life takes people down different paths.

He had sailed when he was young, a small single sail craft he had constructed as a school project. He had even crewed on a couple of trips across the Atlantic on fifty-foot yachts, but he was not a charming man, quite the opposite, and he did not make friends easily. He had tried the merchant navy, officer class, but they needed academic qualifications, not a desire to see the world, and Fogarty knew he was not bright. In fact, that was his only redeeming feature: his ability to recognise the truth of what he was.

He had always lived near to the River Thames, and the advert to work on a boat that plied the Thames, dredging the bottom, aiming to maintain the navigation channels, seemed his best hope. He applied, was accepted, and started work. That was seven years ago, and now he was the captain that he had always longed to be.

Normally it was silt and the rubbish of society that they brought up, even the occasional bomb from the last war.

'What the –?' one of Fogarty's team shouted as they made their daily run down the river. 'Stop the dredge!'

'What's the problem?' Fogarty shouted back.

'You'd better come and have a look.'

Fogarty took one look and called the police.

Isaac Cook and his DI boarded the boat at East India Docks. They had only received notice that there was something that may be of interest late in the day. The vessel was impounded as a crime scene, with Fogarty complaining that he wasn't paid to work extra hours.

The local DI who had attended first, and aware of the torso in Regent's Canal, had phoned Isaac after eliminating all other possibilities.

Isaac had walked down the gangway resplendent in a new suit and a white shirt with a tie.

'I hope you brought some old clothes,' Fogarty said.

'I've protective gear,' Isaac replied. The stench was noticeable, and he held a handkerchief to his nose.

'You get used to it.'

Isaac was sure he never would, but the dirty, smelly boat had something of interest.

An officer from the local station introduced himself. 'It looks like one of yours,' he said.

Isaac and Larry walked across the deck of the boat and peered under a tarpaulin. Isaac walked away and phoned Gordon Windsor. 'You're in for a long night,' he said.

'The one night of the week when I wanted to get off early,' Windsor's reply.

'Not tonight. There's not much for you to work with, but I have my suspicions.'

'Pinto?'

'Judging from what I can see, I don't believe it is.'

'Very well. Give me ninety minutes to round up the team.'

***

Crime Scene Examiner Windsor arrived within the hour, even though he had driven through the centre of London. Grant Meston, his principal CSI, accompanied him. Some of the team had brought floodlights as it was dark.

Once the two crime scene men were kitted up, they walked down the gangway and over to where the body was.

'Why don't you think it's Pinto?' Windsor asked as he peered at the body.

'It looks like it's been in the water for a long time,' Isaac replied.

'I don't know how you could tell that from what remains.'

Windsor moved closer to the body, carefully removing the rubbish and silt that surrounded it. Grant Meston took photos of the scene. 'Not very pleasant, is it?' Windsor said. His voice gave no indication of emotion about what lay in front of him.

'What are your thoughts?' Isaac asked.

'You're a bit premature.'

'I just need to know who it may be.'

'I'll not be able to tell you that here.'

'There are two possibilities: Rodrigo Fuentes or Vicenzo Pinto.'

'It could be either,' Windsor said as he carefully continued to expose the body.

'Is the head there?' Larry asked.

'What remains of it.'

'What do you mean?'

'The fish and the crabs have been at it, and I'm sure this dredger is none too fussy in bringing up everything pristine.'

'Arms, legs?' Isaac asked.

'It's a complete body, but unrecognisable. Have you noticed the legs?'

'What about them?'

'What's left of one still has a chain around its ankle. This person was murdered, and they intended the body to remain undiscovered. If the dredger hadn't found it, it would have not existed in a few months' time. Even now, there is precious little to go on. Have you noticed the maceration of the skin, the exposed bone?'

Isaac moved closer to the body. He felt bile in his throat, the need to vomit. He backed away and cleared his throat. 'How will you identify it?'

'DNA. There's no other way.'

'Are you able to give a cause of death?'

'With the body in this condition, it's almost impossible, although a chain around one ankle is fairly conclusive that it was weighted and thrown in.'

'Are you certain it's male?' Isaac asked.

'Pathology will confirm, but I'd say so.'

***

Alex Hughenden had prepared well for his visit to Challis Street Police Station. Outwardly he portrayed a prosperous and pious man. It was those aspects of his character that he intended to show when he met DCI Cook.

He had prepared carefully for the interview, although he knew they had no proof against him.

What had he done? he thought. *He had been friendly with O'Shaughnessy, even rented a house to him, and the man had turned out to be a murderer involved in the drug trade. How could that be related to him?*

He was supremely confident that the police would be swayed by his elegant manners and his respectability. There was nothing to connect him with the death of Dougal Stewart, although he had to admit he had enjoyed the sight of the man hanging from the ceiling, and Pinto pleading for his life in the corner of a dirty warehouse.

He had expected Devlin and Steve to kill the two men, not to kill one as they did and then cut him up. Devlin had admitted to a phone call and to be acting on instructions, which surprised him as in the past he had been their only contact.

He had thought at the time that someone was usurping his position, but the man had phoned and told him that he had made the phone call.

Alex had said that he understood, as earlier in the day he had been out of contact meeting up with some friends, close friends, and his phone was off, but phoning Devlin direct…

Hughenden wasn't totally sure but had discounted his misgivings. Hadn't the man phoned him up to wish him well for his visit with the police?

He did not know the man's real name, although he suspected who he was. He was certainly well connected and had plenty of money, but Hughenden had never checked further, knew he would not unless the man aimed to cut him out of the picture. Then he would find out who he was, who his contacts were, possibly take the man's position in the organisation. Hughenden realised that he was visible, yet the man was hidden from view and taking all the profits.

What did he receive? he thought as he waited for his appointment at Challis Street. *A lousy three hundred thousand pounds each month. What did the man receive? It must be a lot more judging by the car the man drove, and the suit he wore.*

He decided to find out more about him, just in case.

***

Isaac had to admit the woman was a knockout, dark but not as dark as him. She wore a blue top with a short skirt, even though the weather outside was chilly. She was the sort of woman who men were drawn to like bees to a honey pot.

'My Rodrigo, have you found him?' she asked.

Isaac recognised the accent as Brazilian. 'Are you a friend of his?' Isaac asked.

'We were lovers.'

Isaac realised that friend and lover were not always mutually compatible, but in this case, they probably were. 'And your name?'

'Maria Cidade.'

Isaac moved with her from the entrance to the police station to his office. The woman was nervous. He assumed she had probably overstayed her visa and was working somewhere for cash in hand. He discounted the possibilities of what she did to make money.

Maria Cidade did not look poor, and if she were indeed the lover of Rodrigo Fuentes, then she would have had money, drug money.

'We are conducting investigations,' Isaac said.

'He was with me four weeks ago, and then he disappears without saying anything.'

'What did you think?'

'I thought he had another woman, but he was not like that, my Rodrigo.'

'A good man?' Isaac asked.

'To me he was.'

'But you knew what he did?'

'He always said he would stop, and then we would buy a house in Brazil and make lots of babies.'

'We have recovered a body from the River Thames. Why do you think it may be him? Why have you not come forward before?' Isaac asked. He had been joined in his office by Wendy Gladstone.

'I wanted to, but I knew what he was.'

'A drug dealer?' Wendy said.

'My Rodrigo is driven by ambition.'

'How long have you been in England?' Isaac asked.

'Two years.'

'Legally?'

'Yes.'

Isaac did not intend to follow that line of enquiry. If Maria Cidade had overstayed her visa, he would report it to the authorities another time. The more important matter was the current case, and if the body recovered from the river, and now with Pathology, proved to be Rodrigo Fuentes, then the woman who sat in his office was the closest person to him.

'Tell me about Rodrigo,' Isaac said. 'Describe him.'

'Tall, the same colour as me.'

'His age?'

'Thirty-seven.'

'His medical history. Was he in good health?' Wendy asked.

'He broke his arm about six months ago,' Maria said. 'He fell off his motorbike.'

Isaac knew that he needed to talk to Graham Pickett, the pathologist.

***

Four Old Etonians met. It was unusual for them to meet often. Typically all communication was conducted by phone and email. This time there was to be an extraordinary meeting.

'We agreed on condition of our anonymity,' Fortescue, the parliamentarian said. There were others in Westminster who would say he was anonymous there as well.

'I have always respected that,' the fourth man said.

'That may be, but if they catch you, they'll find us,' Fortescue said. The other two men in the room nodded their acknowledgement.

'I don't see how.'

'There's another body,' Griffiths, the businessman, said. He was not as firm in his criticism. He had used the money that he had gained to stave off impending financial disaster. The supermarket chain that had been attempting to undercut him, to force him out of business, had failed to do so. Every time they lowered the price of an item, he would go lower. In the end, the competitor, realising there was nothing to be gained, had backed off, and discussions were underway to form an alliance to their mutual benefit. Or, at least, the benefit of the two supermarket chains. With them working in collusion, they would become a monopoly in some parts of the country. Then there would be a price war to drive out anyone else who threatened them. Griffiths was delighted that he had accepted the fourth man's offer, but his anonymity was still threatened; he knew that.

Lord Allerton was also concerned, but still pleased with the arrangement. The extra money had secured him financially, and he no longer needed to admit the obtrusive tourists into his home.

None of the four had any concern about the financial viability of the venture, although none relished their good life being affected by their identities being revealed, and three of them knew that to be a distinct possibility.

'This man you're using,' Allerton asked. 'Can he be trusted?'

'He's done a good job,' the fourth man replied.

'That's not what I asked.'

'I've trusted him up till now.'

'But…'

'He may need to go.'

'Another death?' Griffiths asked.

'It's always possible.'

'But why? Each death brings the police closer to us,' Fortescue said.

'May I remind you that I have made every one of you rich,' the fourth man said.

'We were rich before,' Griffiths reminded him.

'You all had your reasons for joining with me.'

'That's as may be,' Allerton said, 'but we didn't count on people dying.'

'That's sheer hypocrisy, and you know it.' The fourth man was angry.

'I don't see why.'

'So if someone dies of a drug overdose, a drug that you supplied, you're not concerned.'

'They don't connect back to us.'

'But if they do? What did you expect when you became involved with this, that it would be a bed of roses? We're dealing with illicit Class A drugs here, not running a chain of supermarkets, or pontificating in Parliament, or prancing around a stately home in a deerstalker hat and shooting poachers. We're dealing with the underbelly of society, the scum, not the members of a club for gentlemen.'

Three men sat stunned. In all the years since they had formed the pact at Eton College, they had never raised a voice in anger at each other.

Griffiths spoke for the three. 'You need to protect us,' he said.

'I am. Believe me, my friends, I know what I'm doing.'

Lord Allerton sat quietly. He was not sure what to do next. He only wanted to be back at home with his family. 'I want out,' he said.

'It doesn't work like that,' the fourth man said.

'Why?'

'You three are my protection.'

'How?'

'If this doesn't work out, if the police get too close, I need you three to get me out of the country and to ensure that I live to a ripe old age.'

'And if we don't?' Griffiths asked.

'You know the answer to that question.'

'You'll tell the police all about us.'

'If I'm going to prison, I'm not going alone. I need people of my own class as cellmates.'

'You're blackmailing us,' Allerton said.

'It's not blackmail, it's survival. All three of you were pleased to go along when the money was flowing and you were isolated in your ivory towers. Now the heat's on, you're all chickening out.'

The meeting ended badly. All four shook hands, offered words of friendship, but it was all a pretence. Only one man knew the way forward. He needed to act decisively and soon.

Chapter 12

Maria Cidade had spent three hours at Challis Street. Isaac had phoned the pathologist to pass on the information about Rodrigo Fuentes' broken arm. Eventually she had left; Isaac would pass on the inevitable news at a later time.

The pathologist, after checking, confirmed that the body on his autopsy table was almost certainly the missing Brazilian, but one hundred per cent confirmation would only come when a DNA sample from his parents in Brazil arrived.

The Homicide team needed no official report to know that they had Fuentes' body.

Alex Hughenden arrived at Challis Street on time. The interview room had been booked for him. Isaac and Larry would represent the police. Hughenden declined legal representation.

Isaac conducted the formalities before commencing. 'We are interested in your relationship with Devlin O'Shaughnessy,' Isaac asked.

'There's nothing to tell you. The man was a friend, and I rented a house to him.'

'A friend who is involved in drug dealing and murder?'

'I don't judge my friends on what you may say they are guilty of.'

'The man had money, yet you never asked where it came from?' Larry asked.

'Why should I? Do you judge your friends, decide if they're worthy to let into your house?' Hughenden replied.

'We are asking the questions,' Isaac reminded the man.

'Devlin was an educated man. Of course, he may not have looked it, but he could converse about art and literature. It's not often that you meet people who can.'

Isaac realised they did not have anything on Hughenden. The man sat back in his chair, his arms folded. He knew that he could deal with the two police officers sitting across from him.

They've got nothing on me, he thought. Hughenden knew he had no criminal record, apart from a minor offence in his youth, no involvement with the law apart from the time his place was broken into. He knew he was superior in intellect to the men who were interviewing him.

He did have one worry, but he did not intend to reveal it in the police station at Challis Street. Why was O'Shaughnessy taking instructions from the man, when the arrangement had always been clear? It had always been agreed that he, Alex Hughenden, would deal with the day-to-day running of the business and that the man was not to have any contact with the people he employed. And how did the man have his former friend's phone number. He was certain that was what Devlin was now. Not only was he avoiding his phone calls, but he was also conducting business deals without him.

Hughenden had heard about the vehicle coming over from France from the driver. He had only contacted him when Devlin had short-changed him on the money they'd agreed. Something to do with a short shipment which could only mean one of two things: the driver was taking some of the merchandise for himself, or O'Shaughnessy was on the fiddle. Hughenden was sure of the answer.

He could see that something would have to be done, but he needed to get out of the police station.

'According to the Serious and Organised Crime Command, you are under suspicion,' Larry said. He did not like the look of the man sitting opposite him. His sixth sense suspected the man knew more, and he had met his type before. To him, Hughenden represented the worst kind of criminal: educated and able to use their intellect to fool the police and to organise major crimes. People like Hughenden never dirtied their hands with the grubby side of the business; that was left to others.

'Where did O'Shaughnessy acquire this knowledge?' Larry asked.

'About what?' Hughenden replied.

'Art and literature.'

'He's a great reader.'

'In prison?'

'We never spoke about his time in jail, but it's possible.'

'What did you talk about ?'

Hughenden thought to himself, *stay calm with this buffoon. He's attempting to provoke me.*

'Art and literature.'

'I put it to you that you were masterminding the whole operation, and that you knew full well of O'Shaughnessy's involvement in the drug trade.'

'That's slanderous, and you know it.' Hughenden could feel his pulse racing. He forced himself to relax. One word said incorrectly, and the police would be looking further into his business affairs. There was still enough evidence of his fencing stolen jewellery, if only they looked.

'O'Shaughnessy and Walters are not capable of pulling off an operation of this size,' Isaac said.

'Am I guilty by association?' Hughenden replied indignantly, realising that he was letting the two men get to him.

'You have the intelligence to do it.'

Hughenden cleared his throat. 'Let's be clear. I have no criminal record, no history of violence. I'm a solid member of the community who goes to church every Sunday and gives to charity.'

'So did Al Capone,' Larry said.

'Do you want to repeat that outside of this police station?' Hughenden replied. His blood was seething at this penniless upstart. *If he wasn't a policeman…,* he thought.

'DI Hill spoke out of frustration. If, as you say, you are a pillar of society, your associations are disturbing,' Isaac said.

'DCI Cook is right,' Larry said. 'Defence based on a person's good character will hold little weight in a Court of Law.

It may mediate the sentence, but it does not absolve the person of guilt.'

'Am I defending myself? From what?'

'That you are involved in the importation of large quantities of heroin and cocaine into this country, and that you have set up an elaborate network to distribute them.'

'Preposterous. What proof do you have?'

Len Donaldson had asked to be present. Isaac had put him off as he was interested in bringing a murderer to justice. He now regretted that decision. There was something about Hughenden that didn't ring true, Isaac knew, but there was no proof, only supposition, and as the man had said himself, guilt by association.

Isaac had to conclude the interview knowing full well that they had only raised the hackles of the man opposite, although he knew that could provoke an action, an unexpected move that would prove the man's guilt. And one thing the DCI knew: Alex Hughenden was guilty.

***

The DNA from Brazil had arrived. Pathology had confirmed that the body retrieved from the River Thames was Rodrigo Fuentes, a known drug dealer and trafficker. There were none in Challis Street who were concerned that another lowlife had died, but the man had had chains around his ankles and was a murder statistic. The team had been working on that basis ever since the body had been discovered; now it was official.

Isaac had phoned Maria Cidade to let her know. He had conducted some checks, and she appeared to be a decent person who had fallen in love with a criminal.

She had taken the news calmly and said she would take his body back to Brazil for his parents. Hopefully, she said, they would never find out the truth of what he had become.

DCS Goddard, wanting to wrap up the murder of Dougal Stewart, was again in Isaac's office at Challis Street. The team were already there.

'DCI, another one?' Goddard stated the obvious.

'Yes, sir,' Isaac replied, anticipating the now predictable response from his senior, the man he had once held in great esteem.

'You know who murdered Stewart. Is the latest death related?'

'We believe so.'

'Proof?'

'Vicenzo Pinto mentioned Fuentes' name before he disappeared.'

'Then it's three murders?' Goddard said.

'We do not have proof of Pinto's death.'

'But you're certain he's dead.'

'Until we receive advice to the contrary, then we will treat his disappearance as murder.'

'And the murderer of Rodrigo Fuentes?'

'Devlin O'Shaughnessy and Steve Walters.'

'Can you prove it?'

'It's unlikely. After four weeks weighted down in the Thames, there's not a lot to work with.'

'The body of Dougal Stewart. Can you register a case against O'Shaughnessy and Walters?'

'With Pinto's evidence.'

'But if he's dead.'

'It would've been better to have a live witness, but we have his interview on video as well as a signed confession. His evidence will hold up, and we have a lot of fingerprints from the warehouse where they killed Stewart. We've enough.'

'Then find the murderers soon before I have him onto me again.' Goddard left the office soon after.

'Who's he referring to?' Wendy asked.

'The commissioner.'

'Davies?'

'He's not an easy man.'

'Will Caddick be back?' Larry asked, hopeful that the unpleasant Welshman who had temporarily occupied Isaac's seat would not be returning.

'He will if we don't start solving the case.'

'What did you achieve with Alex Hughenden?' Wendy asked.

'Not a lot. We don't have any proof against him. At the present time, he's not guilty of any crime.'

'But you suspect him?'

'Serious and Organised Crime Command have their suspicions, but no proof. O'Shaughnessy and Walters have been the visible members of the syndicate bringing the drugs into the country, but they're not smart enough for a venture of this complexity.'

'We could keep a watch on Hughenden,' Larry suggested.

'Can I leave that to you and Wendy?' Isaac said.

***

'You should have brought me in when you interviewed Hughenden,' Len Donaldson said.

Isaac and Donaldson were sitting in a café not far from Challis Street Police Station. Both men were relaxed in each other's company, each having mutual respect for the other.

'In hindsight, but I wanted to get the measure of the man. I needed to know if he had the look of a guilty man,' Isaac said.

'And what did you deduce?'

'He's careful in what he says.'

'Slimy, that's how I'd describe him,' Donaldson said. 'I've been into his shop, spoken to the man.'

'Did he know who you were?'

'I made out I was a customer aiming to buy a bracelet for my wife's birthday.'

'Did you?'

'Not a chance. He charges through the roof, and besides my wife ran off with my best friend. She'd be lucky to get the time of day from me.'

'What were you looking for?'

'The man has money, lots of it. I needed to know where it came from.'

'And?'

'No doubt he makes good money, but not enough to buy a three-storey terrace in Bayswater, and a couple of other expensive houses in the area.'

'Pillar of the church, donates to charity. Doesn't that indicate a decent man?' Isaac posed a rhetorical question.

'No doubt he is kind to children, but he staked nearly one hundred thousand pounds for renovations on the church he attends.'

'Guilty conscience?'

'Maybe his generosity allows him to be involved in an odious business.'

'Like taking from the rich to give to the poor, no matter how the money was obtained.'

'Something like that. Besides that, what did you get from Hughenden?'

'Nothing to incriminate him.'

'What do you reckon of the man?'

'He's involved.'

'How do you intend to prove it?'

'I need to solve two murders first.'

'You've solved them already.'

'We have a case against O'Shaughnessy and Walters for the death of Dougal Stewart, but no way of implicating them in the death of Rodrigo Fuentes.'

'That may never be solved unless you have a confession.'

'We should work together on this,' Donaldson said.

'I thought we already were,' Isaac's reply.

***

Larry was out on the street. He was meeting people, slipping them money for information. Wendy was close to Hughenden's shop. She had looked in the window, seen a ring that she positively loved, but the price tag was the equivalent of six months of her salary.

Rasta Joe was not pleased to see Larry, but he was at risk, he knew that, and the news of Rodrigo Fuentes' death had created fear in those who dealt in drugs.

'Rasta Joe, what's the deal with Alex Hughenden?' Larry asked in the Jamaican's favourite pub. As usual, the drinks were on the police.

'What's there to tell you?'

'Do you know him?'

'I've met him a few times, but we don't move in the same circles.'

'Honest?'

'How would I know?'

'Rasta Joe, you know what's going on. They fished Rodrigo Fuentes out of the Thames. Do you want to be next?'

'Are you trying to frighten me?'

'You're already scared. I saw Fuentes two hours after the dredger had scooped him up. After a few weeks under water, it wasn't a pleasant sight. That's what you'll look like if we don't deal with O'Shaughnessy.'

'Did he murder Fuentes?'

'That's what Pinto reckoned.'

'What happened to him?' Rasta Joe asked. Larry noticed that his concern had not quenched his ability to down the pints.

'Vicenzo Pinto is missing, presumed dead. And why are you so frightened?'

'I was buying from Fuentes. You're not going to arrest me for that confession, are you?'

'Dealing with whoever's behind these murders is more important.'

Rasta Joe considered his position. It was either level with DI Hill or run the risk of an untimely death. He chose to level.

'If I work with you on this, you've got to promise you'll keep me out of prison,' he said. It was the first time he had trusted a policeman; he knew it would raise the ire of his criminal compatriots, but they weren't being threatened, he was.

'That's not a promise I can give.'

'Then no deal.'

'Is what you know crucial to our inquiry?' Larry asked.

'I can finger Hughenden,' the Jamaican said.

'What I can guarantee you is that your past and present crimes will be overlooked, but any in the future, then you're on your own. No protection from me.'

Rasta Joe sat back and sipped on his beer. 'It's a deal. In writing?'

'You know I can't do that. You'll have to trust me on this one.'

'Alex Hughenden is not as clean as he pretends to be.'

'We have strong suspicions that he's not, but it's difficult to prove.'

'I don't know about him and the drug trafficking, although Devlin O'Shaughnessy was drunk one night and he was talking.'

'To you?'

'After a few drinks, no way.'

'Why's that?'

'Sober, he's decent enough, but after a few drinks he starts getting unpleasant, making comments.'

'What sort?'

'The ones I've heard all my life. Ask your DCI, he'll know what I mean.'

'Go back to where you come from, you black bastard. That sort of thing?' Larry asked. 'He still gets it occasionally.'

'At the police station?'

'They wouldn't say it to his face, but some wouldn't be sorry to see him go.'

'There are still racists out there,' Rasta Joe said.

'And people who deal in drugs.'

'Point taken. Besides, I intend to be an honest citizen from now on.'

'Remember, I'll only protect you as long as you're straight with me. Any further criminal activity, I'll not protect you.' Larry knew the Jamaican would not leave crime, no more than he would give up policing. Rasta Joe represented the worst in society: people who prey on the vulnerabilities of others.

Larry looked round the pub. He remembered in his youth, when he used to drink more than he should, that a public house was an Englishman's enclave, but now in a pub close to Notting Hill he could only see people from elsewhere. In the far corner, he saw a couple of young lovers oblivious to their surroundings; at the bar, a group of migrants in from Eastern Europe speaking one of the Slavic languages. Larry assumed it was Polish, as they were everywhere in London. Most were decent people trying to make their way, but an undesirable element had come in with them.

Larry had to admit that he liked Rasta Joe as a person. The man was entertaining, and now that he needed him, affable. It did not excuse the man from the fact that he made a living out of the misery and addiction of others.

The two men organised a pub lunch. Larry knew that after five pints there would be no food for him at home that night. Not that he blamed his wife, as she only cared for him, but sometimes there had been some furious arguments, at least from her side, about why he needed to drink as part of the job. Larry was confident she understood, but it did not stop her complaining, although she was not a woman to dwell on it for too long. The next morning his breakfast would be on the table, and she would be back to her cheerful self.

'What's the deal with Hughenden?' Larry asked as he proceeded to eat his steak and chips.

'You need to check out the merchandise in his shop.'
'I know it's expensive.'
'Ask him where it all came from.'
'What do you know?'

'One of my mates, he's a thief.'

'I thought all your friends were good citizens.'

'He is. Anyway, what's the difference between someone who steals from the rich and those rich bastards who never pay their taxes.'

Larry had to admit he had a point, but he was not there to discuss social inequalities. 'Your friend, what does he say about Hughenden?'

'Hughenden will buy the expensive stuff from him.'

'Are you certain? Will your friend put that down in writing?'

'What do you think?' Rasta Joe said.

'No, but I'll need details,' Larry said.

'Then my friend will be in trouble with Hughenden.'

'Is Hughenden the man in charge of the syndicate?'

'I don't know. I've never seen him involved, but O'Shaughnessy's involved and Hughenden's crooked. What do you think?'

'We have our suspicions that Hughenden is a senior man, but no proof.'

'I can't get you proof. Too much risk for me.'

'But you're here.'

'I've people watching out for me. If anyone makes a move towards me, they'll see them.'

'Part of your gang?'

'Don't look, you'll not notice them.'

Larry knew full well that a black man in London did not look out of place, although there were certain areas where a white man would. He was aware that Rasta Joe had supplied the information necessary to pressure Hughenden, but without proof, the man would slide out from under.

Chapter 13

Alex Hughenden had walked from the Challis Street Police Station a confident man. He knew they had nothing on him, although he had allowed them to get under his skin a few times. He determined to take care not to let it happen again. He could never understand why others allowed themselves to be caught, although greed seemed likely. He had always been careful to keep his criminal activities at a moderate level, knowing full well that the occasional illegal activity would not be visible.

Over the years he had made a fortune, but was always careful to conceal it: no rash purchases of expensive cars, no overt signs of obscene wealth. The houses he had purchased could be seen as the wise investments of a successful businessman and certainly within the realms of possibility from the takings of his jewellery shop. It was small, but it only dealt in the best, to an exclusive clientele who were more concerned with the beauty of the object than its cost. Nevertheless, they would always brag to their socially-paranoid acquaintances about how much they had paid; almost a badge of honour to show that money meant little to them.

He knew these people for what they were, and he did not like them very much. He much preferred the humble people at his church. Hughenden had grown up in a strictly Methodist God-fearing family: the patriarch, the manager of the local bank. He had advised the young Alex well. 'Look after your money, invest wisely and don't show it off to others. They will only be jealous.'

His father had forgotten one lesson, don't get involved in crime, which is what the young Alex did as soon as he was able to figure the percentages on the deal.

'To give you a good religious grounding,' his father had said when the young Alex had complained at being sent to a cold and dusty boarding school. Two years later, when he was ten, Alex learnt the truth during an unexpected visit to his father's bank. He had caught him sitting on his desk with his personal assistant kneeling in front of him. His father had made light of the matter, said he had a stomach ache and she was attempting to massage the sore area.

Young Alex, only ten and unknowledgeable of such matters, remembered later the magazines of some of the older boys at the school and then realised what he had just seen.

From that day on, the relationship between father and son had deteriorated, and no more was mentioned about what had occurred. His mother, oblivious to her hypocritical bigot of a husband, went to her grave believing in him totally. Alex had wanted to tell her when he was older, but never did. He knew he had made the right decision in at least ensuring that one member of his family was blissfully ignorant of the realities of life.

His mother had believed in good and bad, heaven and earth, and her husband. Her son had only one belief, the percentage and what was in it for him. He knew that at the church he was as insincere as his father, but he never cheated them, and he certainly did not indulge in blowjobs with his secretary, not that he had one, and although the lady who helped him at the weekend was attractive, he never made a play for her.

Hughenden was a celibate man. The roughness of O'Shaughnessy had tempted him, although he knew full well what the man's reaction would be, and besides, he liked his life the way it was: alone and self-contained.

***

Wendy, alerted by Larry after his conversation with Rasta Joe, maintained her vigil, although she could not stay indefinitely waiting for the first sign of criminal intent on Hughenden's part, and besides it could be weeks, months before he made a move.

She was sitting in a café opposite observing his shop, but there were only so many cups she could drink in a day.

Larry joined her. 'Anything?' he asked.

'What do you expect? That he's buying stolen jewellery every five minutes?' Wendy said tersely. The caffeine was starting to get to her, and her DI's breath stank.

'Of course not. What do you suggest?'

'What are we trying to achieve? I thought we were after a murderer, not someone who deals in stolen goods.'

'We need a lever on our man opposite. He's squeaky clean, too clean, and he knows something.'

'No criminal record?'

'Nothing of importance, and that's bugging us. Hughenden's fencing stolen jewellery, and he's too smart by half. He made mincemeat of DCI Cook and me.'

'He's the Mister Big?'

'Not sure, but probably not. It would need more than one individual.'

'Hughenden doesn't fit the bill?' Wendy asked.

'The man rarely travels out of the country, and it would need personal meetings to pull off the scale of the drugs being imported.'

'We can't sit here indefinitely. If you want to get this man, we need to research stolen goods, known thieves. Then we might stand a chance. I could work with Bridget on this,' Wendy said.

'I'll concentrate on where O'Shaughnessy has gone. If we can find him, then he may rat on Hughenden. Either we wrap this up soon, or DCI Caddick is back.'

'I suggest we work overtime then. Nobody wants him back in the office.'

'Agreed.'

'If you don't mind my bluntness, DI,' Wendy said, 'buy some mints, the strong ones, or your wife is going to have apoplexy.'

Larry knew she was right. Too many times he had returned home drunk, and he could see it becoming a habit. He had seen too many police officers' marriages confined to history due to a predilection to drink too much, work too many hours, and associate with criminals, and Rasta Joe was a criminal, the worst kind. In fact, he had to admit that many criminals were charming, even Hughenden with his superior manner, but Larry wasn't sure if O'Shaughnessy would be. The man was literate, but he had gone at Stewart's body with a chainsaw: hardly the manner of a charming man.

'Across the road!' Larry said.

'Hughenden,' Wendy said. 'Where's he going?'

'No idea, but it's not the time to be closing up.'

Both the police officers observed the man as he fastidiously secured the metal grille over the windows and set the alarm. He was moving quickly as he completed the task, which seemed unusual, especially to Larry, as the man had been, if anything, in the interview at Challis Street, slow and measured.

'Something's flustered him,' Wendy said. 'We need to follow him.'

'You're better than me. You'd better do it.'

Soon after the two police officers left the café, Larry careful to conceal himself as he turned to the right. Wendy turned to the left, her eyes very firmly on Hughenden's back. She hoped he would not walk fast as her legs were giving her trouble, or jump in a car, as hers was fifty yards away.

Hughenden continued to walk at a brisk pace. Wendy realised she could keep up if it were only for a mile or so. The man did not look to the left and right, and certainly not behind him, which was as well, as a red in the face woman would have been suspicious.

Four hundred yards from his shop, Hughenden came to a halt. A man approached him from a side street. Wendy ducked into a shop doorway to observe. The owner of the shop came out to ask what she was doing. 'Sergeant Wendy Gladstone,' she said. She showed her police identification. 'Give me a couple of minutes.'

'Take as long as you like,' the shop owner said.

Wendy, momentarily distracted, could see the two men in discussion. It seemed to be an amenable conversation. Wendy took out her phone and made a call. 'DI, it's O'Shaughnessy.'

Larry, alerted to the development, started to put plans into place.

Isaac was contacted and could see one murderer charged if they could only capture him. DCS Goddard, who was in his SIO's office at the time of Larry Hill's phone call, was elated. 'This will keep Commissioner Davies off my back,' he said.

'Still causing trouble?' Isaac asked.

'The man looks after his own.'

'Caddick,' Isaac said.

'Davies wants me out, too.'

'Can he do that?'

'If he can prove incompetence.'

'We're not incompetent,' Isaac responded.

'Davies knows that, but that's hardly the point, is it?'

'Throw enough mud around for long enough, some is bound to stick.'

'That's it,' Goddard said. The man had entered Isaac's office ten minutes earlier, and for him, he was in a remarkably good mood. Rarely seen with a cheery smile, he had positively been beaming when he had entered.

Isaac had asked why, although had not received a satisfactory answer. Knowing his DCS as well as he did, it could only mean a new political connection either within the police service or without. He was playing a dangerous game, and if the commissioner discovered it, whatever it was, then Detective Chief Superintendent Richard Goddard would be hung out to dry. Isaac knew that office politics was not a game he played well or even wanted to, but the DCS revelled in it. With the previous commissioner, it had worked well, but with Commissioner Davies it was a risky gamble.

'I want the man charged by tonight,' Goddard said.

'We've got to catch him first.'

'Don't give me that negativity. Sergeant Gladstone's got him in her sights. How can he get away?'

'You're right. We don't intend to let him slip through the net.' Isaac picked up his phone. 'Larry, mobilise whoever you can. We want O'Shaughnessy.'

'He's just driven off with Hughenden.'

'Damn,' Isaac said. 'Any idea where?'

'We know where.'

'Where? I've DCS Goddard in the office with me,' Isaac said. Larry took the hint to be careful in what he said.

'O'Shaughnessy's old house. I had an officer out there as soon as Hughenden closed his shop.'

'Well done,' Goddard said over the phone.

'Thanks, sir,' Larry replied.

'Are they both in the house?' Isaac asked.

'Yes.'

'Storm it and grab O'Shaughnessy.'

'Not so easy. It's best if we wait it out.'

'It could be a long wait. We need O'Shaughnessy today.'

'Very well,' Larry replied.

Chapter 14

Inside a house, a smart terrace house in a good part of Bayswater, two men spoke. One a jewellery shop owner, the other, a known murderer.

'Devlin, the police are looking for you. Why are you here?' Hughenden asked. He was feeling distinctly uncomfortable with the situation, unsure whether to trust his former tenant or not.

'I need to get out of the country.' O'Shaughnessy sat in a comfortable leather chair, his favourite to recline in when listening to classical music when he had been living there.

'Where to?'

'I can't stay here.'

'Why not?' Hughenden asked. The man sitting across from him was edgy, and Hughenden knew he was dangerous. They had been friends, good friends, but now…

'Get real, Alex. We're both in trouble.'

'I'm not.'

'I've had a phone call.'

'From who?'

'Our mysterious master, that's who.'

'And what did he say?'

'He wants me to kill you.'

Hughenden, the colour in his face draining rapidly, took one step back and sat down hard on a wooden chair on his side of the room. 'Why?'

'I never asked.'

'Are you going to do what he says?'

'Killing someone is not the problem, not even you, but you've been a friend, done right by me.'

'And our leader?'

'Who is he? What is he? If he can dispense with you, then he can have me killed.'

'What did he promise you?' Hughenden asked. He had to admit he had gained pleasure from watching Dougal Stewart's death, had even relished Devlin's account of how Rodrigo Fuentes had pleaded for his life in a mix of accented English and Portuguese. He imagined that it had been him instead of O'Shaughnessy who had secured Fuentes' ankles with a chain, the other end secured to an old anchor, and then thrown him off the side of the boat, but now it was him who was to be on the receiving end, and he did not like it.

'He said I would take over from you.'

'With more money than you're getting now?'

'I don't trust him. If he gets me to kill you, then if he's cornered, he'll throw me to the wolves.'

'Am I safe?' Hughenden asked, slightly more relaxed than five minutes previously.

'From me you are, but if I don't kill you now, he'll make sure someone else does, and he'll also deal with me.'

'Then I need to get out of the country as well.'

'And leave all this,' O'Shaughnessy said, looking around the room with its exquisite furnishings.

'You're right. I can't leave. If I am to die, then it will be here surrounded by what I treasure.'

'I still need to go.'

'What do you want me to do?'

'I need two hundred thousand pounds.'

'From me?'

'Who else?'

'You must have earned that.'

'I need an extra two hundred thousand pounds to see me out.'

Hughenden tensed again. He realised that his friend was desperate. 'I need one day,' he said.

The money was not the issue as it only meant disposing of one or two paintings, but they were important to him. He did not want to let them go, knew he could not keep them.

'Fine. Can I stay here?'

'If you want, but the police know this address.'

'I'll take my chances.'

'The police will find you in time,' Hughenden said.

'Not where I'm going.'

'And where's that?'

'Somewhere very remote.'

'And warm?'

'Maybe. I'll make sure I have company for a few years.'

'And then what?'

'Cancer. It's not apparent yet. I may last three or four years, and I intend to live it up. Slammed up in prison or floating face down in the Thames does not appeal.'

'Steve Walters?' Hughenden asked.

'He's gone up north.'

'Is he coming back?'

'I doubt it. It's you and me now.'

'And our leader.'

'Have you met him?' O'Shaughnessy asked.

'Once.'

'Do you know his name?'

'I never asked.'

'You must have an idea who he is.'

'I do, but I've kept it to myself. I'm the only person who can connect him to what we're doing, as well as the murders.'

'That's why he wants you dead. And killing Fuentes and Dougal Stewart were not good moves.'

'Fuentes can't be connected back to us.'

'To me, you mean,' O'Shaughnessy said.

'To you. What about Pinto?'

'Still frozen.'

'You'd better dump the body.'

'Why? No one will find it where it's hidden.'

'The police are smarter than you think.'

***

Two hundred yards from where the two men conversed, a group of police officers gathered. Wendy had relinquished her duty outside Hughenden's house to a younger officer in plain clothes.

Larry addressed the group. 'We need O'Shaughnessy,' he said. He passed a photo around.

'They're still in the front room,' Wendy said.

'Any idea what they're talking about?' Larry asked.

'We've not had time to conduct any monitoring.'

'There's no time now anyway. We want O'Shaughnessy today.'

In the group of eight assembled officers, four were heavily clad in body armour and carrying weapons. Larry and Wendy were not armed and would be standing back from the initial assault. Once the house was secured, they would enter and arrest Devlin O'Shaughnessy. Alex Hughenden would also be taken into custody as a witness.

Isaac had already outlined the plan back at Challis Street. O'Shaughnessy would be in one interview room, Hughenden in another. Two officers outside would be monitoring both interviews, listening for inconsistencies between the two men's statements.

With the briefing completed by the side of the road, the eight police officers made their way to Hughenden's house. Two officers would enter through the front door, two through the back. Another two would monitor in case one or both of the men attempted to jump from a window.

At the house, the two men continued to talk, unaware of the impending action. Wendy phoned the officer watching from outside. He confirmed that the time was optimum.

Two police officers rammed the rear door, breaking through on their second attempt. Another two police officers rammed the door at the front. O'Shaughnessy was known to be violent and probably armed, and ringing the doorbell would have been regarded as risky, though smashing two doors was perhaps excessive.

The two men at the rear moved quickly through the kitchen and along the hallway. The two men at the front were quickly into the room where O'Shaughnessy and Hughenden sat. Both men were on their feet, the more timid of the two in one corner.

O'Shaughnessy, full of Irish adrenaline and not willing to be captured, was shielding himself behind a sofa. 'Come one step closer, you bastards, and I'll let you have it,' he said.

The police officers held back.

'Devlin, you can't hold out,' Hughenden said.

'I'll not let them take me.'

'Please, sir. You are surrounded,' one of the officers said.

'There's no way I'm going to let you take me,' O'Shaughnessy shouted.

The police officer's instructions were to arrest, not to kill, the man who was waving a gun at them. They knew he was an easy target to take down, but they had been told that the man had vital information.

The lead armed response officer, Inspector Jeff Freestone, was glad of the instruction, cognisant of the paperwork afterwards if a gun had been fired.

Larry and Wendy stood outside some distance away. A small crowd of onlookers was forming. The uniforms were trying to move them along, although they were having difficulty. One person was videoing the proceedings. Larry knew that it would be on social media before the television. In the world of instant communication, not only would the news-seeking public be aware of what was happening in Bayswater, but so too would the villains, the Mister Big who the team at Challis Street wanted to bring in. Not that he was guilty of carrying out any murders personally, too smart for that Isaac had reasoned, but the man would have known what was going on, had no doubt given the order for the killing of two men, three if Pinto was ever found, and others, although they were unknown.

Len Donaldson was aware of the events in Bayswater and soon on the phone to Isaac. 'What's going on?' he asked.

Isaac, satisfied with the way things were proceeding and confident that one murderer would be behind bars that night and charged with murder, was ebullient. 'O'Shaughnessy,' he replied.

'Hughenden?' Donaldson asked.

'We've nothing on him.'

'Is he in the house?'

'He's there. We know that O'Shaughnessy picked him up not far from his shop.'

'Have you been staking out his shop?'

'Only today.'

'We've had people watching him for weeks and nothing. You've been lucky.'

'Not luck, just good policing,' Isaac said smugly.

'That's as may be, but this time I want to be present when you interview Hughenden. I could make it official.'

Isaac could understand the man's sentiments. There he was, a senior man in the Serious and Organised Crime Command, and the Challis Street Homicide team, Isaac's team, were stealing his thunder. 'I'd be pleased to have you there,' Isaac replied.

O'Shaughnessy would talk when threatened with a life sentence in prison, and he would point the finger at Hughenden, Isaac was sure of that, but the jewellery shop owner was going to be harder to crack, and Len Donaldson had more knowledge of how the drug syndicate operated.

'I'll be in your office within thirty minutes,' Donaldson said.

One minute after Isaac had terminated his call with Donaldson, his phone rang. 'We've got Hughenden,' Larry said.

'And O'Shaughnessy?'

'Stalemate.'

'Bring Hughenden down to Challis Street. We can start with him. This time he's going to talk. And remind those attempting to arrest O'Shaughnessy that we want him alive and unharmed.'

Larry moved over to the house and spoke to one of the team members who passed the message on.

Freestone, still holding his position just outside the room where a desperate and increasingly irritated man cowered, received the instruction given by Larry. He acknowledged with a nod of his head.

'Our instructions are not to harm you,' Freestone shouted to O'Shaughnessy.

'You'll need to.'

A desperate man considered his position. If he surrendered, he would die in prison. The cancer that racked his body would see him succumb in three or four years. If he fought it out in the house, one of the policemen would shoot him. He could see no solution to his dilemma. He regretted coming to the house as he kneeled behind the sofa, keeping a clear view to his front and rear. He was surrounded, and he knew it. He realised that with the education he had received in prison and his intelligence, he could have come out of there and found a decent job and a decent woman, but what had happened: the inevitable. A friend of a friend offering to help him get on his feet with just one little job, no risk and the money's good, and he was back into crime.

He knew he would not surrender, the odds were not in his favour. There was no way that he was innocent, and the police had a watertight case. He was sure that Alex would eventually break.

Inspector Freestone relinquished his position to another policeman and walked out through the front door of the house.

'What's the situation?' Larry asked him.

'He's determined.'

'What's the plan?'

'Give him a few hours, just wait until he's got an empty belly. He'll not remain alert for much longer, and come nightfall, he'll start falling asleep. We've got him eyeballed from the front and rear of the house.'

'Before midnight,' Larry said. 'It's important.'

'I hope so,' Freestone replied. 'I don't fancy waiting around for that long.' He looked around and saw the crowd watching their every move. He retreated back inside.

Resuming his position, Freestone spoke calmly to O'Shaughnessy. 'Devlin, our instructions are to wait for you to surrender.'

'I'll not surrender.'

'That's fine, we've got time. We've got plenty of hot food, even cigarettes and beer. We'll make ourselves comfortable, not that you will. Once our people are tired, we'll bring in a fresh team. We're taking bets on how long you'll last.'

'Forever.'

'I've got my money on four hours.'

'And the others?'

'One of them reckons you're good for two, another officer reckons six, but there's no way. If you make six, it'll be a new record.'

With one of the team keeping a watch on O'Shaughnessy from the front of the house, Freestone sipped coffee, the smell pervading the air where the desperate man crouched. O'Shaughnessy knew his stomach was rumbling and he was desperate for a visit to the bathroom.

He wet himself, although he did not associate it with the jocularity that he and Steve Walters had felt when Pinto had done the same thing at the warehouse.

Meanwhile, Alex Hughenden was down at Challis Street Police Station. Isaac knew he could not keep him there for long, as ostensibly the man had committed no crime and had put up no resistance to the police storming his house, although he was mighty angry, demanding compensation for the damage done to his property and for sullying his reputation.

Isaac gave little credence to the man's protestations. He knew Hughenden was guilty. Len Donaldson was in the office, excited that there was progress.

Wendy had left Bayswater and returned to Challis Street. Larry did not intend to come back until the police had their man, which according to Freestone shouldn't be too long, as O'Shaughnessy was starting to fall asleep.

Larry understood how he felt. He had drunk four pints with Rasta Joe, and he was feeling the after-effects. At least, by the time he got home, they would have worn off, and his wife would be pleasant, although when that would be was unclear. With both O'Shaughnessy and Hughenden in the police station, it was bound to be the following morning before he arrived home, probably after daylight, but he would be able to take the children to school.

Inside the house, O'Shaughnessy's eyes were closing. Freestone made a tentative move forward, only to watch the man wake up with a start.

'I'm going to lose my bet,' Freestone said.

'You'll not take me.'

'You'll not last three. I give you another fifteen minutes.'

'Not a chance.' O'Shaughnessy attempted to move his legs, but one was cramping. His throat was parched after drinking two beers before, and his stomach was aching. Freestone watched as he attempted to stretch and to force his eyes open.

'Ten minutes.' The instruction was relayed to the team at the front and rear of the house.

Within five minutes, the man behind the sofa was asleep. 'Now,' Freestone commanded.

From both doors into the room, the police entered. The man who was never going to give in was arrested with barely a murmur. His hands were pulled behind his back, the handcuffs applied. The gun was placed in a plastic evidence bag.

Freestone, pleased that the arrest was successful, would deal with the paperwork the next day. However, Larry did not have such a luxury. O'Shaughnessy was bundled out of the house and into the back of a waiting police van. Larry phoned ahead; Isaac would be ready on their arrival.

Chapter 15

The pact that had served all the four Old Etonians for so long was unravelling, and they were meeting for the second time in as many weeks. The fourth man, the acknowledged leader of the group was neither a politician or a businessman or an aristocrat. His friends knew that well enough when they had joined with him in his latest criminal venture.

He had brought them in when he needed them, ensured they were well compensated. He had respected their wishes not to be involved, other than to supply the necessary cash in the early days and to reap the financial rewards later on, and now, when it was becoming precarious, they were ready to isolate him.

'What you wanted was all the profit, none of the risks,' the fourth man said.

'That was what we agreed to,' Griffiths said.

'The agreement's changed. If I go down, so do you three.'

'That was never the agreement,' Allerton reminded him.

'Where does it say that in writing?' demanded the fourth man, angry that his fair-weather friends were willing to sacrifice him.

'You know there's nothing in writing,' Fortescue said.

'That's because we trusted each other. You're only interested in protecting yourselves.'

'And what's wrong with that?' Allerton asked.

The fourth man stood to one side of the other three. He was a good-looking man who had taken care of himself, not like Miles Fortescue with his safe electorate, Jacob Griffiths with his supermarkets, and certainly not like that upper-class snob Lord Allerton, with his stately home and his seat in the House of Lords. The fourth man knew why he had been at Eton: his parents had worked incredibly hard, and he had received a partial scholarship due to his academic brilliance. Also, as the son of a cousin of Allerton's father, he was blue-blooded enough for the prestigious Eton College.

'Is that a threat?' Fortescue asked.

'Take it whichever way you like. I'll take you three sanctimonious bastards with me.'

Allerton sat up, Fortescue adopted an expression of disbelief. Griffiths, a tough man who had dealt with equally tough men in trade, felt the need to respond. 'Are you certain you want to take us on?' he asked.

'If I must. I've put at least thirty million pounds into each of your pockets, and now it's getting dangerous, you're willing to pull out.'

'I don't think anyone mentioned our pulling out. We're still a team,' Griffiths said, although he had enough money now and the risk was too high, he knew that. He did not fancy the idea of a prison cell any more than the others.

Fortescue nodded his head in agreement, although the politician recognised a serious threat. Allerton sat mute, hoping only that the nightmare would go away.

'That's good,' the fourth man said. 'However, there's a problem.'

'More deaths?' Griffiths asked.

'The money you made came at a cost.'

'But murder?' Allerton asked, resigning himself to the situation.

'There is one person who can threaten us.'

'Don't you mean you?' Fortescue said.

'I thought we were clear on this matter. If I go down, so do you three.'

'Not if we deal with you first.'

'Fortescue, if your threats are as impotent as you and your parliamentary career are, then I've got nothing to worry about.'

'We could expose you, strike a deal with the police,' Fortescue said, aiming to secure a way out, knowing full well that any deal would result in their facing charges. The 'impotent' jibe had struck home. He had been married for nearly thirty years, and no children had resulted from the marriage, although they had ceased to sleep together after the first two years. One or two of his subsequent mistresses had wanted children, but he had failed to fulfil their requests, not that it had stopped them taking his money. There was one who had become pregnant, said it was his, but he knew the truth. A doctor in Harley Street had checked him out, declared him fit and able to make love, but incapable of giving a woman a child.

After the woman had bled him for a few more weeks, he had wished her well and left her to her own devices. His parliamentary career had been the same. Initially, he had tried, and had stood up in Parliament on a few occasions to take part in a debate, but each time his arguments had fallen short, and the last time he had made a fool of himself by stuttering. The Speaker had had to tell him to spit it out and then sit down. After that, he attended when his vote was needed, but apart from that he did not impact on the regular business of Parliament.

'Strike a deal with the police! With what? The three of you aren't smart enough, and besides you're all guilty. It won't take much for me to send them a complete dossier of your activities either. Mind you, I'll make sure I'm out of the country before then,' Allerton's cousin said.

Jacob Griffiths, the most successful financially of the three, knew the man was correct. The man was a bona fide genius, as well as the organising force behind the most audacious drug trafficking syndicate in England. Jacob Griffiths had to admire the man even if he was a criminal who was willing to murder. Griffiths knew that he had been tough in business, bankrupted a few, one had committed suicide, but to give the order for someone to be killed – he knew he could not do that.

Allerton, unsure how to proceed, spoke. 'We're doomed whatever happens.'

'Rubbish. That's defeatist nonsense. I'll get us out of this. Once the loose ends are wrapped up, we'll close the business. I've got a few other ideas,' the fourth man said.

'How long?' Fortescue asked.

'Three weeks and then we're out of the drug business.'

Allerton sat back in his chair, hopeful that the nightmare was concluding. He had enough money now to live the life he wanted, as did the others.

Griffiths was not so sure; he needed proof. 'Why three weeks?'

'There's a shipment coming over, the biggest so far.'

'You can stop it.'

'With the people I'm dealing with, not a chance. Either we accept the shipment and pay them in full, or they'll come looking for us.'

'You,' Allerton said.

'Us. Do you think I've not put a contingency plan in place in case you lily-livered cowards chicken out?'

'What right have you to talk to us like that?' Fortescue bellowed.

'Sit down and shut up. The same as you always do in Westminster.'

Fortescue, red in the face, did as he was ordered.

Griffiths, the savviest of the three, still needed details. 'Lay out your plan.'

'Very well. There is one man who's met me. He has to be dealt with. But first, we need to take this last shipment and ensure its distribution.'

'You need this man?'

'If he stays out of police custody, then he can continue to work for us.'

'And if he doesn't?'

'He'll have to be dealt with.'

'Killed?' Allerton asked.

'Do you imagine he'll keep his mouth shut if he's in for a ten-year stretch in prison? And now he's with the police,' the fourth man said.

'Are there any charges against him?'

'He's been associating with a known murderer, but he'll probably walk clear of the police station. At least today he will.'

'But the police will be looking out for him,' Griffiths said.

'You're right. Are you suggesting that we deal with him now?'

'Are you asking if we should kill him?' Fortescue asked.

'It's time you three took part in the decision-making process if I'm to save your skins.'

'He needs to be dealt with,' Griffiths said with a glum expression.

'That's the way. It's easy once you get used to it. Just think of him as a number, not a person.'

'Anyone you have in mind?' Fortescue asked.

'To kill him, or to replace the man?'

'Both.'

'I've got someone who can deal with a murder. Replacing him is not so easy. '

'But you'll find someone,' Fortescue said.

'How about you, Jacob?' The fourth man looked over at Griffiths. 'You know all about distribution and marketing.'

'Not a chance.'

'I'm just testing, and you're correct, I do have someone; someone who'll do very nicely to move the merchandise.'

'And when it's finished?'

'He'll need to be dealt with.'

'Then it's two more murders,' Allerton said.

'Don't be stupid, Allerton. We're not schoolboys now. It's called risk management.'

***

Alex Hughenden sat in the interview room at Challis Street Police Station. He had been supplied with a meal and a hot drink.

'He's too calm,' Isaac said as he observed the man, courtesy of a video camera mounted in one corner of the interview room.

'Slimy, that's what I say,' Len Donaldson said, reminding DCI Cook of an earlier conversation when he had mentioned his disdain for the man waiting to be interviewed.

Hughenden's interview had been delayed for two hours while a lawyer was brought in. The first time, Hughenden had declined legal representation; this time he had not.

Relax, Alex, relax, Hughenden thought. *They've nothing on you that will stick.*

'O'Shaughnessy?' Donaldson asked Isaac.

'He's down in the cells.'

'Has he been charged?'

'He has for the murder of Dougal Stewart.'

'His reaction?'

'Surprisingly calm.'

'He knows he'd be wasting his time proclaiming his innocence.'

'Will he talk?' Isaac asked.

'It's hard to say. He's guilty of murder, and the evidence is tight, but talk about what?'

'Hughenden, the drug syndicate, Rodrigo Fuentes, and there's still Vicenzo Pinto.'

'Maybe, but I wouldn't hold out too much hope. The man knows the drug syndicate's reaction if he grasses.'

'The Stewart solution.'

'Exactly.'

The initial plan had been to interview Hughenden and O'Shaughnessy concurrently, looking for discrepancies in what they said, but that had been dispensed with. Isaac had felt that a few extra hours behind bars would remind O'Shaughnessy of what he had experienced in the past, what was to be his foreseeable future.

Len Donaldson and Isaac entered the interview room where Hughenden sat. He had been joined by Adam Galbraith, his lawyer. Isaac knew the man, having grown up in the same part of London.

'DCI Cook, pleased to meet you.'

'And you, Mr Galbraith.'

Neither man acknowledged their childhood friendship. Isaac rectified the situation. He went through the formalities and to his first question. 'Mr Hughenden, I have known Mr Galbraith for many years as a friend. Do you have any objection to his representing you?'

'No.'

Isaac knew that it had been necessary to state a possible conflict which may have been used in Hughenden's defence at a later time.

'Very well. We have formally charged Devlin O'Shaughnessy with the murder of Dougal Stewart.'

'Why am I here?'

'There are no charges against you yet, but you are a known friend of O'Shaughnessy, and he was apprehended in your house.'

'He was a friend, no more. What he does or did is none of my business.'

'Until proven otherwise.'

'My client is here voluntarily to assist the police,' Galbraith, a short man with horn-rimmed glasses, said. 'It is not for you to imply that he is by default, due to a friendship, guilty of any crime.'

'That's understood. However, it is this friendship that continues to give us concern. Why was O'Shaughnessy at Mr Hughenden's house today?'

'He stopped me in the street,' Hughenden said.

'You could have phoned us.'

'How? Devlin was standing in front of me and insisting we go to my house. You've seen him. He's not the kind of person to argue with.'

'What did he want?' Donaldson asked.

'Money.'

'Did you agree?'

'What else could I do? He had a gun.'

'Your friend?'

'He was desperate, not thinking straight. And besides, the police came barging in. You could have knocked on the door instead of breaking it down.'

'We'll deal with that later,' Isaac said. Hughenden sat back on his chair, aiming to maintain the look of self-assuredness.

'Mr Hughenden, I put it to you that Devlin O'Shaughnessy made contact with you not out of friendship but due to your both being involved in a major drug trafficking syndicate in this country.'

'You are not in a position to make such remarks without proof,' Galbraith said. Isaac remembered him as a little underweight child, not as the sharp lawyer that he had matured into.

'O'Shaughnessy was one of the foot soldiers, not an officer,' Isaac said. 'He will be interviewed soon. The man is about to go to prison for first-degree murder. He has every reason to tell us all that he knows.'

'You'd strike a deal with him?' Galbraith asked.

'If he cooperates it will go in his favour at his trial.'

'My client is innocent of all charges. Your aspersions are ridiculous.'

'Mr Hughenden, do you wish to make a statement?'

'Yes. I have a jewellery shop in Notting Hill. Due to its success, I have managed to purchase several investment properties, one of which is the house in Bayswater that I rented to Devlin O'Shaughnessy. He was a tenant who became my friend. I admit that it is an unusual friendship in that he is obviously a hardened criminal, whereas I am not.

'I was unaware of his return to crime after leaving prison the last time, and his apparent involvement in the death of a man came as a complete surprise. I have not seen him since then, and his meeting me today was unexpected. I can tell you no more.'

'I believe we've exhausted this interview. Is my client free to go?' Galbraith asked.

'Not yet,' Isaac said. 'We will need to conduct a full search of Mr Hughenden's shop.'

'What for?'

'Stolen merchandise,' Donaldson said. 'There will be a warrant issued.'

'I've got nothing to hide,' Hughenden confidently said. Isaac could see beads of sweat on the man's forehead.

'Is my client free to go after that?' Galbraith asked.

'He will be required to stay here until we have concluded our interview with Devlin O'Shaughnessy,' Isaac said.

'This is preposterous. My client is an innocent man who was forced by another to go to his house. The subsequent police siege resulted in significant damage to my client's home, and now you say that you are going to search his shop. This amounts to police intimidation.'

'Unfortunately, this amounts to good policing. We will hear from Mr O'Shaughnessy first before we decide on your client.' Isaac said.

Len Donaldson knew he had something to report back to his senior at Serious and Organised Crime Command. He had seen the perspiration on Hughenden's forehead as well, a sure sign of nervousness.

Chapter 16

Devlin O'Shaughnessy was calm when he entered the interview room, not fifteen minutes after Alex Hughenden had left it. Isaac went through the formalities, Larry sitting to his left.

O'Shaughnessy had been charged with murder. The interview was related to that, not drug trafficking, and Len Donaldson was not required. Not that Donaldson wanted to be as he had plenty to be getting on with. First, he had to see his detective superintendent and to brief him on the situation, which for once looked promising.

Donaldson knew that once they had a crime they could pin on Hughenden, then the drug syndicate would be his next target. If Hughenden was charged and in custody for possession of stolen goods, then he could be further pressured. 'You help us, we'll help you,' the usual format to loosen the tongue of the most resolute.

The extent of the involvement of the punctilious jewellery shop's owner in the drug trafficking was unclear. There was a Mr Big, and that was who Serious and Organised Crime Command were after. DCI Cook and his team could have the accolades for solving the murder of Dougal Stewart, a minor drug smuggler, but Donaldson knew the big fish was still out there, waiting for him to bring him in.

He had been dealing with organised crime for eight years, and each year its inroads into the crime of London increased. What had been the trafficking of a few women from Eastern Europe for prostitution had transformed into drug smuggling amounting to hundreds of millions of pounds a year, and now criminal gangs were smuggling illegal refugees into the country as well. Donaldson did not dwell too deeply on such matters. He had one job to do, and that was to bring down whoever was controlling Hughenden.

The visit to the jewellery shop was to be a joint effort between Isaac's team and Donaldson's. A warrant had been arranged, and it was only waiting for the teams to meet up.

Not that this concerned Isaac Cook and his DI. They were both in with O'Shaughnessy and his lawyer.

'My client strenuously denies all charges,' Adam Galbraith said. O'Shaughnessy was using the same lawyer as Hughenden. Isaac could see that the man was not going to be successful this time.

'Mr O'Shaughnessy, you have been charged with the murder of Dougal Stewart, commonly known as Dave.'

'You can't prove it,' O'Shaughnessy said, his tattooed arms folded in an act of defiance.

'Unfortunately for you, we can.'

'How? I barely knew the man.'

'We have a signed confession from Vicenzo Pinto identifying you and Steve Walters as the two people who murdered Stewart.'

'And you believe him?'

'We also have your fingerprints on record. They match those found at the murder scene. The evidence is overwhelming. Either you or Walters killed Dougal Stewart in a warehouse not far from here.'

'You're framing me.'

'There are only two alternatives for you,' Isaac said.

'What are they?' O'Shaughnessy asked.

'I suggest caution in what you ask,' Galbraith said, directing a look at the man sitting alongside him.

'Why? I'm not guilty.' From what Isaac could see, this apparently intelligent man was reverting to type, criminal type, in denying everything.

'Today, you held off the police with a loaded weapon. Do you deny this?'

'I'd drunk a couple of beers. They caught me at a bad time.'

'An innocent man would have come down to this station and answered all questions. I put it to you that you are a guilty man and you know it. This posturing of yours in this room is non-productive. Mr Shaughnessy, you are going to jail for the murders of Dougal Stewart and Rodrigo Fuentes.'

'I never killed him.'

'Who?'

'That Brazilian.'

'Are you admitting that you were a major player in the distribution of large quantities of illegal drugs?'

'I'm admitting to nothing.'

'DCI, how much longer is this going to continue?' Galbraith asked.

'Until your client starts telling the truth.'

'My client has said all that he can on this matter. He is innocent of all crimes.'

'He can deny them,' Larry said, 'but we've got enough proof to put him away for the next fifteen to twenty years.'

'Five, ten, fifteen, what difference does it make?' O'Shaughnessy said.

'Why?' Larry asked.

'Cancer, that's why. I'd rather spend my last few years enjoying myself, but if the police are determined to lock me up for a crime I didn't commit…'

'But you did commit these crimes. We have enough proof. Your continuing procrastination will serve no purpose.'

Galbraith could see that the interview was not going well. 'Could we have a break, say twenty minutes?' he asked.

'Fine,' Isaac replied.

***

'Devlin, I can't defend you here,' Galbraith said after Isaac and Larry had left the interview room.

'I'll not grass.'

'Not even to save yourself?'

'They're right. They've got me fair and square. Whatever I say, I'll be convicted.'

'What about Steve Walters?' Galbraith asked.
'What about him?'
'Where is he?'
'Up north somewhere.'
'You've had no contact?'
'He's phoned me once or twice, but he's staying where he is. I can't blame him. I should have taken what money I had and made a run for it.'
'Then why didn't you?'
'Greed, I suppose. I knew Alex Hughenden had plenty and I thought some of it would be better in my pocket. He's always played fair by me, and I knew he'd agree.'
'You could have phoned him.'
'I wanted to see the house. For once in my miserable life, I was living well there.'
'Are you going to continue to maintain your innocence?'
'I'll not grass, especially not on Alex.'
'Then you will not walk on the street as a free man again.'
'It looks that way.'

***

Once the two police officers had returned, Galbraith made a statement on his client's behalf. 'My client maintains his innocence of all charges and will strenuously defend himself in a Court of Law. He will not speak further on these matters and will devote his time to his defence.'

Isaac had hoped for more, but if the man intended to remain silent, then so be it. He would at least stand trial for murder, with a one hundred per cent certainty of conviction.

To Isaac, he and his team had solved the murder of the man whose torso had been found in Regent's Canal. Richard Goddard was elated and phoned Isaac to offer his congratulations.

'There's still Pinto and Fuentes,' Isaac said.

'You've already stated that it'll be hard to pin Fuentes' murder onto O'Shaughnessy.'

'He killed him; I'm certain of it.'

'At least the man's inside for one murder. Whether you prove Fuentes' murder or not, it doesn't matter.'

'And there's Pinto's.'

'You've no proof.'

'His body's got to be somewhere,' Isaac said. He still wanted O'Shaughnessy to crack and to tell him where Pinto was and how the drug syndicate operated, but he knew that could wait.

***

Len Donaldson may have been an expert on illicit drugs, but he knew nothing about jewellery. Neither did Wendy Gladstone, who had accompanied him on the Homicide team's behalf. Both had to admit that Alex Hughenden, regardless of what he might be, knew the value of silver and gold. The shop was stocked with the most exquisite items at prices neither of the two moderately paid police officers could afford. The jewellery that Wendy had so admired in the shop window on a previous occasion was locked in a safe at the rear of the shop.

Hughenden, when he realised that the search was going ahead, had given the police all assistance, including the combinations to the safes and how to disable the alarm, which was as well as the police would have still entered and opened the safes, although it would have taken longer.

'I don't want you messing up my shop the same as you damaged my house,' Hughenden said. He was allowed to be present while the search was being conducted, but not to interfere.

'It'll be fixed,' Donaldson said. He had seen the house and had been appalled at the mess left by the police. Someone was going to pay, he knew that, but they had apprehended a murderer, and now he had the heat on the shop owner. Not that it showed as Hughenden was calm, assisting where he could, advising on what each item in his store cost: its silver mark, how many carats, its history, and most importantly, where he had bought it and for how much.

'We'll not find anything,' Donaldson said. He had brought a jewellery expert with him to validate whatever Hughenden said.

'Why do you say that?' Wendy asked. She was attempting to focus on the work in hand, but she was also bedazzled by such beauty.

'He's a meticulous man. His records will be the same.'

'Forged?'

'Some may be.'

'Are you saying we need his records checked by a forgery expert?' Wendy asked.

'We need something on this man,' Donaldson said. 'He's the key to the drug trafficking, I'm sure of it, but he's not going to crack. Not unless we have a lever.'

'He may know about Fuentes and Pinto.'

'Do you know how many people die each year in England because of people like Hughenden and O'Shaughnessy?' Donaldson asked.

'A lot more than the three deaths we're dealing with at Challis Street.'

'Over two thousand five hundred last year. That's three times the European average.'

'It puts it into perspective,' Wendy admitted.

'The deaths of a few criminals are nothing compared to the harm they cause to society. Frankly, I'm not bothered with Dougal Stewart, not even your Vicenzo Pinto, or the Brazilian, if their deaths lead us to whoever's running this syndicate.'

'I can understand your sentiments. I had a friend whose son became addicted. It killed him in the end.' Wendy reflected on her oldest son who for a while had smoked marijuana.

'Don't worry, Mum. It's harmless, no worse than beer,' he'd said.

Thankfully, in his case, it had only been a passing fad, and he soon migrated back to beer, although at the time his coming home drunk had caused her sleepless nights.

The jewellery expert could only praise the quality of the items in the shop. 'Nothing to note here,' he told Donaldson and Wendy. 'Excellent quality.'

'Is any of it stolen?' Donaldson asked.

'The well-heeled don't always report it.'

'Why not?'

'Unless it has special significance, they'll not bother. And most people inflate the price for insurance.'

'But for precious items, they'd need to be valued,' Wendy said.

'A valuation at retail prices, which means the owner would be unlikely to receive that much if they sold them on the open market. They'd be forced to sell through a place like this, and they want their commission.'

'You'd better take the records,' Wendy said.

'I'll have them checked out by Fraud and Forgery,' Donaldson replied. He informed Hughenden, who maintained his air of infallibility.

The search had taken three hours, and Len Donaldson realised he was no nearer to solving his case. Wendy returned to Challis Street Police Station.

Both knew there was a lot more work before their respective cases could be closed.

***

Wayne Norman was a smart arse, always on the periphery of crime. He was a thin young man of twenty-two, and whereas he should be forging a career in the city or in trade, he was doing neither. Not that either option interested him anyway. He was what society would deem a useless layabout. A definition his hard-working mother would only concur with.

'Find yourself a job,' she had said the previous night in the flat that they called home, although others would call it a slum. The woman worked two jobs to pay the rent and to put food on the table, and a twenty-two-year-old child who bled her dry emotionally and financially was not something she needed. She had reasoned with him, even kicked him out a few times, but after a week he had come back reeking of living on the street, dossing down where he could, sleeping in a charity clothing bin or down an alley.

He was her son and she could not kick him out again, even if she did not love him the way a mother should love a child.

'Jobs are for fools,' Wayne Norman would always reply. 'Look at you, working day and night for a pittance.'

'And what about you?' she'd ask.

'I get by.' And get by he did with petty thieving: handbags and mobile phones mainly.

For once, he had left the flat early. He wandered down Acklam Road, not with any purpose, only looking to cause mischief: an unlocked car where the owner had left it the night before when he had come home drunk, a parcel left on a doorstep, some clothing hanging on a line. It was not often he walked along that road, and the sight of a run-down garage off to the railway side of the road intrigued him. He moved closer, tested the lock, looked around him. It was still early, and it was cold. He pulled at the lock, and it came away from the wooden door. He entered, once again checking to see no one was watching. Apart from some old boxes and car parts, there was nothing of interest except for an old freezer in the corner. He opened it, hoping to find something of value, something he could sell down the road, no questions asked.

He moved the ice that had formed with a metal rod that he found in the garage. Wayne Norman, a lazy man, jumped back, falling over as he rapidly retreated from the garage. A local man walking his dog saw him exit. 'What are you doing in there?' he asked.

'It's a ...' Norman's only reply as he ran down the road.

The old man looked inside the garage. He took one look in the freezer and made a phone call.

The team at Challis Street were alerted, and within minutes were in the car, moving towards the location. They brought a couple of uniforms to secure the area.

Isaac, usually office bound, led the team into the garage. They had been forewarned of what was inside and had put on foot protectors and gloves. They kept to one side of the garage, as there were clearly footprints in the middle. Isaac reached the freezer and lifted the lid.

'Vicenzo Pinto, I presume,' he said in an attempt at levity, emulating the immortal lines of Henry Stanley when he first met Dr Livingstone in remotest Africa in an earlier century.

One phone call from Larry, and Gordon Windsor and his team of investigators were on the way. The three police officers retreated from the garage. The curious onlookers were starting to gather. A collection of police cars and police officers was not an everyday occurrence, although there was a good collection of third rate rogues and villains who lived nearby. However, Isaac did not believe any of them were responsible. He knew who had put the body there, and he was in custody for one murder. Another one would not faze O'Shaughnessy, although it may Alex Hughenden. Isaac was determined to nail the man. He didn't believe him responsible for the death of Dougal Stewart or of this victim, almost certainly Vicenzo Pinto – the clothes matched his parents' description from the day he was last seen – but Hughenden was instrumental in them, had possibly given the instructions for two men's deaths, possibly a third with Rodrigo Fuentes.

Once Pinto's cause of death was confirmed, Isaac intended to force Hughenden to speak. The evidence, although not conclusive, was adding up, and was enough at least to charge the jewellery shop owner as an accessory to murder. He knew Galbraith would try to wriggle his client out of a conviction, but it was enough to hold the man in the cells at the police station.

Chapter 17

It only took Gordon Windsor and his team one hour before he was able to give a verbal report. 'It's Pinto,' he said.

'Is the body intact?' Isaac asked over the phone from his office.

'Yes. He was stabbed in the chest.'

'Is that the cause of death?'

'Pathology will need to confirm, but it seems conclusive to me. He's only been in the freezer for a short time. He's still recognisable. DNA checks will confirm it's him, as well as identification by a relative.'

'When can that be done?'

'We'll take the body to the pathologist in the next couple of hours. Give it another few hours for him to defrost, and it should be fine.'

'I'll make it for five this afternoon,' Isaac said. 'Fingerprints?'

'O'Shaughnessy's.'

'Any sign of Hughenden's?'

'None. Just O'Shaughnessy's, although my people will stay on and check further. It looks as though Pinto was dead when he was brought here.'

'We could ask the neighbours if they saw anything.'

'Around here? Are you joking? They're not the friendliest, and besides, it's clear who put him in the freezer.'

Isaac ended the phone call. Wendy and Larry were in the office. 'Wendy, a job for you,' he said.

'The worst job for a police officer: telling the next of kin their loved one is dead,' Wendy said.

'It's either you or a local police officer where they live.'

'I'll do it, and besides, you need them for an identification. I'll bring back one of his parents with me.'

'Larry, check out if anyone saw anything.'

'I'll get some uniforms to do it. We'll need to talk to O'Shaughnessy again.'

'I'll phone up Galbraith,' Isaac said.

'If you don't mind me saying, you have some unusual friends,' Larry said.

'What do you mean?'

'Rasta Joe and Galbraith.'

'Believe me, neither are friends. I grew up with them: one of us became a criminal, another a smart-arse lawyer, and the other a police officer.'

'An excellent police officer,' Wendy said.

'Thanks, but I don't think that is how Commissioner Davies would refer to me.'

'Then he's a damn fool.'

***

Devlin O'Shaughnessy, even after time in the cells, was no more agreeable than the previous time. Adam Galbraith was present. Larry and Isaac represented the police.

'We've found Vicenzo Pinto,' Isaac said.

'What's that to me?' O'Shaughnessy replied.

'It seems you have a preference for freezing your murder victims.'

'I've killed no one, so don't try and put his death on me.'

'We'll make sure you're convicted for the death of Dougal Stewart first. If you worm your way out of that, we'll then charge you with Pinto's death.'

'Do what you want. I'll not be around to see it.'

'Why? Are you going somewhere?'

'Galbraith will get me out.'

'He's that good, is he?' Isaac asked.

'He said you went to school with him.'

'That's true.'

'Then you know he's a smart man. He'll deal with your charging me. Down on your arrest quota this month, are you?'

Isaac could see that the man had nothing to lose and was baiting him.

'My client is innocent of all crimes,' Galbraith finally spoke after his client had said his piece.

'Mr O'Shaughnessy will have his day in court,' Isaac said. 'How he's going to wriggle out of either murder when his fingerprints are everywhere is hard to see.'

'You do know Acklam Road?' Larry asked O'Shaughnessy.

'I drive down it sometimes,' O'Shaughnessy answered in a vague, disinterested manner. 'What about it?'

'Do you own or lease a garage there?'

'Not likely. The bastards will steal anything up there.'

'Then why did you leave Pinto in a freezer in one of the garages.'

'That is a prejudiced question,' Galbraith said. 'Mr O'Shaughnessy does not need to answer.'

'Maybe he doesn't,' Isaac said, 'but his fingerprints are all over the place, and there are shoe prints as well. We're aiming to match them with footwear that Mr O'Shaughnessy owns. He may have disposed of the bloodied footwear from murdering Pinto, but we've got all the records we need. Also, there are tyre marks in the driveway. We will be checking them as well. One way or the other, regardless of whether your client wishes to talk, we've got him. You know that.'

Galbraith sat still, looking Isaac straight in the eyes. *He's got enough evidence,* he thought.

'I'll answer,' O'Shaughnessy said. 'Three words, maybe four. I've got nothing more to say.'

'That's six,' Isaac replied.

'Always so smart, aren't you? I'm dying, and you're going to slam me up in prison for the last few years of my life. You're a bastard and whatever I say will make no difference. Do what you like. I'll say no more.'

Isaac could see that they had drawn a blank with the man, although he was guilty as charged. 'Alex Hughenden is involved,' he said.

'In what?' O'Shaughnessy asked.

'The importation and selling of large quantities of illegal drugs.'

'You're after him as well. He's a successful man, you're just a policeman. Jealous, are you?'

'Did he give you the orders to kill three men?'

'Why do you keep reiterating the same old tired questions? Galbraith, do I have to sit here?'

'If you have no more to say, then no.'

'Okay. I've got no more to say.'

'So be it,' Isaac reluctantly agreed and terminated the interview.

Outside, his senior, DCS Goddard, asked what he thought.

'Fifty years ago, he wouldn't have had to worry about another five years with cancer.'

'Capital punishment, last hanging in 1964.'

'Yes, that's it. The man's guilty and no smart defence lawyer, certainly not Galbraith, will get him off.'

***

Later that day, Wendy phoned in. Pinto's father had formally identified the body. In the meantime, there was still the unresolved matter of Alex Hughenden. Len Donaldson insisted on being present when he was interviewed again. Larry, for once at a loose end, went home early. He had not seen his children for three days as he arrived home late and left early. He knew his wife would be pleased to see him.

Hughenden was known to be at his shop. Sergeant Wendy Gladstone and DCI Len Donaldson went to pick him up. The front door was locked when they arrived even though it was still early afternoon. Wendy remained at the front while Donaldson went around the back.

'What the –?' Donaldson shouted on arriving at the back door.

Wendy, hearing the commotion, rushed to join him.

'It's not looking good,' Donaldson said.

'We need some uniforms.' Wendy took out her phone and called for a crime scene to be set up.

The two police officers entered through the back door. There was a general sense of chaos, with one chair upended and a box of bracelets spilled over the floor.

'We should wait in case someone else is here,' Wendy said. Donaldson chose to ignore her.

He moved along through the small corridor towards the front of the shop. He knew something was wrong; he could sense it. Two uniforms arrived within five minutes. Wendy phoned Isaac to update him. He recommended caution, but Donaldson, a man desperate to break the drug syndicate, was throwing caution to the wind.

'Up here,' he shouted back. 'The man's here.'

Wendy moved forward, unsure of what she was going to find, but conditioned by her work in Homicide to the sight of a dead body, although she had not wanted to see the dismembered torso of Dougal Stewart.

'At least two hours, I'd say.' Donaldson looked a disappointed man.

'How did he die?' Wendy asked, looking at the man sitting in a chair. He looked as if he was asleep.

'Look at his neck.'

On closer examination, Wendy could see the piano wire wrapped around the man's throat. 'Not a good way to go,' she said.

'What that man could have told us,' was Donaldson's only comment.

***

The situation at Challis Street had become frenetic. They had started with a torso in Regent's Canal, and now they had four bodies. Only two of them had the name of a murderer against them – Devlin O'Shaughnessy – and that man was not willing to talk.

One thing was clear to Isaac: whoever had murdered Alex Hughenden, it was not O'Shaughnessy; the man had a cast iron alibi as he was locked up in a prison cell.

'His death is inconvenient,' Donaldson said on his return to Challis Street Police Station.

'Any ideas?' Isaac asked.

'On who killed him? None.'

'Why was he murdered?'

'I'm floundering here. Unless those he reported to were scared that he would speak.'

'He was going down for a few years after you found proof that he had been fencing stolen jewellery.'

'I don't reckon he would have squealed on his superiors,' Donaldson said. He sat on a chair in Isaac's office, dejectedly looking down at the floor.

'The CSIs are checking out the murder scene. Maybe they'll come up with something.'

'There had been a scuffle of some sort.'

'We should get a preliminary report from Windsor in the next couple of hours. In the interim, we should deal with what we've got.'

'Apart from a lot of dead bodies.'

'If O'Shaughnessy killed Dougal Stewart and Vicenzo Pinto, then who killed Rodrigo Fuentes and Alex Hughenden?' Isaac asked. He was not as dejected as his fellow DCI, but he was worried. Once again, a case he was involved in and the bodies were piling up. He knew it would not be long before the commissioner of the London Met, through his mouthpiece DCS Goddard, made his presence known. This time there may be validity in his reaction, due to the number of bodies. Isaac knew that yet again he had to pull out all the stops.

'We're assuming Fuentes was killed by O'Shaughnessy and Steve Walters,' Donaldson said.

'And we don't know where Walters is.'

'You have a case against him?'

'Enough to get him convicted.'

'Then we'd better find him.'

'Could he have killed Hughenden?' Isaac asked.

'It's possible, although so far his murders have only been messy. With Hughenden, it looked professional.'

'But there was a struggle. As if the man who killed him delayed, allowed his prey to get away. A professional would have just carried out the hit without warning.'

'Are we deducing that he may have known his killer?'

'It's a theory.'

'A good theory,' Donaldson said. 'We need to find Steve Walters.'

***

Wendy Gladstone and Larry Hill were brought into the office. Larry's early finish to spend time with his children was curtailed due to the importance of wrapping up the deaths of four people.

'What do we know about Steve Walters?' Isaac asked in the office at Challis Street Police Station.

'He's a thug. No idea why Hughenden would have used him,' Larry said.

'Do we have his criminal record?'

'There's little to recommend him. Incarcerated at fourteen in a borstal for knifing a fellow pupil at school. At seventeen he's sentenced to two years for shooting a shop owner, a minor wound.'

'It's not a long sentence,' Donaldson said.

'Mitigating circumstances according to the trial report.'

'What do you mean?'

'The usual: deprived home, an alcoholic father, his mother had just died. He's out after serving less than two years.

Then there's a period of seventeen months where there are no reports of him, apart from a drunken brawl outside a pub.'

'After that?'

'He joined the army; served in Iraq and Afghanistan.'

'What as?'

'Special forces. He received a few medals as well,' Larry said.

'He'd know how to kill someone with piano wire then.'

'He may be a war hero, but Walters is still a nasty piece of work,' Larry said. 'Six years later, he's demobbed and back out on the street. That's about it for Steve Walters. The next time we hear of him is when he turns up here.'

'And where is he now?' Isaac asked.

'We've no idea.'

As the group sat in the office, Isaac's phone rang. 'No fingerprints although we picked up a shoe print outside Hughenden's back door,' Gordon Windsor said.

'And?'

'It matches a set of prints we found at the first murder scene.'

'Steve Walters?'

'That's the name you have. I only know him by a shoe. Whoever he is, he murdered Alex Hughenden.'

'Now we know who killed Hughenden. Another murder solved,' Isaac said. 'Larry, Wendy, find the man.'

'Yes, DCI,' they both said.

Chapter 18

Lord Allerton, a timid man who had only joined the drug syndicate out of financial necessity, paced up and down the drawing room in his ancestral home. The red rope cord barriers that had kept the tourists' children away from the family heirlooms were long removed. If he could relax, he would have to agree that the room, as well as the house, looked resplendent. He analysed all that had transpired and the trouble he was in.

On the evening news he had recognised the shop where a man had been murdered. He knew that his relative had been responsible. The aristocrat wondered where it was all going to end. The promise had been three weeks, and then there would be no more drug trafficking, an insidious business more in tune with the lower and middle classes. Not with him, a true blueblood who could claim an ancestry dating back eight hundred years. An Allerton had fought and died bravely in every war the British had fought in. Allertons had risen to high office in politics, in business, in diplomatic circles for generations, but he knew he was unique: he was a criminal, no better than a person who does not pay for their bus ticket or someone who cheats an old woman out of her life savings.

He looked up at the walls of the room, lined with paintings of his illustrious ancestors. He knew his portrait would not adorn those walls.

His wife was disturbed by the way her husband paced up and down the room, deep in thought. 'What is it, Timothy?' she asked as she gave him a reassuring hug.

'I have done something wrong, terribly wrong. It gives me great anguish.' His wife knew it was not adultery; she knew him well enough for that.

'Will it help to talk?' she asked.

'It is not something I can live with.'

'What is it?'

'I cannot tell you. It is too sordid. It will destroy us.'

The wife, an elegant woman, the daughter of a Duke, knew when it was a time for silence, a time for speaking. She decided to let him talk.

'I became involved with a group of people during our darkest days,' he said.

His wife knew exactly which days he was referring to. She had hated cheapening themselves as much as he had when they had been forced by an uncaring, overtaxing government to let in the proletariat.

'But you saved us,' she said.

'The cost was too high. I must confess,' he said.

'To God?'

'No. I must confess to the police.'

Lady Allerton shot up from the chair where she had been sitting. 'What!'

'My dear wife, you have to know that I have become a criminal.'

'I cannot believe this,' she said.

'It's true, all true. Out of necessity, I entered into a business venture with my oldest friends. It was a pact which we made over twenty-five years ago, to always help each other.'

'Why is that criminal?'

'I thought it would save us financially. I did not understand at what cost.'

'But we are all fine.'

'There are others who are not.'

'What do you mean?'

'One of our group, my relative, is not a good man. We knew he was devious, even criminal, but we did not know of his ruthlessness.'

'What type of crime?' Allerton's wife asked.

'I helped to finance a smuggling operation. In return, I received a substantial cash benefit.'

'Smuggling what?'

'Drugs.'

The woman, who had been supportive, put her head into her hands. 'How could you?' she said.

'I had no option: the pact. This house and all we own have been saved because of what I did.'

'Do you think that excuses it. I could deal with the gawking tourists, even the shame of losing this place, but crime, drugs. It's so working class.'

Lord Allerton, realising that the life he had known was over, left the room and walked out of the house and to his car. He was aware that it would be many years before he returned.

He made two phone calls from his mobile. The first was to Jacob Griffiths. 'You've seen the reports of the death on the television?' he asked.

'Yes,' Griffiths' reply.

'What do you think?'

'We allowed Keith three weeks to fold up the business.'

'Another murder,' Allerton said.

'He always said there were a few loose ends to tie up. Obviously that was one of them.'

'You're not concerned?'

'I'd prefer for no one to die, but I'm more concerned with my freedom and my family's well-being.'

'I cannot agree,' Allerton said.

'What are you going to do?'

'What I should have done after the first death. I intend to hand myself in to the police.' Allerton hung up. He made another call. 'DCI Cook, I have some information. I will be in your police station within the next two hours.'

'Your name,' Isaac asked.

'Lord Allerton. I will reveal all that I know of the death of Alex Hughenden and the drug syndicate.'

'And who's running it?'

'Yes. I will give you his name.'

'Can you give it to me now?'

'No. I'll only talk in the presence of my QC. Thank you.' The phone line went dead.

Isaac sat back on his chair. He knew he had just received the most bizarre phone call. He called Wendy and Larry back, as well as Bridget.

'Thirty minutes,' Isaac said to Bridget. 'Research everything you can on Lord Allerton. Wendy, Larry, focus on what Bridget finds out.'

'What about Steve Walters?' Wendy asked.

'It depends on what Allerton says, but leave Walters for the moment.'

'What is it with this lord?' Larry asked.

'He's coming here, and he's going to tell us everything, even who is running the drug syndicate.'

'Wow.' Larry's only remark.

Isaac then phoned Len Donaldson. 'Get over to Challis Street. I believe we have the breakthrough you've been looking for.'

***

Jacob Griffiths' first act on ending the phone conversation with Allerton was to phone Miles Fortescue, the notoriously incompetent politician. 'Allerton's going to blow it,' Griffiths said.

'What do you mean?' Fortescue replied, pushing his mistress to one side.

'He's going to confess.'

'To the police?'

'You realise Keith has had Hughenden murdered?'

'He said he had loose ends to tie up.'

'Tim Allerton's lost it,' Griffiths said. 'If he confesses we'll be arrested as well.'

'Hell. I thought this was going to be wrapped up.'

'What do we do?'

'Phone Keith.'

Griffiths put Keith, the fourth man and Allerton's relative, on a group call. 'Your cousin is on the way to the police.'

'He must be stopped. Where is he now?'

'On the road to the police station.'

'We need to meet him before he gets there.'

'And then?' Fortescue asked. His mistress had lost interest and gone into the other room to watch the television.

'It depends,' the leader of the quartet said.

'Would you…?'

'It's up to him. If he can't keep his mouth shut…'

'Why did you have to kill Hughenden?' Griffiths interjected.

'I've only done what is necessary, and besides, each of you has an extra million pounds in your bank account. I'm wrapping this business up as we agreed. The police are getting too close, and I intend to make myself scarce.'

'And what about us?' Fortescue asked.

'From what I know you're invisible in the Houses of Parliament. You'll be fine.'

'I've dialled in Allerton,' Griffiths said.

A nervous voice answered. 'Allerton,' it said.

'We need to meet,' Fortescue said.

'I am resolute. I can no longer continue with this.'

'And what about us?'

'It's each man for himself.'

'What about our pact?' Keith asked. He had lifted himself out of the leather chair which was in the corner of the sitting room in his house.

'My wife was right. It was only four schoolboys aiming to be mysterious and grown-up,' Allerton said.

'You've told your wife.'

'Not the details, and not your names.'

'But the police are not fools. They'll check you out. It won't take them long to fit the pieces together. Allerton, you've stuffed us,' Griffiths said.

'Not at all. I am doing the only honourable thing left to me. I will not reveal your names.'

Keith sat down and weighed up the situation. He knew Allerton's wife would not talk. Her position in society was more important to her than the lives of a few criminals. And if she had to choose between her lifestyle and her husband, he knew which one she would choose. As for Allerton, he could only feel contempt. Keith knew that he had come from the impoverished side of the family – no stately home, no title, no silver spoon – and he had pulled himself up through his own brilliance and sheer willpower. Allerton had just muddled through, and Fortescue was an incompetent lecher. At least Jacob Griffiths had some backbone.

'Can we meet?' Keith asked.

'Very well,' Allerton reluctantly agreed. Regardless of his wife, an agreement he had made with three other men, boys then, still meant something to him.

'Fortescue, your place?' Keith suggested.

'If we must.'

'Is that okay by the other two?'

'Okay by me,' Griffiths replied.

'I'll be there,' Allerton said. 'Give me sixty minutes.'

'Give me ninety,' Fortescue said. He still had unfinished business with the mistress.

***

Len Donaldson was at Challis Street Police Station. Allerton was due soon. Isaac called a meeting in his office. 'What do we have on Allerton?' he asked.

'He inherited the title on the death of his father,' Bridget said. 'He's married with two children. Apart from that, there's not a lot to tell you.'

'There must be more. A peer of the realm.'

'There's plenty, but it's all good. There were some positions in the city when he was younger, but on inheriting the title and the stately home, he located there. There's no dirt on the man, and I've found no information regarding his movements. From all reports, he seems to be a decent man.'

'Yet he's willing to come in here and confess to being a leading figure in a drug syndicate. It makes no sense,' Isaac said.

'It does,' Donaldson said. 'We've never been able to get a handle on its leadership. We've focussed on known criminals, whereas Allerton has no record of crime, which means the others, assuming there are others, may not either.'

'Schooling, financial status. Anything there?' Isaac asked.

'I've checked in *Burke's Peerage*. He attended Eton College,' Bridget said.

With little more to say, the team went back to their desks. Larry worked on some reports that he needed to prepare. Bridget continued to research Allerton, and Wendy sat close to Bridget watching what she was doing. Everyone was on tenterhooks awaiting the arrival of Lord Allerton.

Len Donaldson and Isaac sat in Isaac's office discussing the case. Both men knew it was going to be a long night.

'Could this man be capable of pulling off an operation of this magnitude?' Isaac asked.

'I can't see how,' Donaldson said, 'but then who would? Typically, we'd be looking at the major criminals, the overseas crime gangs, but this time we've been baffled.'

'If it was so successful why didn't other crime organisations aim to take it over?'

'They may have, but if everyone, including the other criminals, were making money, then maybe they were left alone.'

'You believe they were paid off?'

'Someone had to be supplying the drugs in Europe.'

'Any luck finding out who they are?' Isaac asked.

'We know who they are.'

'Who?'

'Bratva, the Russian Mafia in Moscow. They're shipping large quantities of heroin out of Afghanistan. And then there are some Albanians who are trafficking as well, although they're small fry compared to the Russians.'

'What does that mean?'

'The Albanians keep a low profile. If you want vicious bastards, try the Bratva. The Albanians know this, and they're careful not to tread on anyone's toes.'

'Allerton and his people have been sourcing from these two groups?' Isaac asked.

'If the syndicate took enough from the Russians, they'd make sure there was no competition.'

***

Miles Fortescue was not pleased to see the other three at his place. He had always regarded it as his sanctuary away from the rigours of public life and from his wife. He had to admit that she had played her part in the intervening years, presenting herself as the dutiful wife of a politician. To most people, or those who were interested, he and his wife were the perfect blend of political duty and personal unity. The three who were now in his house, an elegant terrace not far from Westminster, were under no illusion. The smell of the mistress's perfume was still apparent, and the politician had been looking forward to more of her time.

'Where is she?' Griffiths asked.

'She's not staying around for you to see,' Fortescue said. He failed to mention that she was married as well, and her privacy was paramount.

'Miles's peccadillos are not important, are they?' Keith said.

'Not really,' Griffiths agreed.

'Allerton, what is it with the police?' Keith asked. The man being questioned sat on a stool in the kitchen. He was downcast and pale in the face.

'You should not have killed that man.'

'I've never killed anyone. I told you there were some loose ends to be dealt with. From what I could see at our last meeting, all three of you were in agreement.'

'Yes, but…'

'There are no buts. If you play with the big boys, you have to learn to play by their rules.'

'Then I was wrong to go in with you,' Allerton said.

'And wrong to accept all the money I put your way. I assume your conscience is not that severely affected that you're willing to return your share of the money?'

'It solved a financial crisis, but has destroyed the lives of my family.'

'Rubbish. It's your stupid old-fashioned sense of right and wrong.'

'You may be right, but I cannot live a lie.'

'So you're going to confess all to the police. Do you know what they'll say inside the prison when they know your story?'

'No.'

'They'll regard you as the biggest fool in Christendom. The man who had everything and gave it away due to a guilty conscience. Your wife is right in one respect. The pact we made all those years ago was a childish fantasy. The fantasy of four young boys wanting to be men. And now we are men, and the world is not so idealistic. It's dog eat dog, and I intend to be the top dog. You've got your fortune, your loving wife and family, your stately home. What did I get as your relative? Nothing.'

'Keith, one thing you should have received was the sense of right and wrong.'

'Stop acting as if you were that little boy again. This is the real world, and it's for the strong and resolute, not the feeble and honourable. How much money would you have made if you had had to work for it, if there had been no inheritance? Hell, man, you would have been lucky to have afforded a house in the suburbs. And what did I get, apart from the Allerton connection and a history of noble ancestors? I received nothing, but I did not complain and go weak at the knees when someone was threatening me, us. I'll tell you what I did; I acted decisively. Hughenden was a liability. I couldn't risk him talking to the police again.'

'He's right,' Griffiths said. 'It's not something I could have done, but Keith has saved us. If you go blabbing to the police, we'll all be in prison together.'

'Why?' Allerton said. 'We did not know what was going to happen. We didn't know that people were going to be murdered.'

'Murder?' Keith said. 'That's what the police call it. With the business we're in, people die every day. Some on the street from the products we sell; others because of their treachery.'

'Hughenden?'

'Eventually he would have done what was necessary to save his own skin. I had nothing against him personally, but business is business. Griffiths understands.'

'That I do,' Jacob Griffiths said. He had helped himself to coffee and was sitting comfortably on a chair to one side of the kitchen. He looked around the house, and he had to admit it looked good. Fortescue, they all knew, was not a man of any great skills, but he knew how to live well. Even Griffiths had to admit that the idea of a mistress appealed, but then he thought that was more likely a middle-aged itch. He had been married to the same woman for over twenty years, good and bad, and he knew his conscience would not allow it. Still, it was good to daydream.

Miles Fortescue was not sure which way to turn. The money had been great, and he had no strong morals, only an innate desire to do what was best for himself. He knew that as a politician he was no Disraeli or a Churchill, but he knew how to ingratiate himself with his constituency, and how to ensure he was a member of various select committees, especially the one addressing the escalating supply of illegal drugs in the community. Committees always allowed him to get his name in the papers and on television, and that was all he wanted, apart from his mistresses. He did not envy Allerton with his obsession about title and duty, or Griffiths with his need to deal with trade. Fortescue knew that politically he was savvy, and the bumbling politician, more often than not, was an engineered affectation.

Keith, he knew, even in their time at Eton, was a dishonest person. It was he who would steal cigarettes and sell them around the dormitory of a night-time. It was he who would sneak them into the emergency exit at the local cinema to watch the latest risqué movie, and somehow he would always have a few

X-rated magazines for hire to the boys who could not afford to partake of one of the obliging ladies in the area.

'Allerton, you're a bloody fool,' Fortescue said. He could see political expediency, the need for drastic action if a disaster was to be avoided, a need for compromise. 'Keith, it's up to you,' he said.

'Allerton, Tim, what are you going to do? Keith asked.

'I will wait one more week. If there are no more deaths and this whole sorry business is wrapped up, then I'll do no more.'

'And the police?'

'I'll not talk to them.'

The four men, all relieved after resolving the issue, went out to a restaurant favoured by Keith. No more was said of the events that had led to their unexpected meeting. At eleven in the evening, Lord Allerton left their company for the drive back to his home and his family. He was a man at peace with the world.

Chapter 19

Isaac, along with his team and Len Donaldson, waited in the office at Challis Street for Allerton. Bridget had done some preliminary work on the man. They had a dossier of his friends, past and recent, as well as a complete rundown on the man's history, his family, a provisional statement of wealth. The one thing they did not have was the man, and he was not answering his phone.

'It's suspicious,' Donaldson said.

'The man said he would be here and he was willing to blow this case wide open.'

'He's not going to show, you know that.'

Isaac phoned Richard Goddard to keep him up to date. The death of Hughenden had raised the issue of additional help for Isaac, and yet again he and Goddard had blocked anyone else joining the team. With the murderer known for three of the four murders, the situation in the office was looking much better. Hughenden was almost certainly killed by Steve Walters, but the man was not around. If Allerton was not going to appear, there were two things to do: find him and Walters.

Lord Allerton's address was well known, an elegant stately home in Derbyshire; it even had its own website, and it was impressive. Isaac wondered why a person who had so much would become involved in crime. The website showed Allerton with his wife and two daughters, all photogenic, although Isaac had dealt with members of the upper class before on previous cases, and there were always skeletons in the cupboard.

Isaac, a man who liked to live well, to have a good woman at his side, although he was bereft of that luxury at present, did not envy those who had plenty. They seemed to have endless problems, and a stately home, he well knew, may be picture postcard but it would be excessively expensive to maintain and draughty in winter.

Isaac called Larry back into his office as he was preparing to leave. 'Steve Walters, any luck?'

'There's an APW out for him, and the local police in his home town are looking,' Larry replied.

'Not really good enough, is it?'

'I would agree, but we've no idea where to look. We know he was here when he killed Hughenden, but since then, nothing.'

'Tomorrow, first thing, you and Wendy resume your search for him.'

'Yes, sir. What about Lord Allerton?'

'Make sure there's an APW out for him before you leave.'

'I've already done it. Also, I've phoned the local police where he lives. I know the officer in charge from a long time back. They know the man, like him as well. They're going to station a car on the road leading up to his home. If they see him, they'll give us a call.'

Isaac left the office with Larry. The day had shown promise, but in the end it had disappointed. Allerton was the key to breaking the whole case wide open, although having the guilty man in custody for two murders out of four was not a bad tally.

***

Steve Walters had found solace in a restaurant not far from the hotel where he was lying low. He reflected on what had happened with Hughenden. How he had entered through the back door after the man had opened it. At first, the man had been surprised to see him, and more than a little nervous.

Walters remembered how he had soothed his fear with words supplied by the mysterious voice on the other end of their short phone conversation. In the end, Hughenden had fetched a drink for the two of them.

'Why are you here?' Hughenden had asked.

'I need to get away. Somewhere I won't be discovered.'

'That's what Devlin wanted to do.'

'He's in prison.'

'And you'll be if they catch you here.'

'They won't.'

'Why are you so sure?'

'I've disguised myself well,' Walters said. His hair was dyed jet black and cut very short, not straggly as it normally was and he was dressed well in a suit, not an old jacket and faded jeans.

'That's true,' a frightened man pretending to be brave said. 'What do you want from me?'

'Only the money outstanding.'

Hughenden had walked to the safe and opened it, remembering to obscure the combination from the man who watched his every move. 'Here you are. Fifty-five thousand pounds.'

'With that and the extra bonus I'll be receiving, I'll have enough.'

'What bonus?'

'One last task and I'm heading off to the sun.'

'What bonus?' Hughenden repeated.

'For killing you.'

'Why?'

'It's nothing personal, purely business,' Walters said, paraphrasing Hughenden when he had given the order for the death of Rodrigo Fuentes.

Hughenden, sensing the change in Walters' mood, had backed away from the safe and the man who was threatening him.

Walters pursued him, the jewellery shop owner upending a chair in his attempt to get away. He rushed to the front door; it had been locked. With Hughenden forced into a corner, Walters grabbed hold of his prey. Hughenden fought, but he was a slight man whereas the man wrapping the wire around his neck was strong.

Walters tightened the wire; Hughenden gasped and died.

'You'll be comfortable there,' the murderer said as he sat the dead man on a chair.

***

Allerton Hall, the ancestral home of the Allertons, had been built four hundred years earlier. It sat on five hundred acres of prime agricultural land on the edge of the Derbyshire Moors. As Lord Allerton approached the imposing brick structure, he wondered what his reception would be like.

He had left that morning with the certainty that his next place of abode would be a prison cell, not the family home. He had phoned his wife to tell her he was returning.

'Are we going to survive?' she had asked.

His answer, he remembered, had been noncommittal. Their future was in the hands of another man, his cousin. He well remembered them playing together as children; he the wealthy son of a lord, Keith the son of a village doctor. They had been friends then, even friends at Eton College, the elite school for the sons of gentlemen and royalty. Their friendship had lasted until today, he was sure of that. He knew he had broken the code that held former pupils of that august centre of learning together. The Lord knew he had been right to do so. An Allerton does not get involved with trade or crime; it was the unwritten code that had lasted for centuries, the code that had allowed the family to weather the inevitable crises that occur in life, and yet he had broken that cardinal rule. He knew that if his wife forgave him, if Keith kept his side of the bargain, he could go back to his comfortable existence; he knew equally that he could never forgive himself. He was damned, and he knew it.

As he approached the last corner before driving through the metal gates at the entrance to Allerton Park, he looked out at the view. His ancestor had chosen well. The house and grounds sat high over the surrounding countryside. The road was sometimes tricky, especially in winter, with a steep drop on one side, but he was driving a Bentley – one of the benefits of his ill-gotten gains – and it was purring along nicely. Keith had been right: he was a hypocrite in that he enjoyed the financial benefits of a criminal venture, not giving much thought to it, only to be concerned when the murders had become too much. Timothy Allerton knew he was a pacifist and death, violent death, did not sit comfortably with him. The death of Dougal Stewart had not concerned him, nor the death of the Brazilian, but Hughenden's had.

Was it because he was a cultured man, the same as him? Was he a snob? he thought. He knew the answer to that question.

Allerton casually reached over for the remote control to the gates. He did not notice the Land Rover that came out of nowhere. He looked up too late. The Bentley, which was travelling slowly, bore the full brunt of the four-wheel drive as it hit the driver's door. Momentarily stunned, Allerton attempted to extricate himself and the car. Again and again the Land Rover kept coming forward, pushing hard on the door. A hand reached out of the Land Rover and shot out a front tyre and then a rear tyre of the Bentley. With no further control over the vehicle, Allerton tried to get out of the car but it was not possible. The Land Rover, with one final push, its engine straining against the immense weight of the Bentley, managed to tip the vehicle over the low stone wall beside the road. Once the car had left the road, the Land Rover sped away.

All that Timothy Allerton remembered was the vehicle tumbling over and over down the steep slope as it headed towards the edge of an old stone quarry. If he had been conscious after the car had fallen the last one hundred feet, he would have had the answer to the question he had posed that morning: when and if he would ever return to his home. The answer was never. An old Land Rover had resolved that question.

***

The first notification of Allerton's death came thirty minutes after his Bentley had gone over the side of the quarry. The local police station that had been keeping a watch out for him had discovered the car at the bottom of the quarry ten minutes after it had landed there. Three local boys out hiking had seen the events at the top of the hill. They dialled the emergency services on 999 at once.

'Another death,' Isaac said when he phoned Len Donaldson.

'Who is it?'

'Lord Allerton.'

'You know why he's dead? I assume it's murder.'

'It's murder.'

'He died because he was going to talk to us,' Donaldson said.

'I'm going up there,' Isaac said.

'I'll come with you.'

'Fine. We leave in twenty minutes.'

Isaac phoned DCS Goddard. The man was not pleased. 'Every time you get involved in a murder case, the bodies keep piling up. Are you jinxed?'

'Of course not,' Isaac retorted. He did not like his senior's comment, but it was true. In his previous cases – the missing actress, the body in the fireplace, the female serial killer – the body count had continued to rise even when the case was virtually solved. Isaac discounted the probability that he may be fated, but his parents had come from Jamaica, and they had a healthy if guarded respect for forces beyond a person's control.

However, Allerton had not died as a result of a phantom hand. The reports coming through indicated death by intent. The question was, whose intent?

Isaac called Wendy and Larry into his office. 'I'm off to Allerton's home. Find out all you can about Allerton's friends and business acquaintances. Someone knew his movements and the fact he was coming to see us. We've got twenty-four hours on this one before DCS Goddard is baying for our blood.'

Isaac and Len Donaldson made the trip up through the heart of England in record time. Isaac, not known for his light foot on the accelerator, was only a slow driver compared to Donaldson, who was driving. 'Used to race Go Karts when I was younger,' he said when Isaac had told him to ease up.

Still, Isaac had to admit he was a good driver and time was of the essence. Allerton's death had not been expected and it had thrown all their investigations into turmoil.

'Pretty country,' Donaldson said as he drove up the road towards Allerton's home. There had been a police car blocking the road below, but Isaac had flashed his badge and they were quickly through. The quarry was their first port of call.

'Not much to see,' a dour man said on their arrival. He introduced himself as Inspector Trevor Corker.

'What can you tell us?' Isaac asked. The weather was biting, with an arctic wind blowing. Isaac pulled up the collar of his coat and shrugged his shoulders in an attempt to keep warm.

'It's a bit brisk today, I'll grant you that,' Corker said. Isaac estimated him to be in his mid-fifties and close to retirement. He had the healthy glow of someone who enjoyed the outdoors, and would positively hate a holiday in the south of France or even the Caribbean where the weather was anything but arctic.

'Lord Allerton,' Isaac said to bring the conversation back to the reason he and Donaldson were freezing.

'We've got three local lads who witnessed it all. One's a bit shaken up, but the other two are fine.'

'It's clearly murder?' Donaldson asked.

'No doubt about it,' Corker replied. 'Apart from the boys, the skid marks are easy to see. Strange, really.'

'Why?' Isaac asked.

'I don't hold much with titles,' Corker said, 'but I knew the man personally.'

You should meet Wendy, Isaac thought, knowing full well her ambivalence to the concept of privilege based on who's bed you were born in, who your parents were.

'And?'

'His Lordship revelled in it, although once you got past the veneer, he was a decent person. If anyone in the local village was in trouble, he was always willing to help out with advice, sometimes money. There are others of the landed gentry around here who wouldn't deem to acknowledge that you existed, but not so with his Lordship.'

'Beautiful car, or at least it was,' Donaldson said.

'He bought it new about five months ago,' Corker said.

'How do you know that?' Isaac asked.

'He gave me a ride in it just after he bought it. As I said, he was a decent man as long as you gave him the necessary respect.'

'His death?' Donaldson asked. Allerton's death, regardless of whether he was well-respected or not in the local community, did not affect the fact that he had had information the police wanted. The man knew something, and he had been silenced. The question was who had been responsible and where were they.

'If the vehicle rolling over before it reached the quarry edge had not killed him, the impact with the quarry floor would have,' Corker said.

'Is the body still in the vehicle?' Isaac asked.

'It's still there. We'll have to cut him out.'

So far, the three men had not approached the vehicle as it was precariously balanced on a rocky outcrop in an area of the quarry deemed unstable. However, they approached gingerly by a route determined as safe by the crime scene investigation team brought in from Derby, the main city in the county.

Isaac crouched down and peered inside. The man who had phoned him was pinned between the steering wheel and the roof.

'Almost decapitated him,' the crime scene examiner said.

'DCI Isaac Cook, Challis Street in London, and this is DCI Len Donaldson, Serious and Organised Crime Command.'

'Are you saying Allerton was involved with crime?' the CSE asked.

'He's part of an ongoing investigation,' Isaac admitted.

'There's not much more to see here,' Donaldson said as he marched up and down on the spot, trying to keep the circulation flowing in his legs.

'Where are the three boys?' Isaac asked Corker.

'They're up at Allerton Hall, in the housekeeper's cottage.'

'We'd better go and see them. Has Allerton's wife been informed?'

'I dealt with it earlier. She took it well.'

'No tears?'

'Women like her do not show their emotions.'

***

The four friends were now three, and the agreement made twenty-five years previously was now broken. Four men who would look out for each other, no matter what, and now one of the four had killed another of their group. The news of Allerton's death had been on social media before the news agencies and the television channels had picked it up.

'Keith, you've had Tim Allerton murdered,' Griffiths said over the phone.

'Did you trust him?' the leader of the group said.

'He was reluctant, but yes.'

'The risk was too great.'

For once Jacob Griffiths was speechless. He had seen a flaw in the character of the person he was talking to. The man, even as a boy, had been brilliant but he should have known that the police would double their efforts to find out who had killed a member of the aristocracy. The man was one of the elites of society, not a tramp on the street.

'You've killed one of us,' Griffiths said.

'Before he destroyed us.'

'How long before the whole sorry saga is concluded?'

'Ten days.'

'And then?'

'You will never hear from me again.'

'You're leaving Fortescue and me to deal with the aftermath?'

Keith sat down and looked out of the window of his penthouse overlooking the River Thames. He thought of how far he had come, how much he had achieved. It was good that all that he owned had been purchased through offshore companies, and that whatever happened he would be able to realise his assets. It was remarkable, he thought, that he had gone through life being liked, pretending to like others, but the reality was that he cared for no one other than himself. Even that agreement with those silly boys had meant nothing.

Sure, it had ensured they covered for his illegal activities at Eton, and that Fortescue, fool that he was, had ensured his identity had remained unknown when he was swindling some locals in Fortescue's constituency. If either Griffiths or Fortescue decided to weaken as Allerton had, then their fate would be the same. Keith knew that where he was going, no one would find him. He decided to shorten the ten days to eight, and woe betide anyone who got in his way.

'Are you listening?' Griffiths asked.

'Jacob, my dear friend Jacob. You worry too much. What was Allerton to us? Is your freedom more important than his life?'

'It was unnecessary.'

'It no longer matters. I give you my word. There will be no more killings. Ten days is all I ask.'

'Ten days.'

Jacob Griffiths ended the phone call knowing one thing: Keith had lied through his teeth.

Griffiths called Fortescue to let him know about Allerton and the previous phone call.

'Good God, we're done for,' Fortescue said.

Griffiths could only agree. Keith would be gone, and he would cover his tracks well, but Tim Allerton's friends and acquaintances would be checked.

'There's no hope.'

'Can you get out of the country?' Fortescue asked.

'Not a chance, and I don't want to. I've my businesses and my family here.'

'But you'll be arrested.'

'How about you, Miles?'

'The same as you. I can't leave, can't stay. We're doomed because we trusted Keith.'

'It's hindsight. What can we do?'

'Nothing, just nothing.'

Chapter 20

The housekeeper's cottage, located close to the main house, was warm when the two policemen arrived there. Mrs Townsend, the housekeeper, a middle-aged woman, kept the humble abode meticulously clean. 'It's so sad,' she said.

Isaac could see she had been crying. 'We have a few questions,' he said.

'Warm yourself by the fire while I fetch some tea.' Even though the woman was obviously distraught, she was still able to deal with the basics.

The two men stood in front of the blaze for two minutes until it became too hot.

'One thing his Lordship appreciated was an open fire. Mind you, it can be perishing cold up in the big house. For me, I'd rather be here, snug and cosy.'

Both men sat down and enjoyed a respite from the investigation.

A uniformed officer came in. 'The three boys are ready in the other room,' he said.

'Thanks,' Isaac said. 'Are they okay?'

'They're fine now. Their parents are here as well.'

'Fine,' Donaldson said. 'We'll interview all three at the same time.'

Five minutes later, the boys entered accompanied by two of the parents. Mrs Townsend brought another pot of tea for the police officers and the two parents, hot chocolate for the boys.

'I'm Detective Chief Inspector Isaac Cook and this is Detective Chief Inspector Len Donaldson,' Isaac said as both men shook hands with the three boys. The parents sat to one side.

'I'm Billy Smith, this here is Frank Fogarty,' the first boy said. The third boy, younger than the other two, introduced himself as Terry Smith.

'He's my brother,' Billy said.

All three boys were dressed in clothes designed for the weather: jeans, heavy jackets, and sturdy hiking shoes. Isaac knew he was not.

'It's warm in here,' Billy said as he removed his jacket. The other two boys followed his example.

'According to Inspector Corker, you all saw the incident when his Lordship's car went into the quarry.'

'Uncle Trevor. He's our uncle,' Terry Smith said. He did not seem to recognise the seriousness of the matter.

'Very well,' Isaac said. 'According to your uncle, you saw what happened.'

'We were up here hiking.'

'Do you do that often?'

'Sometimes. There's not much else to do around here.'

'Tell us what you saw. Billy, maybe you can tell us first, and then after, Frank and Terry can add in anything you missed.'

Billy and Frank acknowledged their understanding of how the interview was to proceed. Young Terry looked out of the window.

'He's not all there, our Terry,' Billy said. Isaac could see that the youngest of the three was drifting. At best, he was an unreliable witness, whereas Billy and Frank seemed to be focussed.

'Billy, please start.'

'We were walking up here on a track off to the side of the road. It's hidden by bushes so no one could see us from the road.'

'What were you doing up here?' Donaldson asked.

'Just walking.'

Donaldson, who had grown up in the country, knew that was not the truth. They were up to mischief. He let it pass. They had bigger issues to deal with.

'Continue, Billy,' Isaac said. 'We'll not interrupt again,' giving a subtle hit to Len Donaldson to keep quiet.

'We'd seen the Land Rover, but we took no notice. Anyway, we carried on up the hill. We could see Lord Allerton coming up the hill in his car, so we ducked down low. We didn't want him to see us. He slows down to enter his place, and the Land Rover comes out from a track nearby and rams the car. We rushed up the hill to get a closer look.'

'Did anyone see you?' Isaac asked. He deemed it was a relevant question to interrupt the young boy.

'Lord Allerton may have, but the man in the Land Rover didn't.'

'I saw him,' Terry Smith said.

'Who?' Isaac asked.

'The man in the Land Rover.'

'Don't listen to him,' his elder brother said. 'He makes up stories.'

'I still need to hear it,' Isaac said.

'He was a little man.'

'Anything else?'

'He had tattoos on his arms. I could see that, even if Billy thinks I'm lying. Mister, I'm telling the truth.'

'I believe you,' Isaac said, the description suspiciously similar to a prime suspect.

'He had a gun,' Frank Fogarty said.

'Could you identify it?' Isaac asked.

'No. We only heard it being fired.'

'That correlates with what they found at the crime scene,' Donaldson said.

'Then what happened?' Isaac asked.

'The Land Rover pushes Lord Allerton's car off the side of the road,' Frank Fogarty said.

'We could see the man shouting,' Billy Smith added.

'Who?'

'Lord Allerton.'

'Then what?'

'We rushed up here and phoned the police.'

'Is there any more you can tell us?' Isaac asked.

'Nothing. The Land Rover drove off, that's all,'

'Did you get a registration number?'

'No, I didn't.'

'I did,' Terry Smith said.

'What was it?'

'Is there a reward?' the young boy asked. Isaac realised he had probably been fed a diet of American cop shows on the television.

'We'll arrange something,' Isaac said. He'd let Uncle Trevor deal with that.

'HDE 59F,' Terry blurted out. Isaac had to admit if the boy was a little slow for his age, at least his ability to remember car registrations was unbeatable.

Isaac picked up his phone and dialled Bridget back in Challis Street. He then called his DI and his sergeant to follow up on the car and its occupant.

***

There was one more interview to conduct before Isaac and Donaldson returned to London. They found Lady Allerton in the main house. Mrs Townsend had taken them over. It was apparent that the two women were fond of each other.

After a few minutes when the two women comforted each other, the housekeeper left. Isaac looked around the room; it was magnificent. It wasn't the first stately home he had been in, but it was one of the best. Apart from the portraits on the walls, there were hunting trophies from a bygone age and an elephant's foot footstool near the fireplace. Isaac did not like the idea of it but did not comment.

'My husband was a good man,' Lady Allerton said. She was dressed conservatively in black.

'I'm very sorry about this,' Isaac said, 'but I must ask some questions.'

Isaac remembered Inspector Corker's statement that women such as Lady Allerton keep their emotions in check. The man had been right, as the woman maintained her composure.

'Thank you. I believe his body has been removed,' she said.

'You will be required to formally identify your late husband. Will that be acceptable?' Donaldson asked.

'Perfectly acceptable.' Given that her husband had just died, Isaac marvelled at the woman's self-control. Not only had she maintained a steady voice devoid of emotion, but she had also managed to order tea for all three. A woman entered carrying the tray.

'Lily, please pour,' Lady Allerton said. It was the first opportunity that Isaac had to study the woman. He knew from Bridget's check of *Burke's Peerage* that she was forty-two. She was slim and well proportioned. Isaac, a man with an eye for beauty, could only declare her beautiful.

Donaldson, if asked, would have said that he had taken no notice, and that after his wife had taken off with his best friend, he had given women a wide berth.

'I must ask,' Isaac said.

'Please do. I will answer your questions to the best of my ability.'

'Do you know the reason for your husband's death?'

'No.'

'Are you aware that he was in London?'

'He told me he had some business there.'

'Did he tell you what kind of business?'

'I did not ask. My husband is free to conduct his affairs without an inquisitive wife.'

'Affairs?' Donaldson asked.

'Not the sort you are referring to. My husband did not become involved with other women.'

'He phoned me earlier today,' Isaac said. 'Do you know why?'

'I've no idea.'

Isaac thought he had seen her move imperceptibly in her chair. The woman was distraught; it could be the only logical reaction after the man she had shared a bed with for the last twenty years had died violently not three hours before. It was clear that she believed in a stiff upper lip, especially in front of the staff, and especially in front of two police inspectors. He gave her the benefit of the doubt and a willingness to accept all that she told them as true.

'Lady Allerton, do you believe your husband capable of an illegal act?' Donaldson asked.

'Timothy? No way. You'd never meet a more honest man.' Lady Allerton was firm in her rejection of Donaldson's aspersion.

'My apologies if I offended you.'

'Your apology is accepted.'

'But we have reason to believe that he was.'

'How dare you come into my house and accuse my husband, a man who died only a few hours ago, of criminal activity.'

'I'm sorry,' Isaac said, 'but he phoned to tell me he wanted to confess.'

'Go, please go. I will not speak to you anymore without my lawyer being present. My husband was a good man, adored by his wife and his children. Your accusations are scurrilous.'

'I'm sorry to be impolite,' Isaac said, knowing full well that their time at Allerton Hall was about to conclude. 'A vehicle intentionally ran your husband's car off the road. It's not a random hit and miss, it's murder. The question is why?'

Outside the house, Donaldson spoke. 'At least she was polite enough when she showed us the door.'

'Too polite,' Isaac replied.

'Do you believe her?'

'I want to, but she could be lying through her teeth.'

'Why?'

'She's aristocracy. Don't try to reason it too closely. They run with a different set of moral barometers: position and respect are more important than the mere machinations of a murder inquiry.'

'Are you saying that if she knew something, she'd keep quiet just to protect the good name of the Allertons?' Donaldson asked.

'Yes,' Isaac replied.

***

Bridget traced the Land Rover with no difficulty: a 2007 Defender.

The timing of Allerton's death indicated that someone knew of his movements. And the two officers were familiar with the description of the driver. If it was who they thought it was, then he was in the north and possibly nearby, although that was far from conclusive.

'We need to find Walters,' Larry said to Wendy.

'Easier said than done.'

'Someone knew how to contact him.'

'No one we know.'

'Allerton may have. Do we have his phone?'

Larry called Isaac as he was about to leave the Allerton property. 'We need Lord Allerton's phone.'

'I'll see what I can do. We're off to see Terry Smith, the youngest of the three boys, again. He's at his home in the village not far from here. He's been correct with the vehicle's registration; he may be able to tell us more.'

Isaac phoned Inspector Corker after ending his call with Larry. 'Do you have Allerton's phone?' he asked.

'Yes. It's still working.'

'I need it.'

'It's evidence. You'll need authority.'

'I'll get it.'

Isaac phoned Goddard, his senior, explained the situation. Within fifteen minutes the phone was released.

'Quick work there,' Corker said.

'We're off to see Terry Smith. Can you bring the phone to his house?'

'No problems. Terry's the hero.'

'He was accurate with the vehicle. We need to see if he can assist in proving who I think the driver is.'

'It'll do him good to be the centre of attention. The other children tease him mercilessly, but he's harmless, just slow. Oxygen starvation at birth.'

'You owe him a reward,' Isaac said.

'Do I?'

'I promised him one. You'll need to deal with it.'

'Don't worry. I'll think of something.'

***

The unexpected death of a member of the aristocracy was bound to cause a ruffling of feathers in Scotland Yard. It was not long before the expected reaction.

'Lord Allerton. What's going on?' Goddard blasted down Isaac's phone.

Isaac and Donaldson had just left young Terry Smith's house. He had not been able to add much more to what he had seen. Billy, his elder brother, remembered that the driver of the Land Rover crunched the gears on the vehicle.

'Allerton was involved,' Isaac responded to the man he once admired, but could only feel contempt for now.

'How do you know this?'

'He told us.'

'And it's proven?'

'It would have been, but someone beat us to him.'

'Explain yourself, DCI. I've got the commissioner breathing down my neck, and the former commissioner is asking what's happened.'

'You mean Lord Shaw, your mentor?' Isaac replied, remembering the close relationship his DCS had had with the previous commissioner; the same as he had previously had with his DCS.

'As you say, my mentor. But the man's in the House of Lords and one of their own has been murdered. It is murder, isn't it?'

'Yes.'

'I need something to keep Davies off my back.'

'Very well,' Isaac replied. 'Earlier this morning, Lord Allerton phoned me to say he was coming into Challis Street to confess.'

'Did he arrive?'

'No. We were all here, and he had been clear that he would give names, including the person who has been running the drug syndicate.'

'When he didn't turn up?'

'There wasn't a lot we could do. It was only a few hours, and we had no information on where he was, or what car he was driving. Our assumption was that he had been delayed or had chickened out.'

'And that's it?'

'No. We phoned the police station close to Allerton's home to keep a watch for him. They saw him pass by, but fifteen minutes later, the man's dead.'

Goddard let out an audible sigh of exasperation. 'Keep me posted. I'm off to another earbashing.'

'Commissioner Davies?' Isaac asked.

'Who else? Sometimes I wonder if it's all worth it.'

Isaac felt sympathy for the man who had guided his career, a willingness to see the best in his DCS. 'Good luck,' he said.

'And you. Wrap this up soon or else.'

'Or else the commissioner will wrap us up.'

'You know the procedure.'

'By now I should,' Isaac replied. 'As long as it doesn't involve that obnoxious DCI Caddick.'

'It probably will. The man hangs around like a bad smell.'

***

With no information to the contrary, Isaac and the team moved forward on the premise that Steve Walters had driven the Land Rover. Isaac, in possession of Allerton's mobile phone number, had passed it on to Bridget who was accessing the records of calls made, calls received.

As Isaac was driving on the return journey to Challis Street, it would not be as quick as the trip up. Even so, they still expected to be back in the early hours of the morning. He knew the team would still be working, but he needed at least a couple of hours sleep. He agreed to meet up at seven the next morning in his office.

The phone which Inspector Corker had given him was in his pocket. The numbers in the phone's memory could be of some interest, but whoever had arranged for the death of Allerton, or who Allerton may have spoken to, would almost certainly be recent and on record.

Wendy and Larry were in the office going through the spreadsheet that Bridget had supplied them. Most phone calls made from Allerton's phone had been trivial and easily discounted. What was important to the team was that they did not alert Allerton's criminal accomplices to what was going on.

It was clear that Hughenden's and now Allerton's deaths were the acts of desperate people. Larry was confident they were closing in, and he intended to stay in the office until they had something to tell their DCI in the morning. His wife, as usual, complained about the hours worked.

Wendy, on her own after the death of her husband, had no one complaining about her; she wished she had, but realised she never would. All she had were her two cats, the legacy of a cat-loving woman in a previous case who had died after seeing her dead son. Wendy had never been a cat person, but she had become fond of them. Larry had taken another of the cats, and it was well ensconced in the Hills' household, so much so that he had to push it out of his chair every night when he got home.

Of the thirty plus numbers on the spreadsheet, several were deemed suspicious. It had been possible to identify Allerton's family, as well as his lawyer and local tradesmen, yet some remained unclear. Why would he have been phoning an MP, and a well-known businessman? The men on the other end of the phone numbers could have been innocuous and completely innocent, but the team were very suspicious of everything and everyone.

Lord Allerton had appeared to be beyond reproach, but he had been willing to come in and confess. What about the MP, the businessman? Could they be innocent or was there something more?

'Bridget,' Wendy asked, 'any correlation with the records from Eton College?'

'Allerton went to the college with the two men.'

'So they're innocent.'

'I'm just the office worker, you're the police sergeant,' Bridget replied with typical late-night humour.

'Larry, how do you fancy a day hobnobbing with the upper classes?' Wendy asked.

'A trip to Eton College? When?'

'Tomorrow morning.'

'What about the meeting here?'

'That's fine. We'll be here at 7 a.m. After that we'll drive down to Eton, it's not far.'

'Agreed. Do you know anyone down there?'

'Eton College? It's hardly likely. Maybe the janitor,' Wendy said.

Chapter 21

'You bastard, you stinking bastard,' Lady Allerton screamed down the phone.

'Laura, I don't know what you're talking about,' Keith Codrington replied.

'You were always trying to get him involved in some lame-brained scheme or other, and now he's dead.'

'I'm sorry for your loss, but I don't know what you're talking about.'

'Did you kill him? Tell me that.'

'Of course not. I may be a rogue, but I'm not a murderer.'

'You lying bastard. You had him killed to protect whatever shabby business you're involved in. Tim was a good man, even if he was a soft touch. Believe me, I should know.'

'He married you.'

'I loved the man for all his faults. Is this revenge because I refused you?'

'That was a long time ago, and besides, I couldn't give you a title.'

'Tim said it was drugs.'

'The police, did you tell them?'

'And bring the family name into disrepute?'

'Not you,' Keith Codrington said. 'You would have fed them a line about what a good man he was. No doubt some tears.'

'Timothy told me everything,' Laura Allerton said. She knew she was talking to the responsible person; a person callous enough to have someone killed. She remembered when they had been lovers all those years before. She remembered his arrogance, his unfailing belief in himself, his desire to show that even though he was only a distant cousin, he deserved the title and her. He knew she would have gone with him if that had been the case, but the cards had been stacked against him. The one person that he could not have, and she was on the phone berating him for killing her husband.

'What did he tell you?'

'He told me about the smuggling of drugs into the country, and how it had saved us from financial ruin.'

'Did it?'

'Yes, of course it did.'

'Then was the cost worth it?'

'If I had known before I would have said no.'

'But you didn't. And now? Are you willing to give all the money back?'

'What do you think I am, stupid?'

'Anything but stupid. You'll hang onto the money, as Tim would have. The man may have gone soft, but he wanted the money, not the risk.'

'Is that an admission of your guilt?'

'Not an admission, just a statement of fact.'

'You murdered him because he was going to talk to the police. Don't deny it.'

'You know me better than that.'

'Yes, I do. You're guilty. Did he tell you he had already phoned the police?'

'When?'

'Before you killed him.'

The phone went silent for a few moments. 'What do the police know?' Keith Codrington, former lover of Lady Laura Allerton and murderer of her husband, asked.

'They knew he was involved, but he had given them no names.'

'That's why they were up there with you so quickly.'

'They're not dummies. They'll put two and two together.'

'And you, Laura? What's your position?'

'I will protect the Allerton name.'

'Even if that means lying.'

'And whatever else is necessary. You're the murdering bastard who destroyed us.'

'I saved you. What if you had been forced to leave Allerton Hall? You're a snob, the same as Tim was, the same as me, but I don't have a fancy title, only my ability to make money. One day you'll thank me.'

'It won't be today,' Laura Allerton said as she ended the phone call. It was time to mourn her husband.

***

The meeting in the office at Challis Street the following morning took less time than expected. Len Donaldson was spending so much time in the office that Bridget had bought him his own coffee mug from a shop down the road.

Apart from a debriefing on Isaac and Donaldson's trip north, not much was said. Wendy and Larry were ahead of the game and were ready to make the trip to Eton College.

A local inspector had phoned the college to arrange an appointment with the administration office.

Upon arrival, they were ushered into a warm room. They had not brought any uniformed police at the request of the college. 'Doesn't look good,' Maureen Goode, the head of admissions said.

Wendy thought that it may look even worse when the truth of what some of their ex-pupils had been involved in became general knowledge. So far, Lord Allerton's death was being reported as murder, cause unknown, although that did not stop the speculation on social media, ranging from close to the truth to the bizarre. Not that Wendy took any notice of it. Apart from the occasional email and her limited attempts at typing a report, she saw no need for the technological age. She had grown up in a small farming community, and there had been no technology apart from a black and white television, a crackling radio and a black Bakelite telephone.

'Mrs Goode,' Wendy said, 'you are aware of the death of Lord Allerton.'

'Yes. Tragic. They said a few words in assembly this morning about him.'

'Did you know him?'

'Oh no. I've only been here ten years. He left long before that.'

'We are here because of his death. We need to find out who may have borne a grudge against him.'

'He's an Old Etonian. Nobody would.'

'That's as may be,' Larry said, 'but someone murdered him. You are aware of that.'

'He's one of our boys. They're such good people, good citizens. You're conscious of the quality of the young men we admit, their families?'

Their bank balances, Wendy thought but kept it to herself. Larry had checked on Wikipedia. They had had their fair share of villains as well, regardless of Mrs Goode's statement to the contrary.

'Is there anyone here who would remember Lord Allerton? Possibly a member of the teaching faculty,' Larry asked.

'Mr Weston, one of our chemistry teachers. He was a pupil here at the same time as Lord Allerton. He made a speech at the early morning assembly about his memories of the dead man.'

'When can we meet him?'

'He'll be free within an hour. I'll make sure he comes over to meet you both.'

***

'That damn fool had already told the police that he was going to see them,' Keith Codrington said.

'And you still went and killed him,' Fortescue said.

The three remaining men met in the centre of London at a café they frequented.

'What can we do?' Griffiths asked. He knew there was no way out. The trail was too hot now, and it was only a matter of time.

'You two can claim ignorance,' Codrington said. His previously unshakable belief in his infallibility was crumbling, and the other two men could see that: the shirt that he wore, the jacket, the trousers, the shine on his shoes, none were as sharp as on previous occasions.

'Ignorance will not protect us,' Fortescue said.

'You're innocent of the murders. You took no part in the business other than to finance me when I asked. What's the most that can happen?'

'Keith's right,' Jacob Griffiths said. 'The most we'll get is five years.'

'That's what I mean,' Fortescue retorted. 'We'll be social lepers. I'll lose my comfy seat in Westminster.'

'And your mistresses,' Griffiths said. 'What will happen to me? The banks will renege on their loans.'

'Allerton may have been a lily-livered coward, but he didn't complain as much as you two. And now, when it's falling down around our ears, you're hoping that it will all go away. Well, it won't. The only question is what do we do?'

'What are you going to do?' Fortescue asked.

'This will be our last meeting,' Codrington replied.

'You can't do that.'

'Why not? What are you going to do? Have me murdered?'

'What about us?' Griffiths asked.

'Do what you like.'

The meeting ended badly, with Codrington taking a taxi, the other two men walking down the road.

***

'I knew Allerton,' Cyril Weston said. The man was dressed in a tailcoat, the standard wear for pupils and staff alike.

'What can you tell us about him?' Larry asked.

'Likeable fellow. He married the Duke of Ashby's daughter.'

'Was he ever in any trouble at Eton?'

'Not that I recall. As I said, I knew him, but I was not one of his circle.'

'Do you remember who was?' Wendy asked.

'It's a few years back now, but if there was a photo, I could probably pick them out. One of them became a politician, I know that.'

Mrs Goode quickly procured the annual photo for the year in question. 'That's Tim Allerton,' Weston said, pointing to a boy standing in the second row.

'Anyone else who is familiar?'

'That's me. I was a spotty individual then, not the person you see now.' Wendy could see what he meant.

'Anyone else? Lord Allerton's friends?'

'That's the politician. Miles Fortescue. The other friends are the one to his left and the one standing at his rear.'

'Mrs Goode, any way to identify them?' Larry asked.

'Five minutes. I've a record of every one of them.'

'Is there any more that you can tell us?' Wendy asked.

'Not really. I was friendly with Allerton but nothing more. I remember that I didn't like Fortescue very much, but for the other two, nothing. I certainly don't remember either of them down on the sports fields.'

Five minutes later, as agreed, Mrs Goode had the information. 'The boy at the back is Keith Codrington. The other one you're interested in is Jacob Griffiths. He owns all those supermarkets you see up and down the country. I have no further knowledge on Keith Codrington.'

'Do you have their last known addresses?' Wendy asked.

'I hope this doesn't reflect poorly on the college,' Weston said.

'Unfortunately, it may. Allerton was murdered, and the other three may be implicated.'

'Sad, very sad,' Mrs Goode said.

'Can you prove this?' Weston asked.

'It's part of an ongoing murder investigation. Lord Allerton's time here and his friendships may be circumstantial, but we need to check all possibilities,' Larry said.

***

Codrington took the taxi to his Thame riverside flat after leaving the two fools, Griffiths and Fortescue, licking their wounds. The man had a broad smile on his face as he entered. He looked around, admiring his lifestyle. He then picked up two suitcases and left. *No coming back*, he thought.

He had to admit to himself that it had worked out splendidly. Not only had he avoided the law, but he had ensured that two others would take the blame. Where he was going there was no coming back, no need to. He had ensured that enough wealth was waiting for him on his arrival, and enough women if that was what he wanted, although he still wanted Allerton's widow, the lovely Laura. He wondered if in time it would be possible. He thought it would, as she was mercenary, the same as he had been. He had been penniless when they had courted, but now she had the title and he had the wealth, at least more than her, and if the police confiscated her share, then he was always there. He knew she would come then.

'Heathrow,' he said, getting into the taxi that had waited for him. Codrington knew he would miss England, especially London with its drizzling rain and slush underfoot when it snowed, which in recent years had been infrequent, but he would not miss it so much that he would come back. His name would soon be known, and the police would be in contact with the overseas police forces to be on the lookout for an Englishman of average height, average weight, going by the name of Keith Codrington, an Old Etonian. The only problem was that once he left the taxi at Heathrow, he would no longer be Codrington and certainly not an Old Etonian. The passport that he would present at the airport had cost him plenty, almost twenty thousand pounds, but he knew quality. A beard, some extra pounds of weight as well as dying his hair and he would be invisible within two weeks. And once that disguise was complete, he would move again until there was no more need to. His life of crime had been fun, but now he intended to be respectable, boringly respectable, and it excited him.

Chapter 22

Wendy and Larry, armed with the information they had received at Eton College, headed back to Challis Street Police Station. It was clear that Allerton had maintained contact with his childhood friends Jacob Griffiths and Miles Fortescue, but so far they had not been able to pinpoint Keith Codrington.

The team were pulled in together on Wendy and Larry's return. DCS Goddard was present.

'We need to interview Griffiths and Fortescue,' Isaac said.

'Are they the people running the show?' Goddard asked.

'We're not certain. Our suspicions lie with another man.'

'Then call him in.'

'Not so easy. He's the mystery man.'

'What do you know about him?'

'Keith Codrington, the second cousin of Lord Allerton, was educated at Eton. He's the same age as Allerton. We've been checking his background. Bridget, what do you have?'

'Keith Humphrey Codrington, age forty-two. His father was a doctor, his mother a housewife. He attended Eton College until his eighteenth birthday and then went to Oxford University. He graduated from there with a degree in applied mathematics. After that, he spent many years in the Middle East as a shipping agent. He returned to this country eighteen months ago.'

'What type of shipping?' Isaac asked.

'Oil, one way. Livestock, the other,' Bridget said.

'As well as drugs?' Larry speculated.

'There are no criminal cases against Keith Codrington. Also, he's a member of Mensa.'

'Smart then,' Goddard said.

'Smart enough to fool us, if he's our man,' Isaac said.

'That's as may be, but we need him and the other two you mentioned in here today. You know the alternatives.'

'That bad?'

'Yes.'

'Larry, an update on Walters.'

'Just one thing,' Bridget interjected. 'They found the Land Rover less than fifty miles from here. The number plate had been changed but the engine number tallies, and there is significant damage to the front of the vehicle.'

'Commensurate with pushing a Bentley off the road?' Goddard asked.

'They're checking now, but the advice I've received is that it's possible.'

'Who's there?' Isaac asked.

'Gordon Windsor is heading out there.'

'Tell the locals to leave the vehicle alone until he gets there. There could still be prints.'

'Do you have an address for Codrington?' Goddard asked.

'The only address is bogus. We believe he was using aliases.'

'But if he was involved with the other three, they must have been visible.'

'We're following up on that now,' Larry said.

'What do we have on Miles Fortescue?'

'We know he's an MP, and that he's financially secure.'

'What do you mean?'

'He owns a house in Belgravia.'

'Have you been there?'

'Not yet. We're going there, or to the Houses of Parliament, after this meeting.'

'Very well. You'd better caution him and bring him to the station.'

'He'll claim some sort of immunity,' Wendy said.

'He has no immunity,' DCS Goddard said. 'He's only an MP and not a very effective one at that.'

'The DCS is right. He's either interviewed in front of his political colleagues or here. It's up to him.'

'What about Griffiths?' Isaac asked.

'Turn on the television every night. He's always there,' Wendy said.

'Apart from his supermarkets, what else do we know about him? Bridget, any updates?'

'Jacob Aloysius Griffiths, age forty-three and the son of a farmer. He left Eton at the age of eighteen and went to agricultural college. He made his first million by the age of twenty, lost it all within one year. After that a succession of businesses, some good, some bad, until he hit the jackpot with supermarkets.'

'Where did you get all that information?' Isaac asked.

'Wikipedia.'

'You've only one more day to wrap this up. Are you certain these are the key people?' Goddard asked.

'It all points to them.'

'Let's hope you're right. Any stuff-ups on this one and you know what happens.'

'I've already been there once, sir,' Isaac replied.'

***

Steve Walters was feeling good. The money he had received for his latest killing had given him enough to plan his future. It had been a few grim weeks hiding out from the police, scurrying around in Manchester, remaining unshaven and not going to the gym. He could feel the flabbiness in his body; he intended to rectify the situation as soon as possible.

It had not been difficult to travel from where he had been staying, a nondescript hotel in a nondescript suburb in Manchester, over to Derbyshire, only forty minutes to drive if he had been driving a decent car. The man on the end of the phone introduced himself as Zachary. Walters knew it was not his correct name, but what did a name matter; it was what he had to say that was important. 'Fifty thousand pounds.'

'What for?' Walters had asked.

'For what you're good at.'

'Who?' There was no need for further explanation. Steve Walters knew only one trade: how to kill a man. A trade that Her Majesty's Government had taught him well when he had served with the British Army behind enemy lines in Iraq and Afghanistan. He remembered the advertisement for signing up: 'Join the modern British Army and learn a trade'. He had certainly done that, and it had been most useful. Not only was he adept with a knife and a piece of wire, but he was also good at calculating the force necessary to push a car off the road, and Zachary's description of the target's car, a Bentley, told him that it needed something more substantial than a small Toyota. It needed a four-wheel drive; it needed a Land Rover, not that he fancied driving one of them again. He had driven plenty in the army, and they were uncomfortable, and the gearboxes were a disaster.

'How will the money be paid?' he had asked Zachary.

'Half will be in your bank account within the hour. The remainder on completion.'

'I want it all now.'

'Very well. The full fifty thousand pounds in thirty minutes. You need to be in position within seventy-five.'

'I'll leave now. I'll check my account on the way. No money, no death. You savvy?'

'Yes, I fully understand.'

Codrington then proceeded to describe the area where the accident was to happen. He had visited Allerton's home many times. He was even godfather to the Allertons' first child.

Walters, confident that the British Army had trained him well, took a train to the outskirts of Manchester. He soon found a suitable vehicle and hot-wired it within two minutes. He had to admit that for a Land Rover it was a lot better than the ones he had driven in Iraq, but it was still an uncomfortable trip. Ten minutes later he checked his phone. The fifty thousand pounds was there; the fate of the intended victim was sealed.

He arrived at the scene and parked on a track to one side, glad for once of the four-wheel drive, as it was muddy from the rain of the last few days. Sitting high up on the hill he had time to think, time to look around. From his vantage point, he could see any vehicles ascending the road towards him, and a Bentley would be distinctive, the sort of car he aspired to, although where he was going it would be incongruous. He double-checked his bank account. With the addition of the fifty thousand pounds, the balance stood at one hundred and thirty-two thousand. It was sufficient, but he could always hire himself out around the world if necessary.

An old van trundled by, followed by a young couple in an old car. He could see by the way they were entwined around each other that they were looking for somewhere secluded to park.

He surfed the net on his phone, keeping one eye peeled. It was not long before the Bentley came into view. Even though the day was overcast and it was starting to rain, the vehicle still shone. He saw the car slowing to turn through the metal gates at the entrance to Allerton Hall. He assumed that was the name of the man he was about to kill.

Walters waited until the vehicle was almost at a standstill before pulling out at speed from the concealed track. He remembered the look on the man's face as he hit the Bentley the first time. He saw him attempting to move the car; the gun he carried soon dealt with that problem. The Land Rover, powerful as it was, still struggled to move the Bentley, but eventually, after three attempts, it managed to push it over a low stone wall that had probably been constructed two hundred years ago. Steve Walters watched the vehicle turn over and over, gaining momentum before disappearing over the edge of the quarry.

He then sped off and headed south. He stopped after thirty minutes and changed the number plates. He realised he had about ninety minutes before the Land Rover would be reported missing. At that time, the owner, a doctor that he knew, would be leaving the hospital at the end of his shift. Only then would he realise his vehicle had been stolen and call the police.

***

Miles Fortescue, an important person in his estimation, did not appreciate two police officers in his office at the Houses of Parliament. 'What right have you to be here?' he asked.

Wendy thought him a rude man who had made a point of not shaking DI Hill's hand and hers.

'Mr Fortescue, we are investigating the death of Lord Allerton. We are aware that he was a friend of yours,' Larry said. Both he and Wendy were standing up; Fortescue had his back to the window. He was attempting to look superior; it wasn't working, at least not with Wendy.

'Timothy Allerton was a friend. His death is tragic.'

'When was the last time you spoke to him?'

'Is this important? I'm due in the chamber, a crucial vote.'

'It's not sitting,' Wendy said. She had checked.

'We can conduct this at the police station if you prefer.'

'No,' Fortescue reluctantly said. 'Here will be all right.'

'This interview will be recorded. Is that acceptable?' Larry asked as he looked at the man. He was not impressed. Fortescue was only one year older than him, but he looked closer to fifty than forty. He was dressed well in an expensive suit, but his belly strained against the front of his shirt. It was evident to both of the police officers that this man, this representative of the people, enjoyed the finer things in life: good food, good wines and not so good women. Bridget had found out that useful little nugget about his personal life. It was not widely known, nor was the man. Bridget had also looked at his track record as an MP and found it lacking.

'I'll repeat my previous question,' Larry said. 'When was the last time you saw Lord Allerton?'

'Two weeks ago.'

'And your last communication with him?'

'As I said, two weeks ago.'

'Mr Fortescue, we have his phone records. We know that you spoke by phone with Lord Allerton on the day of his death. Do you deny this?'

'Yes, no…'

'Which is it?'

'My position here…' Fortescue mumbled.

'Sir, your position as a member of parliament is not of interest to us. The murder of Lord Allerton is.'

'And mine. He was a friend. I had known him for nearly thirty years. Of course I'm interested in who killed him, but I need to protect my position from any hint of scandal.'

'We are only interested in the death of Lord Allerton. And what do you mean by scandal?'

'Figuratively speaking, you realise. Proven or otherwise, my friendship with a murdered man will raise concerns, questions about my suitability.'

'Are these more important than the death of your friend?'

'No. What do you want to know?'

Wendy knew the man was feigning interest. It was evident to her that Fortescue was the worst kind of parasite, the type that pretends to be benevolent and caring while sucking its victim dry.

'On the day he died, Lord Allerton was in London. Did you know this?' Wendy asked.

'He never mentioned it.'

'You said that you spoke to him by phone. What did the two of you talk about?'

'Nothing important. He seemed a little tense, but no more than normal.'

'What do you mean by no more than normal?'

'Allerton was a worrier, that's all. He always was.'

'Even at Eton?' Wendy asked.

'Even there.'

'Let me come back to his time in London. Did you meet with him?' Larry asked.

'No.'

'You have a place in Belgravia?'

'That's on the public record. Ebury Street.'

'Lord Allerton's Bentley was parked not more than a five-minute walk from your house.'

'I didn't know that. It's possible. The man knew other people in London.'

Fortescue stood up from the chair he had been sitting in. He moved to the window, looked out at the River Thames. Wendy thought the man was trying to get rid of them. She knew that he felt disdain for them, but if he knew Allerton and had met him, it could mean guilt by association. Fortescue may have thought his rank gave him certain protections, but with her and Larry Hill it did not.

'We have reason to believe that Lord Allerton was involved in the importation of illicit drugs into this country.'

'Rubbish!' Fortescue said. 'He was the most honest man you'd ever meet. He wouldn't last thirty minutes as a member of parliament.'

'Do you need to be dishonest to be an MP?' Wendy asked.

'You know what I mean. Here, you need to play the game, bend with the wind, follow the party line. Not always so easy.'

'Coming back to Lord Allerton's confession,' Larry said.

'What confession?'

'Lord Allerton phoned our DCI and stated that he was coming into the police station to confess and to name names. Was yours one of those names?'

Fortescue approached perilously close to Larry. 'The next time we meet I will be with my lawyer. In the meantime, I will contact Commissioner Davies and make an official complaint. If you're a police officer next week, it will be more by good luck than anything else. Your career is finished.'

'Is that a threat, sir?' Larry asked.

'It's a statement of fact. Now, I suggest you leave before I have you thrown out.'

Chapter 23

Detective Chief Superintendent Goddard reacted with alarm when Isaac informed him of his DI and sergeant's meeting with Miles Fortescue. 'How can I protect them, you?' Goddard said. 'Before it was always Davies trying to exert his influence, look after his own people, but now an official complaint from an MP, no less.'

'He's involved.'

'Can you prove it?'

'Not conclusively. We need him to break first.'

'And how do you plan to do that?'

'We keep the pressure on.'

'I thought Serious and Organised Crime Command were dealing with the drug trafficking,' Goddard said. He was stamping up and down his office on the third floor at Challis Street Police Station. Isaac Cook, his DCI, was standing still, allowing the man the opportunity to vent his spleen. Isaac knew the routine; the man would blow his top for a few minutes and then calm down. Only then could they talk seriously.

Isaac knew that if his DI and sergeant were suspended pending a full enquiry, then he was threatened, as well as his DCS.

'Give me the facts,' Goddard said. He had sat down behind his desk.

'Len Donaldson of Serious and Organised Crime Command is working on the drug trafficking. We're working on the murders. We know who the murderers are: Devlin O'Shaughnessy and Steve Walters.'

'Isn't that the end of your work? Just wrap that up, and our side of the case is complete.'

'O'Shaughnessy's under lock and key; Walters is still at large.'

'Walters killed Allerton?'

'We found prints on the Land Rover. It's him alright, and we can prove he killed Hughenden. So far, there is no one that we can prove for the murder of Rodrigo Fuentes.'

'Then catch Walters.'

'Not so easy. We've not been able to find him yet.'

'Unless you can prove Fortescue's direct involvement in the murders, you'll not win on this one.'

'He's not our primary suspect.'

'Who is?'

'Keith Codrington, Lord Allerton's cousin.'

'And where is he?'

'His whereabouts have always been unclear. We haven't located him yet.'

'What do you want me to do?' Goddard asked. 'Every time you put me on the spot. Have I got to take on the commissioner again to save your skin?'

'Yes, sir. I'm afraid you must. We need the person or persons who ordered the deaths of five people that we know of. They, or he, are more dangerous than those who carried out the crimes. There's one more person to pressure.'

'Who?'

'Jacob Griffiths.'

'The Jacob Griffiths!'

'That's the one.'

'Make it official. Make sure you interview him at Challis Street and make sure he has legal representation. I don't want last year's businessman of the year talking to the media.'

'Yes, sir. By the book.'

***

Jacob Griffiths reluctantly presented himself at Challis Street. The man who accompanied him was tall and thin. He looked expensive.

'Thank you for coming,' Isaac said. Len Donaldson stood alongside him.

The four men entered the interview room. Griffiths sat facing Isaac, the lawyer sat opposite Donaldson. Donaldson was on edge; Isaac could tell the man was anxious to wrap up the case.

'My client has come here of his own free will,' the lawyer said.

'We are aware of that,' Isaac said.

With all four men comfortable, Isaac commenced the interview, remembering to follow official procedures. DCS Goddard stood in another room, observing on a monitor.

'Mr Griffiths, you were a friend of Lord Allerton?' Isaac asked.

'A good friend. We were at Eton together.'

'Along with Keith Codrington and Miles Fortescue.'

'We were all friends.'

'According to our enquiries, there was a special bond between the four of you,' Donaldson said.

'That's correct. It has served us well over the years.'

'My client is here to assist you with your enquiry into the tragic death of his friend,' the lawyer, Andrew Rushton, said.

Isaac studied the man. He was in his early fifties, and he had a formidable reputation, even at Challis Street. It was the first time he had met the man in person, but he knew he would need to be careful in how he phrased his questions.

Griffiths' face was well known from the constant adverts on the television, proudly proclaiming that his products were the cheapest, his vegetables and fruit the freshest. Len Donaldson knew him from his beaming face on the poster at the local supermarket he frequented every week.

'We understand that Mr Griffiths is giving us his valuable time.'

'Can we come back to Lord Allerton?' Donaldson asked.

'Tragic,' Griffiths said.

'We know that on the day of his death he was coming to this station to confess.'

'Confess to what?'

'I received a phone call from him in the morning to say that he would be here,' Isaac said. 'And that he'd tell us who was involved in the drug syndicate and who was the person in control.'

'What drug syndicate?' Griffiths replied.

'If you are attempting to find guilt against my client due to a friendship, then you will need to be very careful,' Rushton said, with steely eyes.

'We're trying to ascertain the facts. We do not believe that Lord Allerton was a major player, although we believe one of his friends is.'

'It's not me,' Griffiths protested. Too strongly for Donaldson.

'Our investigations indicate that Keith Codrington is the ringleader and that Lord Allerton was purely a minor functionary. We are aware that his financial position has dramatically improved in the last twelve to eighteen months, as has yours and that of Miles Fortescue.'

'I'm an entrepreneur. That's the definition.'

'We believe that the scale of the operation required a large cash injection, more than Codrington could manage. Our enquiries confirm that the man was academically brilliant, highly skilled in international trade, and capable of setting up the large-scale importation and distribution of illegal drugs.'

Griffiths was on his feet. 'Are you accusing me of being involved?'

'Sit down,' Rushton said, attempting to grab the man by the arm.

'We are conducting enquiries. We're not accusing anyone, but we are aware of some of the shipment dates, and we are correlating monies into your account and others.'

'My financial records are not for public scrutiny.'

'They will be,' Donaldson said, knowing full well that a man such as Griffiths would have many bank accounts, and not all of them would be easy to trace.

'Without Keith Codrington, we will place charges on those who financed him. Not only is there drug trafficking, there are also the murders of five people. We know the men who killed them, but the person giving the order is also subject to the charge of murder under English law. Believe me, we will continue with our enquiries, including the movements of all those suspected. We will make the connections, we will place charges,' Isaac said.

Jacob Griffiths was sitting ashen-faced. 'My client is innocent,' his lawyer said.

'We've not accused him of any crime,' Donaldson said.

'Just one more question,' Isaac said. 'Where is Keith Codrington?'

'I've no idea,' Griffiths replied.

'When did you last see him?'

'Two weeks ago.'

'Thank you, Mr Griffiths. We will contact you if we have any further questions.'

The beaming face that confronted Len Donaldson at his supermarket every Saturday was not visible as the master shop owner left Challis Street.

'Well handled,' DCS Goddard said to the two police officers afterwards.

'What do you reckon, sir?' Donaldson asked.

'Can you prove it?'

'In time, but without Codrington it's going to be difficult.'

'Time is the one luxury you don't have.'

***

Jacob Griffiths and Miles Fortescue, fearful of being seen together, kept in contact by phone.

'There's no way out,' Fortescue admitted. A quick phone call to Alwyn Davies to register an official complaint had been easy to do, but if there was any hint of his guilt, Fortescue knew the commissioner would pull back.

'What are you planning to do?' Griffiths asked. For once, he was at a loss on how to proceed. In the past, whether it was a takeover of another business or facing financial ruin, there were always options: favours to pull in, pressure to be applied. But now, with an impending arrest due to his involvement in drug trafficking, as well as the crime of murder, he knew full well who would give him support – nobody. And there were some who would put the boot in, try to grab his assets. Even if he was willing to accept a prison term, Griffiths knew there was no way his business empire would survive.

'I've no answer,' Fortescue replied. 'We're damned whatever we do. Codrington landed us with his dirty work. We'll be the ones in prison while he's swanning around the world.'

'Any idea where he's gone?'

'Somewhere that has no extradition policy and is willing to take bribes.'

'That could be anywhere. In the meantime, what do we do?'

'We wait and see. And besides, what proof do the police have? We've admitted to our friendship with the man, although I lied that I had seen Allerton that day.'

'So did I,' Griffiths replied.

'Look, I'm certain the police have nothing on us.'

'If they do?'

'It'll be easy to confess to lesser crimes. What did we really do? We loaned Codrington money. It's not as if we were actively involved.'

'But the money we received? There's no way they'll believe it was the proceeds of honest graft.'

'You can doctor your financial records, I can't,' Fortescue said. A smart political animal, he had a way out, but it was risky, and he would not consider it until the optimum moment. He needed to find Codrington, but failing that, he needed to move the blame from himself. He wouldn't be the first politician to be convicted of a crime; he wouldn't be the last. He knew that his political career would not survive, and his constituency would not endorse his re-election, but that was not important. He had enough money, and if he had to follow Codrington into exile, so be it. All he had to do was to make the case against him go cold while firming the blame on Jacob Griffiths. He knew it would not be too difficult.

***

The team stayed late that night at Challis Street. The conclusion to the case that had seemed so strong was falling apart. Apart from a watertight case against O'Shaughnessy, they had little else to show for their efforts. And although Isaac was still hoping to rekindle his romance with Jess O'Neil, every time they tried along came another twist and turn with the current case and any arrangements to meet up were scuttled.

The death of Lord Allerton was big news, and the media were clamouring for an arrest. Lady Allerton had been on the television, as stoic as when Isaac and Len Donaldson had met her. Isaac, an emotional man, could not understand how she did it, but he realised that his ancestry, Jamaican and black, was very different from being white and privileged. Bridget had found out that not only was Laura Allerton the daughter of a Duke, but that she could also claim descent through a succession of ancestors from a former Tudor ruler of England.

'We need another conviction,' Larry said.

'Steve Walters, anything on him?' Isaac asked.

'We've got an APW out on him. If he's caught, we'll be able to charge him.'

'What do you think has happened to him?'

'Think or know?'

'Either.'

'He can't hide out in England indefinitely. His best bet is to skip the country.'

'All airports, Eurostar, ferries being monitored?'

'Standard procedure.'

'There's not a lot more we can do there. It's no use looking for him in his old haunts. He's not likely to be at any of them.'

'Probably not, but he's not a smart man. O'Shaughnessy is, supposedly, and we nabbed him not far from here.'

'Okay,' Isaac said. 'Let's focus on Fortescue and Griffiths. What do we reckon?'

Len Donaldson, who was also present, answered. 'They're guilty.'

'Of what?'

'They've not been involved with the murders, but they must know something.'

'If they won't talk?' Isaac asked.

'We apply pressure. What's the worst that can happen?'

'Our careers,' Isaac replied.

'You're not saying we back off?'

'Not at all. Wendy and Larry are in trouble as it is. It can't get much worse.'

'It can, but we still go on.'

Wendy shifted uncomfortably on her chair, anxious to get home. If her time as a police officer were to end, she would not be too disappointed. Larry still harboured hopes of promotion, and suspension with a disciplinary warning was not to his taste. He had not liked Fortescue, and the man had been too eager to take offence. A seasoned politician would have handled an aspersion about his character better than he had. He intended to maintain the heat although he would need to be subtle.

'We'll keep the heat on Griffiths,' Isaac said when Larry elucidated his plan regarding Fortescue. 'Bridget, what do we have on Griffiths that we can use?'

'What do you want?'

'Any dirt, dodgy dealings, financial irregularities.'

'I'm checking, but so far the man's clean.'

Chapter 24

An unexpected phone call at Challis Street. 'Manchester Airport. We've picked up someone you know.'

Bridget had taken the phone call. 'Who?' she asked.

'Someone trying to board a flight to Bangkok. He tried to slip through immigration using a forged passport. Our people picked it up straight away.'

'But who?' Bridget had to ask again. The lady on the other end was obviously more interested in the diligence of her people than who they had detained.

'Steven Walters. We have your name as the person to contact.'

'Is he secure?'

'He's not going anywhere.'

'Then make sure he doesn't. No smart-arse lawyer getting him bail. My people will be there soon enough.'

Isaac, who was in his office, had come over to Bridget's desk in response to her waving. 'It's Walters,' she whispered, her hand over the mouthpiece of the telephone while the woman in Manchester continued to talk.

'Secure?' Isaac asked.

'That's what she says.'

Isaac phoned Larry. 'I need you up in Manchester. They've picked up Walters.'

'I could drive. I'm out with Wendy, checking addresses, trying to get an angle on Griffiths and Fortescue. I believe we've enough to push Fortescue again.'

'How long to Manchester?'

'Three hours. Where to?' Larry asked.

'The airport. Bridget will give you the contact once you're on your way. By the way, what do you have on Fortescue?'

'We've proved that Griffiths was at Fortescue's house in Belgravia.'

'At the same time as Allerton?'

'Yes. The times match.'

It was a sorry looking man who confronted Wendy and Larry on their arrival at Manchester Airport. The police cells had been strengthened for terrorists after the attacks on the city in the past. As it turned out, Walters was their inaugural client since the work had completed.

'That bastard,'

'Which bastard?' Wendy asked later when the formalities had been dealt with.

'The bastard who sold me the passport. If ever I get my hands on him…'

'It depends whether he ends up in the same prison as you.'

'O'Shaughnessy's the one you want,' Walters said. Larry recognised the signs: blame someone else, blame life, blame anyone and anything.

'We've already got him, you know that.'

'He killed Stewart.'

'What about Pinto, Fuentes?'

'I know he killed Fuentes. You can't pin that on me.'

'Are you saying that you were involved in the death of Pinto?' Larry knew the truth, but if Walters would give details about Fuentes, it may wrap up that murder as well.

'I didn't kill him,' Walters said, but that was already known by the team at Challis Street. The garage where Pinto had been hidden showed only proof of O'Shaughnessy, although the victim had probably been murdered elsewhere.

The holding cells at Manchester Airport were not the ideal location to conduct an interrogation, but if the apprehended villain wanted to talk, then neither Wendy nor Larry were going to stop him. A local DI was also present to corroborate that all was in accordance with regulations.

'Tell us about Dougal Stewart,' Wendy asked.

'That was Devlin's idea.'

'Devlin?' Larry preferred full names to save any confusion later on.

'Devlin O'Shaughnessy. I thought we were going to rough him up, frighten him. We knew he was stealing, but that's hardly a reason to kill the man.'

'But you were willing to tie him up to a beam with a rope?'

'I'm a hard case, violence comes easily to me. I had no issue with giving him and Pinto a good thrashing.'

'That's been your life, hasn't it?' Larry said.

Walters sat calmly on his side of the cell. Wendy could see that the man had made an attempt at altering his appearance. They had been looking for a smallish, well-muscled man with tattooed arms and straggly hair. The man they were interviewing was certainly on the short side, even shorter than Wendy. She estimated his height at five feet seven inches. He wore a suit with a tie, and his hair had been cut short. He also sported a pair of glasses. They looked prescription, but Wendy thought they were the style that you could buy in any pharmacy.

'I've always looked out for myself.'

'We have your prison record. We know of your convictions for crimes of violence.'

'I've not killed anyone, at least not in this country.'

'Fuentes. What can you tell us about him?'

'I knew what O'Shaughnessy was planning to do. Fuentes had been undercutting us.'

'Why are you telling us?' Wendy asked. 'You're admitting to your involvement in the importation and distribution of Class A drugs.'

'What's the sentence for that? Ten years, out in seven for good behaviour.'

'It's more than that, but you'll get out at some stage.'

'That's how I see it.'

'With sufficient money in your pocket,' Larry added.

'If you say so. I didn't kill anyone. I'm not going to jail for that.'

'We need details about Fuentes. Unless we can prove that you were not involved in any murders, you'll be convicted for the killings of Stewart and Fuentes.'

'And Pinto?'

'We've charged O'Shaughnessy with that murder. However, if you want to confess to your involvement…'

'Not a chance.'

Wendy looked over at Larry. He shook his head imperceptibly. He knew that she wanted to tell him that he had forgotten about the death of Alex Hughenden. He had not.

'O'Shaughnessy told me he needed me to deal with Rodrigo Fuentes,' Walters said.

'Will you testify to that?' Wendy asked.

'If I get a reduction in my sentence.'

'That will depend on the judge.'

'He'll go for it; they always do.'

'You're very confident.'

'I've been there before.'

'They don't like people who grass, on the inside,' Wendy reminded Walters.

'I can handle myself.'

'Coming back to Fuentes,' Larry said. 'What happened?'

'O'Shaughnessy had received instruction that Fuentes had to disappear; give a warning to anyone else who fancied their chances.'

'Where were you the night of his murder?'

'I was shacked up with a woman.'

'Will she give you an alibi?'

'It's hardly likely.'

'Why?'

'I don't know her name. We met down the pub. By the time we got back to her place, we were both drunk. I can't even remember if I screwed her, although she said I did and she was demanding money.'

'What happened?'

'I told her to shut up and gave her a couple of hundred pounds.'

'And O'Shaughnessy killed Fuentes. Did he tell you afterwards?'

'After a few beers.'

'What did he say?'

'He told me that he took him down the river for a few miles, tied chains around his ankles and tossed him over the side. O'Shaughnessy said the man cried like a baby.'

'What was your reaction?'

'Nothing. I just ordered another pint.'

'No sorrow for the man O'Shaughnessy had murdered?'

'I'm a violent person. Maybe I'll end up one day dead in a ditch. I've got no strong views either way on Fuentes or anyone else. I've killed plenty of men in my time.'

'Your time in the army?'

'Then I received a medal, and most of those that I killed in the name of Queen and country were decent people; just on the enemy's side. Kill scum as a civilian, and they send you to prison. Makes no sense to me, but I don't think much about it.'

'You would kill if it was necessary?'

'I'm not answering that question,' Walters said. 'What's your plan now?'

'We're transferring you to London.'

'Not the same place as O'Shaughnessy.'

'We'll keep you apart. What about Lord Allerton?'

'Who's he?'

'He's the man in the Bentley who you pushed over the side of a quarry.'

'I don't know about that.'

'Alex Hughenden, will you deny that you killed him as well?'

'Yes.'

Steve Walters sat still. He may not have been as smart as O'Shaughnessy, but he knew he had said too much.

'It doesn't matter,' Larry said. 'We've enough to convict you. This interview will be admissible at your trial.'

'You bastard,' Walters said. He attempted to get up from his chair to come at Larry.

'Don't do it.' Larry said.

Walters sat down again.

***

'Commissioner Davies is delighted,' DCS Goddard said on the phone.

'You've told him?' Isaac asked, knowing full well that Richard Goddard would be the first to claim credit for Challis Street's Homicide team.

'You're off the hook. That's five murders solved.'

'Five convictions. We've got enough evidence now. We've still not found the people behind the scenes.'

'Are they important?' Goddard asked.

'You know they are.'

'I suppose I was naïve to think you'd let it rest. Okay, work with Serious and Organised Crime Command, but I can only give you forty-eight hours. Will that be sufficient?'

'Yes, sir,' Isaac replied.

'And don't forget the paperwork. I want O'Shaughnessy's and Walter's cases to be watertight.'

'They will be.'

Later that day, the full team were back in Challis Street. Len Donaldson was holding the mug that Bridget had bought him. Larry and Wendy had arrived back from Manchester two hours earlier. The day was drawing to a close, but everyone was on a high.

'Walters?' Isaac asked.

'They'll hold him in a local prison up there; transfer him to London tomorrow.'

'Great work getting his statement.'

'We should thank the people at the airport. I saw the forged passport, it was good. I wouldn't have picked it.'

'Len, do you want to speak?' Isaac asked.

'Thanks. Our attempts to find Keith Codrington have drawn a blank so far. We believe he may have left the country. That's the only likely explanation.'

'Any idea where?'

'Somewhere we can't get him back. And he's probably assumed another identity.'

'We'll focus on Griffiths and Fortescue,' Larry said.

'What do we have on Fortescue?' Isaac asked.

'We can prove that Allerton's and Griffiths' cars were parked in the vicinity of Fortescue's house on the day in question,' Larry said.

'Circumstantial?'

'It's not likely.'

'But can you prove it?'

'No. We also know that Codrington was there.'

'How?'

'We conducted a few door knocks.'

'And?'

'A neighbour identified his photo.'

'Do we have a recent photo of the man?'

'Only a passport photo, but she bumped into him as she left her house. Supposedly her dog's lead became entangled around his legs.'

'What did she say about him?'

'She said he was polite and gracious, not like Fortescue who was always complaining about the dog barking. She also said he often had one woman or another around.'

'If you can prove Codrington was there, and there's enough evidence to lay charges against him, then we've enough to pull Fortescue in.'

'What proof do we have against Codrington?' Wendy asked.

'Phone records from Hughenden to him.'

'We still don't know if they are from Codrington,' Donaldson said.

'Fortescue doesn't either.'

'Are you planning to lie to Fortescue?'
'Are you in agreement?' Isaac asked.
'Totally,' Donaldson's reply.
'Larry, you know what to do.'
'My pleasure. I can't wait to see the face on that sanctimonious bastard who reported us when I visit him next.'

Chapter 25

Miles Fortescue did not expect to see the two police officers that he had reported on his doorstep in Ebury Street.

'Mr Fortescue, we have some questions for you,' Larry said with a sense of joy. He savoured the man's expression when he had opened the door.

'Detective Inspector Hill. I thought you would have had enough after the last time we met.'

'My visit's official. We have some questions for you,' Larry said again. He had ensured a marked police car was parked outside. Wendy could see curtains twitching up and down the street.

'Not today. I'm busy.'

'It's official. I could enforce your attendance at Challis Street Police Station.'

'Very well. Give me five minutes.' The door to the house slammed shut in Larry's face. Not that he minded, as he knew the man was angry.

Inside the house, Fortescue picked up his phone. 'Jacob, the police are here.'

'What are you going to do?'

'I've no option. I've got to go with them.'

'But they've no proof.'

'How would I know? I'm a politician. I can't hide everything.'

'What should I do?' Griffiths asked.

'Make a run for it. If I get free of them, I'm off.'

Ten minutes later, Miles Fortescue left by the front door of his house. 'My lawyer will be at Challis Street. I'll drive my own car,' he said.

'That's fine. We'll meet at the station.'

At Challis Street Police Station, Isaac and Len Donaldson sat discussing tactics.

'We're taking a risk with this man,' Donaldson said.

'We're following the agreed procedures. He's a material witness.'

'This man has influential friends. If we fail to break him, he'll make sure we're dealt with.'

'Are you saying we should go easy on him?' Isaac asked. The fellow DCIs had achieved mutual admiration for each other. Isaac was testing the waters.

'Not at all. I'm just reminding ourselves that with this man it's break or bust.'

'Either he breaks, or we're bust.'

'That's it.'

***

Jacob Griffiths pondered what to do. He had enough funds outside of the country to maintain his lifestyle, but he had a business that he enjoyed and a wife he loved. He was seen throughout the country as a solid businessman who through sheer hard work, a suitable amount of derring-do, and a lot of charisma had achieved great success. He had always given to worthy causes, received honorary doctorates from two universities, and was often recognised in the street, and now he was contemplating throwing it all away.

He did not want to, but what were the alternatives? Fortescue had some protection, he was sure of that. The man was a politician, and they would not want one of their own lambasted in the press and then languishing in one of Her Majesty's prisons. Fortescue was confident that if they convicted him, it would be of the lesser charge of funding an illegal activity: two years at most, and he may even keep his generous politician's pension.

Griffiths knew that Fortescue was secure, whereas he was not. Some competitors would revel in his ignominy; even refer to it in subtle advertising. It was what he would do if the situation were reversed. He knew his options were limited. He would give Fortescue his time with the police. If the man left there unscarred, then maybe he would stay, but Jacob Griffiths was a pragmatist; he knew that Fortescue was his own man, always had been, even at Eton. When the others were bending the rules, the man would be standing back, ready to distance himself, and now when they faced their greatest challenge, Griffiths had little faith in a man who had taken part in that pact all those years ago.

He cursed Timothy Allerton for his lack of backbone, Keith Codrington for running out on them, and Miles Fortescue for what he would do, but mostly he cursed himself for what he had brought on himself.

***

News travelled fast. No sooner had Fortescue left his house than the social media started to speculate about what he was doing with a police car outside his door. DCI Isaac Cook suspected a nosey neighbour had released the information.

By the time the reluctant politician arrived at Challis Street Police Station, the government Whip was on the phone asking him questions.

Fortescue, after putting off the Whip, went into the police station. Isaac met him on his arrival; offered him his hand only to have it rebuffed. 'What's this all about?' Fortescue asked.

'We'll discuss it in the interview room,' Isaac replied. He needed to go hard on this man, and he did not want to be seen as ingratiating.

In the interview room, Fortescue was joined by Archie Cameron, his QC. 'My client has come here at your request. He is willing to help you, but if this is a waste of time…'

Isaac looked at the QC. He saw a little man with a beak of a nose, his spectacles balancing precariously on the end.

Isaac conducted the formalities. Len Donaldson sat to his side.

'Mr Fortescue, you are a personal friend of Lord Allerton, Jacob Griffiths and Keith Codrington,' Isaac said.

'You know that.'

'We have in custody Lord Allerton's murderer.'

'So what's that got to do with me?' Fortescue replied.

'On the day of his death, Lord Allerton was present at a meeting in your house.'

'Was he?'

'We have proof that Keith Codrington was there, as well as Jacob Griffiths.'

'What proof?' Cameron asked. 'Hearsay has no validity here.'

Len Donaldson sat quietly, biding his time.

'We have a witness for Codrington. Allerton's and Griffiths' vehicles were parked nearby. Do you deny that Keith Codrington visited your house on the day in question?'

'Are you trying to imply that my client is implicated in the death of Lord Allerton?' Cameron asked.

'We are not implying anything,' Donaldson said. 'What we do know is that the bank accounts of Miles Fortescue, Jacob Griffiths, and Lord Allerton have received substantial funds in the last year.'

'And?' Cameron asked. Fortescue sat quietly, unsure what to say.

Go easy, Donaldson. We've not proven that yet, Isaac said to himself.

'Is it true that you, Miles Fortescue, along with others were involved in the importation of illegal drugs into this country?' Len Donaldson was tired of procrastination.

'My client vigorously denies any such accusations. He is well-respected in this country. Unless you have something more concrete, I would suggest that you conclude this interview.'

'Mr Fortescue, were you personally involved in the death of Alex Hughenden?'

'I've never heard of the man. This is preposterous nonsense. You may have reason to talk to Keith Codrington, but I've committed no crime.'

'Yet he still visited your house on the day in question,' Donaldson asked.

'Okay, he did visit my house, but that can hardly be construed as an admission of guilt on my part,' Fortescue said.

'Coming back to your previous statement,' Isaac said. He had seen an inconsistency. 'Why did you say that we may have a reason to talk to him? I don't believe we've indicated that he is our primary suspect.'

'Miles, say no more,' Cameron said quietly to his client.

'I request an adjournment for thirty minutes to confer with my client,' the lawyer said, addressing Isaac.

***

'Miles, what's the truth?' Cameron asked. 'What's Codrington been up to?'

'You've known the man as long as I have. He was always pushing the envelope.'

'Are you involved?'

'I might have lent him some money.'

'What does that mean?'

'He was in debt. He was trying to set up another business, and he wanted me as a silent partner. That's all.'

'What type of business?'

'Import. The same as he had been doing in the Middle East.'

'Importing what?' Cameron asked. It was true that he had known Keith Codrington almost as long as Fortescue; they had all been in the same year at Eton College. However, Cameron had never been friendly with Fortescue or Codrington, and he had detested Timothy Allerton, but time had moved on, and Fortescue, an Old Etonian, needed help.

'He said food products from the Middle East.'

'And?'

'It wasn't.'

'Don't tell me what it was.'

'I didn't realise at first the extent of the trade,' Fortescue said calmly. He knew he was in trouble, and Cameron, the snotty little boy as he was at Eton, was his best chance.

'Did he return your investment?'

'Tenfold.'

'A lot of food products,' Cameron said as he sat back in his chair. The man was no fool; he knew what was going on. He just didn't want to know from Fortescue's mouth.

'If this comes out, nobody will understand,' Fortescue said.

You knew what he was up to, you bloody fool, Cameron thought.

'What do you want me to do? What do you want to say?' Cameron asked.

'Codrington's skipped the country.'

'Has he?'

'That's what he said he was going to do.'

'When?'

'I met him with Griffiths a few days back.'

'Where?'

'In the centre of London.'

'Were you seen?'

'It's unlikely.'

'Hell, man. You know that Codrington's involved in something dodgy, yet you still meet him. Have you no sense? And what about Griffiths? I thought he'd know better.'

'Codrington told us he was leaving. Since then he's not been answering his phone.'

'Any ideas where he may be?'

'None. He'll never be seen again.'

***

Thirty minutes later the interview resumed.

'My client wishes to make a statement,' Cameron said.

'I have known Keith Codrington since our teens, and I have always regarded him as a friend,' Fortescue said. 'Eighteen months ago, he approached me with a business proposal. He had just returned from the Middle East where he had lived for many years, successfully running a trading company. He wished to set up a similar business in England trading with the Middle East, primarily food products. After he had outlined the plan, I invested one million pounds in the venture.

'Subsequently, with no further involvement from me, he started to pay me back with interest, and since then I've received regular amounts into my bank account. I became aware recently that Codrington had been trading in commodities other than food. I, along with others, confronted Codrington and asked for an explanation. He did not admit to any criminal activity. The meeting with him ended badly, with all those who wished to sever the relationship unsure of how to proceed. Needless to say, we were confused, knowing full well that if we reported the man we would be by default subject to suspicion.

'These events have transpired in the last two weeks. I am innocent of all crimes and open to your questions. I will give you my full cooperation. I will also remove the official complaint against your two police officers.'

Isaac sat back in his chair, realising they had achieved a breakthrough. Len Donaldson maintained his focus on Fortescue. *You lying bastard. You knew exactly what Codrington was up to*, he thought.

The two police officers glanced at each other. Isaac knew what Donaldson was thinking; the same as him.

'You mentioned that you continued to receive payments after the initial start-up loan had been repaid?' Isaac asked.

'Yes,' Fortescue replied.

'Are you able to tell us the total amount of those payments?'

'In total, close to one million pounds.'

'Verifiable?'

'My bank records will be available.'

What about the offshore accounts in Panama, the Cayman Islands? Donaldson thought.

'You mentioned there were others who financed Codrington,' Isaac said. 'Could I have their names?'

'Timothy Allerton.'

'Anyone else?'

'There was one other.'

'His name?'

'Is it important?'

'Mr Fortescue, you've just made a statement that you are innocent of all crimes.'

'That's correct.'

'Then who else is involved? Was it Jacob Griffiths?'

'Yes.'

'Thank you.'

'Let us come back to the payments. You receive a million pounds, but you don't question how the business is progressing? You don't ask to see financial records?'

'That was the agreement. We'd supply the initial capital, and Codrington would run the business.'

'But a million pounds. You must have been suspicious?'

'Not really. He had a good track record.'

'There was a meeting at your house on the day Allerton died. Are you willing to admit to that?'

'Yes.'

'And Allerton and Griffiths were present, along with Codrington.'

'Yes,' Fortescue replied. He knew that he had opened up a can of worms. He hoped that Archie Cameron could control the situation.

'What was discussed? Donaldson asked.

'Allerton was suspicious. He was always a nervous man.'

'Were you?'

'Not really. In government, you get used to large amounts of money.'

'But not into your personal bank account. Also, we know that Lord Allerton received more than one million pounds.'

'He may have had a different arrangement.'

'We are aware of at least twenty million pounds in Allerton's account that cannot be explained. Are you, Mr Fortescue, telling us that you only received a million? Where is the remainder? How much did you know about Codrington and his drug trafficking? Did you know about the deaths of Stewart, of Pinto, of Fuentes, of Alex Hughenden? I put it to you, Mr Fortescue, that you are complicit in the crimes of Keith Codrington and that you should be charged with murder. How do you plead?'

'My client has nothing to say,' Cameron replied.

Isaac knew he had overstepped the mark and that their proof was flimsy.

Fortescue, an experienced politician, took it in his stride. He was aware that if Allerton had been there, he would have been reduced to tears, but he was made of sterner material. The politician knew that he would deal with this black apology for a police officer another time.

'We met at my house to confront Codrington. To tell him that we were aware of what he was doing and that we wanted out.'

'Let's break that down,' Donaldson said. 'Firstly, what were you aware of, the drug smuggling or the murders?'

'The drug smuggling.'

'How?'

'It was the money. There was just too much, and Griffiths had asked for some financial records on a previous occasion.'

'Did he receive them?'

'No.'

'Why did you assume it was drug smuggling?'

'What else could have generated that sort of money?'

'One million pounds?'

'Yes, that's it,' Fortescue said, fully aware of another thirty million offshore.

'Mr Fortescue, where are you hiding all your money? We will find out in time.'

'I've already told you I will supply you with my bank records.'

Both police officers realised that pursuing Fortescue over hidden financial assets was futile.

'Let's come back to the meeting,' Isaac said. 'Why was Lord Allerton killed later that day?'

'Allerton had told Codrington he wanted out,' Fortescue said.

'What did Codrington say?'

'He made it very clear that if he went down, so would we, that's all.'

'That's all!' Donaldson exclaimed.

'The meeting ended badly.'

'Are you aware that Lord Allerton had phoned me before your meeting?' Isaac said.

'No, but he said he was ready to confess.'

'What did Codrington say?'

'He just repeated what he had said previously. All four of us were guilty and if he went down, then so would we.'

'My client has been open here today. I would suggest that you focus on the guilt of others, not my client,' Cameron said.

Isaac ignored the lawyer. 'You've admitted to a later meeting in London.'

'Jacob Griffiths and I met up with Codrington.'

'Why?'

'What do you think? Allerton's dead, we're implicated, and we don't know what to do.'

'What was said at the meeting?'

'We confronted him over the death of Allerton. He said nothing about it other than he was leaving and we'd never see him again. That's the honest truth.'

'Why didn't you tell us this before?'

'How? Whatever I say, I'm guilty. It's the same with Griffiths. We're respected members of the community without a criminal offence to our names. What were we to do?'

'Are you planning to leave the country?' Isaac asked.

'I will stay and defend myself.'

'We haven't charged you.'
'My political peers will. I'm guilty without a trial.'

***

Back in the office, everyone was delighted. At last they had a connection to Codrington, but no Codrington. It was evident the man was no longer in the country. Bridget had managed to trace where he had been living. He had used the name of Dennis Hennessey when leasing the penthouse flat, subsequently paying cash to purchase it through an offshore company.

Miles Fortescue had left Challis Street Police Station by the back door and in the back of Archie Cameron's car to avoid the reporters out the front. Even though the police had made no mention of Codrington and the drug trafficking, somehow the press knew something.

It was suspicious, Isaac knew, but it was not their primary issue.

Steve Walters was back in London and ready to be interviewed again, but it was clear that he would not add much to the current investigation. Both he and O'Shaughnessy were in the same prison awaiting trial. Bail had been applied for O'Shaughnessy, but denied.

'Any ideas on Codrington?' Isaac asked.

'We've alerted Interpol,' Bridget said. 'Also, we're checking with the airports.'

'What's next?' Len Donaldson asked.

'Jacob Griffiths,' Isaac replied. 'Larry, any idea where he is?'

'In London. I've checked just in case.'

'Okay, you know what to do.'

Seventy-five minutes later, a late model Mercedes pulled into the car park behind Challis Street Police Station. Jacob Griffiths got out of the car, not with the smiling face that was seen on the television constantly but with the look of a man worried about life.

Isaac watched as he walked across the car park and into the building. Larry walked at his side.

'Thank you for coming,' Isaac said as Griffiths walked into the interview room.

'I didn't have many options, did I?'

Andrew Rushton, Griffiths' lawyer, arrived soon after. Isaac had not liked the man the first time; his opinion did not change on their second meeting.

'If this is a waste of time...' Rushton said.

'It is not,' Isaac's curt reply.

With the formalities dealt with, the interview commenced, following the same procedure as with Fortescue.

'Mr Griffiths, we have proof that you received substantial payments as a result of a criminal act,' Isaac said.

'Can you prove it?' Rushton asked.

'We have interviewed Miles Fortescue. He has admitted that you knew that Keith Codrington was importing large quantities of illegal drugs into this country.'

'Not at first,' Griffiths said.

'When?'

'When we met with Codrington at Fortescue's house.'

'The day of Allerton's death?'

'Yes.'

Len Donaldson and Isaac knew immediately that Griffiths had been contacted by Miles Fortescue after he had left the police station. They knew further questioning would only give them parrot responses, with each of the two men aiming to corroborate the other's story, and to prove their ignorance about how Codrington had been able to pay them so well.

'And yet both you and Fortescue chose not to contact the police. It's hardly the action of innocent men.'

'We were not sure what to do.'

'Are you telling me that Allerton's been murdered, and you could not come to the police?'

'Keith Codrington was a vicious man. If he could murder Tim Allerton, he could murder us.'

'And what about all those drugs you sold? Did you ever worry about them?'

'We didn't know.'

'Rubbish. We have records of conversations between you and Codrington. We are aware that you knew of the murder of Alex Hughenden, even reluctantly agreed to its necessity.'

'How?'

'We found a printout of a phone bill with a mobile number at Codrington's flat. We were able to obtain records of conversations. It's only a matter of time before you and Fortescue are fully implicated in the murders of five men, as well as the importation and marketing of illicit drugs. Mr Griffiths, you will be charged with murder at the end of this interview,' Isaac said.

'My client will not answer to unproven allegations,' Rushton said.

'We didn't know. All three of us needed money, and when Codrington put forward his idea, we went for it.'

'Even though it was illegal?'

'We didn't know that.'

'Are you telling me that you, a successful businessman, did not smell a rat?'

'It's the truth.'

'Did you agree to the murder of Allerton?'

'No. We thought it was alright with Allerton, and that he was going to do nothing for another week. Codrington told us he was finished with the business and for us to give him three weeks. Allerton's death frightened us.'

'You and Fortescue?'

'Yes. If Codrington could kill him, then he could have us killed.'

'And still you did not come to the police.'

'To say what? That we were criminals in fear for our lives?'

'Are you in fear now?'

'Keith Codrington, wherever he is, could still deal with us.'

'Are you willing to make a confession?'

'Not to murder.'

'I need a confession stating that Keith Codrington was a major drug trafficker and that five people to your knowledge were killed as a result of his instructions.'

'I will say that we never knew the nature of the business or of the deaths. We were purely men who trusted a fellow Etonian; allowed ourselves to be hoodwinked.'

'That's fine,' Donaldson replied.

'What will happen to me?' Griffiths asked.

'You will be charged.'

'Not with murder.'

'You will be charged with the lesser charge of drug trafficking.'

'But I didn't know. Rushton, what should I do?'

'Give them their confession stating clearly all the facts. They'll not be able to prove that you're actively involved.'

'How long?'

'Two years, maybe five,' Rushton said.

He'll be lucky if it's less than ten, Isaac thought.

***

Miles Fortescue was arrested later that day. For once, he had stood up in Parliament to make a speech. The one day when he should have felt some pride in his political career; the one day when he suffered the ignominy of being led from the Houses of Parliament to a police car, his hands cuffed with police regulation handcuffs.

Two days later, Keith Codrington was walking along the beach in Abu Dhabi. He was aware of what had happened in London with his former friends. He smiled. The extradition laws were weak, and he had contacts; contacts who would protect him for a price.

He did not see the car parked to one side of the beach. If he had looked, he would have seen the window wound down, the barrel of a gun, its telescopic sights trained on him.

The gun fired, and Codrington collapsed to the ground.

The man who fired the shot turned to his colleague in the driver's seat. 'The man never paid us the full amount for the last shipment,' he said in Russian.

The End

ALSO BY THE AUTHOR

Murder is only a Number – A DCI Cook Thriller

Before she left she carved a number in blood on his chest. But why the number 2, if this was her first murder?

The woman prowls the streets of London. Her targets are men who have wronged her. Or have they? And why is she keeping count?

DCI Cook and his team finally know who she is, but not before she's murdered four men. The whole team are looking for her, but the woman keeps disappearing in plain sight. The pressure's on to stop her, but she's always one step ahead.

And this time, DCS Goddard can't protect his protégé, Isaac Cook, from the wrath of the new commissioner at the Met.

Murder House – A DCI Cook Thriller

A corpse in the fireplace of an old house. It's been there for thirty years, but who is it?

It's clearly murder, but who is the victim and what connection does the body have to the previous owners of the house. What is the motive? And why is the body in a fireplace? It was bound to be discovered eventually but was that what the murderer wanted? The main suspects are all old and dying, or already dead.

Isaac Cook and his team have their work cut out trying to put the pieces together. Those who know are not talking because of an old-fashioned belief that a family's dirty laundry should not to be aired in public, and certainly not to a policeman – even if that means the murderer is never brought to justice!

Murder is a Tricky Business – A DCI Cook Thriller

A television actress is missing, and DCI Isaac Cook, the Senior Investigation Officer of the Murder Investigation Team at Challis Street Police Station in London, is searching for her.

Why has he been taken away from more important crimes to search for the woman? It's not the first time she's gone missing, and why does everyone assume she's been murdered?

There's a secret, that much is certain, but who knows? The missing woman? The executive producer, his eavesdropping assistant? Or the actor who portrayed her fictional brother on the Soap Opera?

Murder Without Reason – A DCI Cook Thriller

DCI Cook, now a Senior Member of London's Anti-Terrorism Command, faces his Greatest Challenge. The Islamic State is waging war in England, and they are winning.

Not only does Isaac Cook have to contend with finding the perpetrators, but he is being forced to commit to actions contrary to his mandate as a police officer.

And then, there is Anne Argento, the Prime Minister's Deputy. The man has proven himself to be a pacifist and is not up to the task. She needs to take his job if the country is to fight back against the Islamists.

Vane and Martin have provided the solution. Will DCI Cook and Anne Argento be willing to follow through? Are they able to act for the good of England, knowing that a criminal and murderous activity is about to take place? Do they have any option?

Hostage of Islam

Kate McDonald's fate hangs in the balance. The Slave Trader has the money for her, so does her father and he wants her back. Can Steve Case's team rescue her and her friend, Helen in time?

Three Americans are to die at the Baptist Mission in Nigeria - the Pastor and his wife in a blazing chapel. Another, gunned down while trying to defend them from the Islamists.

Kate is offered to a slave trader who intends to sell her virginity to an Arab Prince. Helen, to ensure their survival, gives herself to the leader of the raid at the mission and the murderer of her friends.

The Haberman Virus

A remote and isolated village in the Hindu Kush mountain range in North Eastern Afghanistan is wiped out by a virus unlike any seen before.

A mysterious visitor checks his handiwork clad in a space suit, and American female doctor succumbs to the disease, and the woman sent to trap the person responsible, falls in love with the man who would be responsible for the death of millions.

Malika's Revenge

Malika, a drug-addicted prostitute waits in a smugglers' village for the next Afghan tribesman or Tajik gangster to pay her price, a few scraps of heroin.

Yusup Baroyev, a drug lord enjoys a lifestyle many would envy. An Afghan warlord sees the resurgence of the Taliban. A Russian white-collar criminal portrays himself as a good and honest citizen in Moscow.

They are entwined in an audacious plan to raise the quantity of heroin shipped out of Afghanistan and into Russia and ultimately the West.

Some will succeed, some will die, some will be resurrected from their plight and others will rue the day they became involved.

ABOUT THE AUTHOR

Phillip Strang was born in England in the late nineteen forties, during the post-war baby boom in England. He had a comfortable middle-class upbringing in small town seventy miles west of London.

    His childhood and formative years were a time of innocence. There were relatively few rules, and as a teenager he had complete freedom, thanks to a bicycle – a three-speed Raleigh – and a trusting community. It was in the days before mobile phones, the internet, terrorism and wanton violence. He was an avid reader of science fiction in his teenage years: Isaac Asimov and Frank Herbert, the masters of the genre. How much of what they and others mentioned has now become reality? Science fiction has now become science fact. Still an avid reader, the author now mainly reads thrillers.

    In his early twenties, the author, with a degree in electronics engineering and desire to see the world, left the cold, damp climes of England for Sydney, Australia – his first semi-circulation of the globe. Now, forty years later, he still resides in Australia, although many intervening years were spent in a myriad of countries, some calm and safe, others no more than war zones.

Printed in Poland
by Amazon Fulfillment
Poland Sp. z o.o., Wrocław